broken
ground

Lu Hersey

Beaten Track
www.beatentrackpublishing.com

Broken Ground

First published 2022 by Beaten Track Publishing
Copyright © 2022 Lu Hersey

Paperback: 978 1 78645 536 9
eBook: 978 1 78645 537 6

Cover Design by Rhi Winter

Beaten Track Publishing,
Burscough, Lancashire.
www.beatentrackpublishing.com

Praise for *Broken Ground*

does feel strangely vivid and pre-industrial. I bought into this world completely, and loved the characters—and I loved how it takes the genre of folk horror and brings it beautifully up to date with a political and satirical edge."

Paul Magrs, author of the LOST ON MARS trilogy

"*Broken Ground* did that magical thing of drawing me into its world—now I'm sorry that I got to the end. It's a great story—likeable and interesting characters, lots of magic and mystery woven into and around a modern horror, with a strong evocation of place and a compelling narrative driving the story forward.

Sara Crowe, author of BONE JACK

"A breathtaking coming-of-age story about the power of friendship and the pursuit of justice, interwoven with folklore, magic and the paranormal. *Broken Ground* is a moving, deeply atmospheric drama that grips you to the very last page."

Mel Darbon, author of ROSIE LOVES JACK

Praise for *Deep Water*

"Outstanding... I raced through it."

Malorie Blackman

"Excellent. Shimmers with Celtic fairy tales, marine marvels, creepy Cornish fishing villages and a fabulous granny."

New Statesman

"Filled with local folklore and a genuine sense of magic, this is right up there for 11+ readers with Margaret Mahy's *The Changeover*, Susan Cooper's *Greenwitch* and Alan Garner's early novels."

Amanda Craig

"Such an accomplished, tightly-shaped book."

Julia Eccleshare

"Has a lovely, mythical quality while still contemporary and right for the audience."

Elen Caldecott

Author Note to *Broken Ground*

This story is set entirely in the landscape surrounding the Neolithic monuments of Silbury Hill and Avebury, in Wiltshire. I changed the placenames simply because I needed to bring villages and landmarks closer together to make the plot work.

Broken Ground takes place around the time of Lammas, or Lughnasadh, and has a background in ancient folklore surrounding the harvest.

Chapter 1

AN UNEARTHLY SHRIEK fills the night air. My skin goosebumps.

I grab Clay's sleeve. "What the hell was that?"

"What?"

"Shh! Keep your voice down. You must have heard it? There's something out there."

We stand stock still and listen. The silence booms around us. Clay sniffs and stares into the dark. I can hear his stomach gurgling. Not surprising, the amount of pizza he put away earlier.

"I can't hear anything, Arlo. You're way too jumpy. I'll find my torch."

I snatch the bag from him. "NO!"

I feel spooked. That sound went right through me.

Clay huffs at me. "How are we supposed to see anything without a bloody torch? We need to measure out the circle."

"I can pace it. We'll reel the tape out as we go."

"That's dumb. It'll take forever."

"Look, I definitely heard something. Something weird."

"You're just paranoid."

"Clay, seriously, you're just deaf. It was super loud!"

"Probably an owl."

"Of course it wasn't. I know what owls sound like. I've never heard any animal make a noise like that."

"Okay, we'll wait another minute or two."

But Clay doesn't think there's anything out there, and he can't keep quiet. He sighs and yawns like a bored dog. I can tell he's staring at me expectantly. After a while, I realise there's no point. I can't hear anything over his stupid breathing, and if we're going to make this crop circle, we need to get going. Creating the pattern is complicated—and takes hours. And these summer nights are short.

I look all around the field carefully to check our position. "Reckon this is a good spot to make the centre—what do you think?"

"Your call, Arlo. You know the field boundaries way better than I do."

He's right. I used to live at the farm, so of course I do.

"Okay, so we'll put the stake in about…here." I jab the sharpened wooden pole into the soil, using my body weight to twist it into the ground. I test how stable it is. "Reckon it'll hold."

"Have you got the graph?" asks Clay.

"Yes, but we don't need to look at the design until we've paced out the radius. It's a hundred and fifty metres to the edge, and I can estimate each step as about a metre. No torches. We can check the measurement when we get there. Pass me the tape?"

Clay mutters about not being able to see anything but manages to find the tape measure in the bag. My ears are super-charged for any noise out in the dark as I loop the tape ring over the stake. As soon as it's fixed in place, I click the tape out a couple of metres.

I can just make out Clay's chipped front tooth as he grins at me in the dark. One thing I really like about him is his enthusiasm for circle making. I try to relax a bit. "Ready? Got your stalk stomper?"

"Of course. I'll take yours for you if you're measuring."

"Thanks, mate."

I hand him my stalk stomper—a plank of wood threaded with rope. Stompers are heavy and cumbersome, so I'm glad he's offering. We need them to flatten the pattern into the crop once we've measured it out.

In the distance, we hear the village church bell chime twelve times.

"Hey, it's gone midnight. It's my birthday!" Clay says.

"Happy birthday! So let's get started. If we both count, we'll get a pretty good estimate of distance, okay?"

"Right-oh."

"We'll head towards the culvert by the bottom gate."

"What's a culvert? Which gate?"

I realise he's facing the wrong way and grab him by his shoulders to turn him around. "Down there. Can you see the gate now?"

"Oh, yeah. By that big black thing?"

"It's an oak tree. Yes, that way."

3

I'm pretty sure that's where the sound came from. I don't mention it to Clay in case it's nothing, but we need to check we're alone out here. Apart from anything else, there could be heavy penalties if we get caught.

"Okay, let's go."

Clay nods and starts counting his steps out loud as he paces.

"One, two, three, four, fi..."

"Shhhhhh! Count in your head, can't you?"

"Okay, okay. It's cool. Don't panic."

"I'm not panicking."

"You're totally overreacting."

"No, I'm being careful. Unlike you. Phelps could hear you coming for miles."

"What's wrong with you tonight? Is this to do with you and Jaz?"

"What about me and Jaz?"

"You want to ask her out but you don't."

"Don't be stupid, of course it's not. It's to do with not wanting to get caught by Phelps, that's all."

"There's no one here. It's gone midnight. Not even Phelps farms at this time."

Clay's right. Phelps is very unlikely to be out here now. But I don't think that eerie sound had anything to do with Phelps.

"Okay, let's get on with it. Quietly!"

I feel him glare at me before he starts counting again. He's annoyed and I can't blame him. It's hard to explain why that noise put me so on edge. But how come didn't he hear it too?

Clay puffs along behind me with the stalk stompers as we follow a tramline between two rows of barley. Tramlines are the straight lines the tractor tyres make when planting the field. Sticking to them as much as we can means we don't leave too much evidence of how we got in the field, and we make less noise crashing through the crop. I keep my eyes fixed on the culvert the whole time I'm walking.

All at once, there's a strange crackling in the air, and the hairs on the back of my neck rise. I'm positive we're not alone. I stop and turn to look at Clay, who's totally oblivious and still counting softly.

"Ninety-five, ninety-six, ninety-seven—"

"Clay!" I hiss as loud as I dare.

"What?" He makes no effort to hide his irritation. "Dammit, now you've made me lose count! What's your problem?"

"Shhh! Get down. There's someone in the field."

He opens his mouth to make some snappy reply, then realises I'm serious. We crouch down silently. The crop's just about high enough to hide us unless someone is walking the same tramline.

A light breeze whispers through the barley. I slowly stick my head up to scan the field. The stars are out, but the moon hasn't risen yet. My eyes are drawn back to the darker areas under the oak, searching for silhouettes.

Then I see it. A faint, greenish light dapples through the crop about a hundred metres from where we're hiding, coming up from the culvert. I focus my attention on the spot, keeping as still as I can.

Clay fidgets and hisses at me, "What can you see?"

"Some kind of torches," I whisper. "Think they're heading this way. Can't you keep still a minute?"

Clay ignores me and kneels up so he can take a look too.

"What the crap?"

We both watch as the lights slowly approach. Out in the dark of the field they look ethereal, like subtly shifting fibre-optic strands. The weirdest thing is that the lights seem to be coming up from the ground and creating some kind of pattern. It must be an optical illusion, caused by the total darkness.

"How are they doing that?" whispers Clay.

"Dunno, but it's amazing."

"Who are those guys? They're just messing with our heads. I don't like it."

"I don't think they know we're here."

"Of course they do, Arlo. Don't be such a dumb ass." Clay's made no attempt to keep quiet, and he suddenly stands up.

The lights go out immediately.

"Let's split now," hisses Clay. "Give me the bag for the stalk stompers."

Clay and I have an agreement. We take it in turns to be in charge of the bag, and tonight it's his turn. First sign of trouble, we split up and head off in opposite directions. That way, it's less likely we'll both get caught.

He grabs the bag off me, we fist bump for luck, and he scarpers. I listen to the sound he makes rustling out through the crop. He's moving fast. A couple of minutes later and I can't hear him anymore. Just the breeze clicking through the barley. I try not to move a muscle.

I should have run when Clay left, but I'm too scared. Heading the opposite way from him means I could run straight into whatever's out there. The surge of adrenalin is making my chest go tight. My left foot's cramped up. I try to concentrate on the pain of that in an effort to bring my heart rate down.

After a few minutes, my senses have become so heightened I can practically hear the crop breathing. The smell of pesticide is overpowering, and it's all I can do not to gag. I know what this means. It happened once before. Another rush of adrenalin pumps around in my blood. Probably the pulsing lights triggered it. My head's beginning to feel like it might explode, just like the first time. If I'm lucky, I'll make it home before the seizure comes on, but I need to leave right away.

I look up cautiously. Nothing. I keep my eyes fixed on the area where I last saw the lights and wonder if it's safe to pick up my graph notebook containing the circle design before I run for it. I dropped it when we crouched down. I feel around the roots of the barley, trying to find it.

Time practically stands still. Finally, my fingers feel the smoothness of the cover and I lift it carefully, wondering if it'll make a scratchy noise if I try to push it into my hoodie pocket. I stare out into the darkness before I risk it.

Suddenly, the sound I heard before fills the night air. The spectral howl is close this time, pulsing up through my legs as though it's coming from the earth under my feet. My heart freezes.

A rustling, swishing sound. Someone is moving, really fast, towards me. Soft green light shimmers under the crop as they get closer. Do they know I'm here?

My heart starts beating so fast, I feel like anyone could hear it. All my senses go into overdrive. I drop the book in panic, and it flaps against the wheat as it falls, the sound crescendoing in my ears. I can't get home in time. It's started already.

Looming out of the dark, for barely a split second, I see a shadowy face above the crop, eyes glinting in the eerie green light. Someone is looking straight at me.

Then everything goes black.

Chapter 2

SOMETHING COLD PRESSES against my forehead. Metal. I open my eyes.

"Nice of you to join us." The barrel of a shotgun is pointing in my face. I say nothing as I stare up at Phelps's angry expression. From this angle, I can see the hairs growing out of his flaring nostrils and the blackheads on the end of his nose. Basically, he's much too close for comfort.

It takes a few seconds to realise where I am. I'm still in his field, near the hedge up by the hawthorn. I'm confused. How on earth did that happen? Last thing I remember, I was close to the culvert at the bottom gate.

Phelps's son Hayden is standing next to him, looking pale and beanpole thin as ever. He avoids eye contact with me, staring at the ground like he hopes it'll swallow him and fiddling nervously with his glasses. The lenses glint in the early morning sun.

Phelps coughs and gobs onto the ground right beside me. I suddenly feel sick. Did I have a seizure last night? I've only had one before, and that was back when they fetched Dad's body in from the barn. Ma and the doctor thought it was probably the shock. Having another one could be really bad news. I feel a cold pit of anxiety forming in my stomach. Does having another one mean I'm going to get them for the rest of my life?

"You're trespassing on my land, Arlo Fry. I might have shot you 'by mistake'. Would have got away with it too. You're lucky Hayden was here, or you'd be another bit of dead vermin."

I blink and give Hayden a grateful glance. He blushes and looks away.

"I've called the police," Phelps says. "They'll be here in a few minutes. You'd better find your tongue before they arrive. You've got some explaining to do."

"Police? Why?" It's the best I can manage. I'm finding it hard to talk. My head feels so fuzzy. It's not my fault I had a seizure. Is he getting me arrested for trespassing?

"Oh, let me see now." Phelps's voice is heavy with sarcasm. "Stand up and we'll take a look, shall we?" He pokes me in the chest with the rifle. "This is going to cost you."

I stand up shakily. My brain's fuddled, and I'm totally disorientated. I squint in the strong morning sunlight. Nine Acre field slopes steeply down from where we're standing, giving a perfect view of Wights Mound rising up majestically from the plain below. Stretching down the bottom half of the field towards the bottom gate is the most beautiful and elaborate crop circle I've ever seen. The sun burnishes the flattened barley an orangey gold, bringing the design magically to life.

"Wow, that's incredible!" I say it without thinking, forgetting the company I'm in.

"Proud of yourself, are you? We'll see what the police have to say about that."

Suddenly I realise what he's getting at. "You think I made that? You must be joking. That's way out of my league."

I bite my tongue, realising I've said too much already. I could be in serious trouble here, but somehow I can't stop staring at the circle. It's mesmerising. I've never seen anything like it, and I've seen quite a lot of crop circles. Me and Clay have made a few ourselves since we started our revival of the art form.

This one is of three horses, done in a Celtic knot style. They look like wild horses, galloping nose to tail, intricately weaving into each other so there's no obvious beginning or end to the design. The detail is beyond fantastic. It would be hard to make in broad daylight, and practically impossible at night. I couldn't even draw it on graph paper, let alone make it on this scale in a field.

The breeze picks up for a moment and the horses seem to come alive. The ears of the barley undulate around them, making it look like they're actually galloping. I almost gasp out loud. How can anyone create effects like that?

"I'll get the combine out as soon as the police have gone." Phelps points the gun in my face again. I flinch. He's a total psycho. I reckon he's more than capable of shooting me and saying it was an accident. Even so, I have to ask.

"Why? Why would you do that? It's a tiny part of your crop and it's beautiful. You could make a fortune charging people to come and see it. The barley isn't even ready for harvesting yet."

"I'd keep my mouth shut if I were you."

"I didn't make that circle. You must know that. Have you ever seen one that detailed before?"

"Frankly, I don't care if you did it, or if it was a spaceship full of aliens. What I see is a good insurance claim." He smirks. "And finally a chance to evict you and your flake of a mother out of Primrose Cottage. Must be my lucky day! I've been waiting for an opportunity like this ever since I bought the farm."

I glance at Hayden. He looks like he's desperate to say something but doesn't have the nerve to open his mouth. Hayden and I aren't friends anymore, and I'm still angry about what happened after Dad died, but I feel sorry for him. Not having a father is painful, but it has to be better than putting up with a bully like Phelps.

The distant wail of a police car siren travels on the summer breeze towards us. Phelps shifts his attention to the lane beyond Wights Mound, and I seize the moment to signal frantically to Hayden. I hope he understands the sign language. I want him to grab some photos of the circle with his phone before his father takes the combine to it. No one is going to believe how good it is unless I can show them some photos. He nods, so I think he's understood. But then he mimes making a phone call, so maybe not.

"What do you think you're doing?" Phelps cuffs the top of his son's head, hard. Ouch. I bet that hurt.

"I wondered if he needed to call—" Hayden is trying to stand up to him, but he looks frightened. He pushes his glasses back on his nose nervously.

"Don't talk to him. Just keep out of this and let the police deal with him." Phelps glares at me. "I hope they lock you up and throw away the key."

He swings the butt of the shotgun around and prods me hard in the stomach. I double up in pain, and my face flushes hot with anger, but I keep my mouth shut. Much as I'd like to punch him, my head's throbbing too much. Probably as well. He might make it an excuse to shoot me.

"Come on. Start walking back to the farm. The police can take you off *my* land, and good riddance." He emphasises the *my* to rub it in.

I stumble along the tramline through the wheat with Phelps poking me in the back with his gun every few steps. I need to stop for a pee but decide I can hold it a while longer. The acrid smell of recently sprayed pesticide catches my throat again.

My head is aching so much, I hope to hell it doesn't mean I'm heading for another seizure. The sweat's getting in my eyes, and I search my jeans pockets for a tissue to wipe it away but can't find one. I reach into my hoodie pocket instead... and almost gasp out loud.

My notebook's in there.

Did I pick it up? Last thing I remember is dropping it when I saw that shadow figure out in the dark, staring at me. Just thinking about it makes me shiver, despite the heat.

I try to piece together the events of last night. What happened to the wooden stake and the surveyor's tape? If Phelps has found them, I'm stuffed. I can get away with the notebook. My graph drawing is a geometric pattern. It looks nothing like that horse circle.

We reach the gate at the end of Nine Acre field. The top of the gate is wound with barbed wire. I hate that. It's so unnecessary. Dad would never have used barbed wire like that. Phelps opens the gate carefully, and it squeals on its hinge like a trapped rat. He waves us through with the shotgun and we're on the track leading back to the farm. The smell of dry bracken overrides the chemical stink of pesticide.

I turn to glance at Hayden. He stares at me like he really wants to communicate something. His eyes are a very intense blue. Forget-me-not blue, Ma used to say, back when we were friends. Anyway, he's got no chance of saying anything while his dad's around. Not unless he wants his brains knocked out.

We walk down the long track that twists around the edges of the fields back to the farmyard, silent but for the crunch of chalk stones under our feet. The smell of the bracken gives way to the stomach-churning stench of Phelps's giant piggery. There's nothing worse than

14

the smell of pigs cooped up in tiny pens, shut away from natural light.

Dad would have hated Phelps's farming methods. Even his crops are grown right up the field edges, with no wild flower strips anywhere or proper allowance for the hedgerows.

The sound of the siren gets louder as the police car bumps closer to us along the track from the road. My head is still throbbing. We stand in the yard as it pulls up and the police get out.

One of them is a policewoman about Ma's age who instantly recognises me and smiles. She was there at the farm. Here, in fact. The day Dad died. I glance at the policeman. Don't think I've seen him before. Maybe he's new.

The policewoman turns to Phelps.

"Good morning, Mr. Phelps. I'm PC Colenutt, and this is my colleague, PC Chopra."

PC Chopra sniffs the air and tries to hide his disgust. No one likes the smell of the piggery.

Phelps grabs the back of my hoodie and pushes me towards them. He's still holding the shotgun in his other hand.

"This is what you're here for. Take him away and lock him up. I'll be prosecuting, of course."

PC Colenutt looks concerned.

"You're Arlo Fry, aren't you? Are you all right? You're very pale."

I smile at her gratefully. "Think I'm okay. I had a seizure last night."

"Seriously?"

I nod. I'm getting this horrible feeling of déjà vu. PC Colenutt was there soon after the first seizure. My legs feel shaky. I daren't look to where the old barn used to be. Where Ma and her friend Mary found Dad.

"Then you need to rest. My youngest sometimes took a couple of days to recover after an episode."

Oh, yes. Her daughter. I try to remember her name, but my head's too fuzzy and I can't. She was several years below Clay, Jaz and me at school. I only remember her because she had seizures and we all had to look out for her.

I smile shakily. "Thanks, I will as soon as I get home." I'm still struggling to find words and my headache's getting worse. "Would it be okay for me to go to the toilet now? I haven't had a chance."

"Don't think you're coming in *my* house for anything, sunshine," Phelps says. "You can use the farm workers' toilet up by the piggery." He turns to the policewoman. "I'd follow him if I were you. He might do a runner."

She frowns. "I seriously doubt it, Mr. Phelps. We know where he lives."

Suddenly I remember her daughter's name. She's called Rose. Haven't seen her since we left junior school, five years ago. I try to recall what she looked like as I slope off to the toilet. Fluffy brown hair and dark eyes. I wonder what happened to her. Something PC Colenutt said made me think she might not be alive anymore, which makes me even more anxious. Some types of epilepsy can be very serious.

The graffiti in the disgusting outside toilet is interesting. Someone's written *Phelps is an arsehole pig* in biro on the wall above the empty toilet roll holder. Someone else has scribbled *Unfair to pigs* underneath, dangerously close to the stained, brown-streaked toilet bowl. Then the first person has written *and arseholes*. I'm guessing Phelps doesn't use this facility.

I wash my hands in the dribble of rusty water that splutters out of the tap into the grimy basin. There's no soap. I decide not to dry them on the filthy towel. I've no idea what colour it started out, but it's now a shade of pig dirt. I wipe my hands on my jeans.

I glance up at the house as I walk back to the yard, wondering if I can spot any changes. Someone ducks back from an upstairs window. I'm left with a fleeting impression of a pale, scared face and halo of wild fair hair. Something about it bothers me. Surely that wasn't Hayden's mum?

My attention is drawn back to the yard, where PC Colenutt is attempting to reason with Phelps.

"But Mr. Phelps, if you want to prosecute, you have to have evidence. You need to let PC Chopra and I inspect your field to see the alleged damage."

"I'm not wasting my time traipsing back up there. I'm a busy man. You'll have to take my word for it, or go see for yourselves."

"I'm afraid we can't do that, *Sir*."

The way she says *Sir* makes me think Phelps is starting to piss them off. I'm not surprised. His attitude sucks. He opens his mouth and starts another rant.

"This country is going to the dogs. You're more interested in the rights of the criminal than protecting my rights as a landowner. I'm the victim here, remember."

"We just need to see the field, Mr. Phelps. Won't take long now, will it? And the more we stand here arguing the point, the longer it will be. Unless you'd prefer to drop the charges, of course."

The last remark is like a red rag to a bull. Phelps goes puce with rage.

"You must be joking! You think I'm going to miss a chance to finally get this vandal out of that cottage and off my land? Come on then…"

Phelps stomps off back down the lane, expecting us all to follow him.

"Just going to check the pigs," mumbles Hayden. He tries to mime something at me when Phelps isn't looking. I hope he's telling me he's going to fetch his phone before he joins us, but I'm still not sure he's got the message about taking pictures.

WE STAND IN Nine Acre field at about the spot where Phelps found me, looking down the slope at the circle of horses. They shift a little as the wind picks up, as if they're flexing their muscles, ready to gallop off. I think both police officers are impressed.

"It's very detailed," observes PC Colenutt, tucking her hair behind her ears as she gazes down the field.

"It's a work of art!" PC Chopra says, quickly glancing at me. I could almost kiss him for the reaction he gets from Phelps.

"Work of art? I'm running a business here, in case you hadn't noticed. It's criminal damage, that's what it is. I'll have to combine the crop immediately, and the wastage will cost me thousands."

There's a brief pause when nobody says anything. The police officers both seem transfixed by the horses, twitching and shifting below us in the summer breeze.

PC Colenutt reaches for her notebook. "Are you sure it's worth cutting down the entire crop?"

"Whose side are you on?" Phelps has raised his voice again. He looks at her accusingly.

She scribbles something in her notebook. "The side of the law, Mr. Phelps. And if you're making an insurance claim, we have to give an accurate assessment of how much of the crop is affected."

"Are you positive you didn't do this, er, damage to Mr. Phelps's crop, Arlo?" asks PC Chopra.

"No, really. I came out last night to look at Wights Mound in the moonlight. This field is a good place to view it from. Then I felt the seizure coming on, and I must have passed out. The formation definitely wasn't here then."

"He's lying!" Phelps says.

I don't say anything. I'm hoping Phelps doesn't find the stake or the surveyor's tape when he combines the field. Things look bad enough for me without him having actual physical evidence.

Officer Colenutt glances at him but keeps her face free from expression as she makes more notes. She looks up at me. "Did you see anyone else out here last night, Arlo?"

"No, sorry. This must have happened after I passed out."

Even as I'm saying it, I picture those glittering eyes in the darkness, staring straight at me.

But I can't tell them what I saw. The whole episode was beyond strange. It was so surreal, just thinking about it makes my pulse rate shoot up.

Chapter 3

MA'S NOT IN when the police drop me back home, which is a massive relief. She's probably out taking one of her herbal remedies to a client. As soon as the police drive off, I message Clay to meet me in the café then shower and change as fast as I can, hoping to avoid Ma until later.

I get as far as the garden gate and run straight into Jaz with her bike. She's a bit breathless from cycling, and her dark skin glistens in the sunlight. She looks amazing.

"You off out?" she asks.

"Going to meet Clay, that's all."

She grins and props the bike against the garden wall so she can give me a hug. Her hair smells warm, like cinnamon. I try not to over-hug back.

"You meeting him in the café?"

I smile. "Where else is there around here?"

"I'll walk up with you, and you can tell me what happened." She gives me a knowing look.

"You've heard?"

"Hayden called me. He said you'd had a seizure and his dad caught you asleep in the field. Are you okay?"

"Bit of a headache, but all right."

"You don't look all right."

"Thanks!"

"I mean you look tired, stupid!"

"Did Hayden tell you the rest?"

"About the police?"

"I'll take that as a 'yes.'"

"He says his father is going to prosecute. Did you actually make the crop circle with Clay? Promise I won't tell anyone if you did."

"No. Wish I had. At least then this trouble might be worth it. Don't know what Ma's going to make of it. Phelps says he's going to evict us."

"He can't do that! Your mum's got more than enough problems as it is!"

Jaz and Ma have always got on really well. It's another reason I can't risk asking her out. I don't answer because I don't know what to say. She's right. Ma has a lot on her plate right now.

Jaz squeezes my arm, and we start walking up the lane towards Corn Flakes, the café by Stanton Stones.

As we pass the gate to Mound field, I notice a girl dressed in black standing close to the Mound, crows circling her head. She's some distance away, but she looks up and stares at us so intently I find myself staring back. Then she suddenly starts running towards us, her long red hair flying out around her. She's moving so fast, it's almost creepy.

I turn to Jaz. "Wonder what's up with that girl?"

Jaz stops pushing her bike and looks into the field. "What girl?"

I follow her gaze. The girl has disappeared.

"That's weird. She was there a second ago." I don't see how she could have vanished like that.

"Maybe it was a sheep?"

"A sheep?" Jaz tries to keep a straight face. "Well there's nobody there now. Apart from those sheep grazing on the Mound. Was she wearing a fluffy white coat?"

We both crack up laughing.

But it's still bothering me. What if seeing things that aren't there is a symptom of having epilepsy?

WHEN WE GET to the café, Clay's already sitting at a table near the window and playing some game on his phone. The place is full of the usual mix of hippies and new-agers, along with a coach party of Japanese tourists who've probably been to see Stanton Stones.

"Good job you're not working here today, Arlo," Jaz says. "It's even more crowded than usual."

Clay looks up from his phone. "Take your time, why don't you?"

"Happy birthday!" Jaz says and hugs him. "I've got you a present for later."

Clay smiles and looks at me.

"Not my fault I'm late. Only just got back when I messaged you. Phelps tried to get me arrested."

"You're kidding? How come?"

"Caught me in the field this morning."

"This morning! What were you doing back there in daylight, you nut job?"

"Dunno. Think I must have had some kind of seizure last night and passed out."

"A seizure? What, like, seriously? You mean you were there *all night*?"

"Must have been."

"Was it a seizure like the one you had before?"

"Yeah."

There's a tumbleweed moment where neither of us mentions Dad.

Clay blinks. "Heavy. That's a long time to be out. But how come Phelps tried to arrest you? Having epilepsy isn't your fault."

"I don't have epilepsy."

Clay and Jaz look at each other quickly.

Clay coughs. "So what happened after the last seizure? I mean, didn't they give you any medicine for it? Like, maybe you need to take some now?"

"No, they didn't. And no, I don't."

Jaz tries to smooth things over. "Didn't your mum find a remedy last time?"

Now I feel awkward. Ma's remedy was major league embarrassing. "Yeah. She made me listen to Mozart every day for three months and forced me to swallow some herbal gunk she made."

Clay snorts with laughter and Jaz scowls at him.

"Shut up, Clay. It's worked up until now hasn't it? Arlo's mum is a brilliant healer. That first seizure must have been nearly two years ago, and he's been fine since then."

Clay looks thoughtful. "Bet it was those stupid lights we saw. Lights can trigger seizures, right? Really bad luck Phelps caught you, though."

"Tell me about it."

"What's the charge?"

"Criminal damage. There's a new crop circle. He thinks I made it."

Clay's suddenly so interested he puts his phone down. "A new circle? Where?"

"In Nine Acre field, where we were."

"Wow. Must have been the hippies with the lights. What's it like?"

"Best I've ever seen. Magical. Like it's alive or something."

"Don't be dumb, Arlo. That seizure must have zapped your brain. You'll be telling me aliens made it next. Is it up on the board yet?"

"Doubt it. And sadly, Phelps will be combining it as we speak."

Clay gets up out of his chair. "I'm going to take a look. Get us another coffee, could you?"

Before Jaz or I can answer, Clay's pushing his way through the crowded tables to get to the massive noticeboard that covers the end wall of the café. It's what a lot of people still come here for. Apparently, back around the millennium, Corn Flakes was like crop circle central. These days, photos of any new circles get posted online straight away, but the board here is still a favourite place to exchange info with others who've already been out in the fields. There are just far fewer of them now. It's why Clay and I are trying to revive the art.

I turn to Jaz. "Do you want a coffee too?"

She smiles and her eyes light up. "Thanks. I'll save the seats. Let me give you some money."

"That's okay. If I'm lucky, Ronnie will let me have them for free. I've been working some extra shifts this week, it's been so busy!"

As I head to the counter, I'm still thinking about Jaz's incredible eyes and wondering if maybe Clay's right and I should actually ask her out.

Clay comes up to me while I'm getting our coffees. He's dead excited.

"It's up there, Arlo! Someone's taken a photo from a microlite, but it's very blurry and there's no coordinates yet. Horses, right?"

"Right. Try not to jog my arm, could you?"

"Not my fault. It's so crowded in here. Oh, can you manage the coffees yourself? I've just seen Josh, and I want my old Nintendo back. It's a collector's item now. Won't be a minute."

He disappears before I can answer. I put the drinks on a tray and weave my way over to re-join Jaz.

As I pass the coffee to her, I get the feeling I'm being watched. I turn towards the window. There's a girl staring at me through the glass. Even from here, I can see her eyes are emerald green. I breathe in sharply. That incredible long, red hair, the black dress—I'm sure it's the girl I saw in the field. Has she followed us here?

Bright-blue tattoos spiral up her arms, even going up her neck and onto her cheeks. Or maybe it's paint: she looks way too young for tattoos.

"Why's that girl looking at you?" asks Jaz. "Do you know her?"

"No. Never seen her before...unless..."

"Unless what?" asks Jaz a little too quickly, a slight edge in her voice. Or maybe that's wishful thinking on my part.

"Could be the girl I thought I saw in the field. Maybe. Not sure."

I don't why I say I'm not sure. I'm positive it's her. My heart's racing, and I'm starting to sweat.

"The sheep girl?"

"Yeah." I attempt a smile.

Suddenly, the café sound system kicks in and starts blaring out some old rock music. 'Stairway to Heaven', Led Zeppelin. Ronnie, the woman who runs Corn Flakes with her wife, Liv, is always playing stuff like that because she says the Germans like it. Somehow, it feels like bad timing.

I jump as Clay clatters back down into his seat. "Who was that old woman?"

"What old woman?"

"The weird-looking one that was staring at you."

"What do you mean old? She's about our age!"

I look at the window. The girl has gone. I feel like I can breathe again.

27

"Well, she looked old to me," Clay says. "At least thirty. Anyway, what do either of you know about Phelps's mining application?"

For a moment, I'm glad he's changed the subject. Then my brain registers what he said. "Mining? Phelps? First I heard of it."

"There's a notice on the board. He's applied for planning permission. Says he's 'bringing wealth to the area to the benefit of all.'"

"Benefit to Phelps more like," Jaz says. "Yeah, we got a leaflet through the door. Mum's going to oppose it, obviously, with the whole area being a heritage site."

Jaz's mum, Caroline, is a Green Party campaigner, so that's no surprise. "Where's he planning this mine?" I ask.

Clay looks at me oddly. "We're talking about Phelps, mate. Where do you think?"

"The farm?"

Clay nods. "Where else?"

"What's he mining for?"

"Dunno. It doesn't say."

I feel like I've been punched in the chest. "Dammit, this is really going to upset Ma. It's bad enough I've got to tell her Phelps wants to evict us. I'd better go home."

"If I know your mum, she'll just be worried about you," Jaz says. "But I reckon Phelps won't prosecute. He'll want to avoid any bad press at the moment, in case anyone opposes his application."

"I hope you're right. But he's wanted us out of Primrose Cottage since he bought the farm."

Jaz smiles. "I'm always right, so try not to worry about it. And give your mum my love. Tell her we'll be over later."

"Yeah," Clay says, which probably means the same. "And it's my birthday, remember?"

I grin at him. "Sure."

As I leave, I glance out of the window again to double-check the weird, tattooed girl has gone. I feel uneasy about the way she looked at me, almost as if she knew me. Hopefully, she's some traveller's kid that's passing through and I won't run into her again.

Chapter 4

MA IS SITTING by the window, watching the bees buzzing around the sunflowers. She spends a lot of time studying bees. Too much if you ask me.

She looks up when I come through the door. "The bees aren't happy, Arlo, but I can't work out what's wrong."

"Maybe they've heard about Phelps's planning application," I say. "Did you know about it?"

"Yes, I saw it in the paper. But surely he won't get it? This whole area is a heritage site."

"That's what Jaz said. There's a notice up on the board in Corn Flakes. Apparently, he wants to start test drilling soon."

Ma immediately picks up her knitting needles and starts casting on stitches with a ball of black wool. She only knits when she's knitting out a problem. Sometimes she knits several metres, a seemingly endless stream of black, shapeless nothingness as she knits the trouble away.

She frowns, deep in thought. "But the way the bees are behaving, there's already some problem."

I guess I'll have to tell her sooner or later. I take a deep breath. "Sorry I didn't come back last night."

She looks up. "That's okay, love. Thought you must have gone to Clay's." She narrows her eyes. "So why are you sorry? What's happened?"

"Me and Clay were up at Nine Acre, where we planned to make the circle. But then something... well, some*one* was up there. Clay managed to run away."

"Why didn't you run too?"

"I couldn't. I felt weird, then I blacked out."

Now she looks really worried. "It wasn't a seizure was it? Like that night we found Dad?"

I try to play it down. "Might have been."

"It was, wasn't it? I thought it was the shock back then." She studies my face in a concerned way, not taking her eyes off me for a second. "How do you feel? Are you okay? You look so tired!"

"I'm fine, Ma. Don't remember a thing and I didn't injure myself. But I must have fallen asleep after. Phelps was standing over me with his gun when I woke up."

She picks up her wool again and knits a little faster. "Phelps caught you? Arlo, you're lucky you didn't get hurt! He's not right in the head—and always strutting about the place with that shotgun."

"He called the police on me."

Ma tuts angrily. "Whatever for? Trespassing?"

"There was a new circle in the field, and he thought I'd done it. He says he'll have us out of the cottage."

The knitting needles clack in the silence as she finishes her first row of black. Then she looks up. "He can't get us out and he knows it. It's ours in perpetuity.

Your dad had it written into the contract when we had to sell up. It was a condition of the sale. It's our land by rights."

"But have you ever seen the contract? Are you sure? Phelps can afford a good lawyer and we can't. Really sorry, Ma. Didn't mean to cause this trouble."

"It's not your fault, Arlo, and it'll probably come to nothing anyway. We can worry about it if it happens. In the meantime, I'll make up some more of that remedy for seizures. It worked well before."

I try not to pull a face. Her remedy tasted disgusting.

"You'd better go and see Doctor Bill as well. I'll make an appointment for you."

She smiles, but I can tell she's still worried. This isn't only about me having a seizure or Phelps threatening to evict us.

I sigh. "So, what else is wrong?"

"Can't put my finger on it, Arlo. It's the crows. They're as restless as the bees. Something is disturbing the land."

I'm so relieved Clay didn't come back with me. Ma's a good healer, but all her 'signs and portents' stuff can be really embarrassing. The only one of my friends who understands her is Jaz. She told me once that her dad's mum, who lives in Ethiopia, is a healer too. I think she still misses her dad and her grandmother, but we don't talk much about the time before her mum brought her to England.

Ma looks at me thoughtfully. "I'd better give the surgery a ring while I'm thinking about it, to make you that appointment. Tell me more about last night. What happened? You made a circle in Nine Acre but had a blackout and fell asleep, and so Phelps caught you. Is that all?"

"No Ma, I told you. We didn't make the circle. I wish we had. You should have seen it. It was amazing—way beyond what me and Clay can do."

Ma drops her knitting into her lap and looks up at me, suddenly interested.

"Is it a proper one?"

"Eh?"

"You don't see so many good crop circles these days, not like back in my day."

I grin at her. "When you say 'proper', I hope you're not asking if it was made by faeries or aliens."

Ma tries to look indignant. "Of course not."

"You are, aren't you?"

She pretends not to hear me. "So what's the pattern?"

"Horses. Celtic knot style. They look almost alive. It's so complex, it's unbelievable."

I realise I've said too much when I notice the glint in her eye. Ma *loves* crop circles. It's one of her things. Dad used to tease her about it, even though that's how they met—in a crop circle back on the farm.

"Sounds incredible! I'd really like to see it."

"Get a grip, Ma! We can't go there now. Phelps will be out in the field—he might have combined it already.

You know what he's like about crop circles on his land. He was only waiting for the police to collect evidence against me, taking photos and the like."

"But we could go and find out. We'll be careful, and we can sneak back straight away if we spot him out with the combine."

I can see there's no stopping her. She knows Nine Acre field better than I do; she'll only end up going without me. And if the circle is still there, it would be a great chance to take some photos of my own.

"Okay," I say. "I'm in so much trouble with Phelps already, it can't get much worse."

She looks at me sharply. "Oh, Arlo, I should have thought! Are you up to this? You look a bit pale. You don't have to come with me. You've had a seizure. You should get some rest—"

"No way. I'm fine. I'm coming."

"Okay, but I'll phone Doctor Bill as soon as we're back."

As we leave the house, I notice she's got another grey streak in her hair at the back of her head. They only started coming after we lost Dad. Sometimes I think they appear overnight.

We walk quickly along the lanes to the nearest gate entrance to the farm, then skirt along the remaining hedgerows towards Nine Acre. We don't talk at all and keep a constant lookout for any sign of Phelps or his farm workers. Whatever Ma says about the lease on

Primrose Cottage being watertight, neither of us wants more trouble with him if we can avoid it.

A crow suddenly flaps over the hedge, cawing loudly. Seconds later, the rest of the flock fly over and land in our field. We both know what this means.

"Someone is in Nine Acre. Keep still!" hisses Ma. She doesn't have to tell me twice.

We strain to hear what's happening on the other side of the hedge, careful not to move a muscle. One of the crows walks up close to us and stands and stares at me. I stare back. Although I poke fun at Ma for her talk about crows, they're clever. Sometimes they really look like they're trying to communicate.

We hear an engine start. A Land Rover.

"Phelps. Sounds like he's leaving," whispers Ma. The vehicle drives off, and we listen until it's gone. The hedge is too high to see over, so we make our way cautiously towards the gate. The crows stay in the field and don't seem bothered, all except the one that was staring at me. He flies onto a branch of the oak near the gate and watches us.

"Coast is clear," Ma says. She's right. The crow would be too smart to stay there if Phelps was still in the field. I read once that crows recognise people individually. And they definitely know about guns.

We clamber over the gate and head quickly up to the place with the best view of Wights Mound, the spot by the hawthorn where Phelps found me this morning. Ma looks down the sloping field and gasps in amazement.

"Arlo, did you see them?"

"Who?"

"Whoever—or whatever—made that circle."

I hesitate slightly. "No. Me and Clay saw some lights, but then I had the seizure."

"There's no way it's manmade."

"Who do you think made it then? Aliens?" I try to keep the edge of sarcasm out of my voice, but sometimes she goes way over the top.

"I don't know. Maybe it's made by beings from *the other place*."

"So you really do think faeries made it?" I'm being openly sarcastic now, mainly to stop myself thinking about the figure I saw staring at me in the dark. It was creepy as hell.

"I didn't say *faeries*. I said beings."

I grin at her. "Sorry. I thought that was the same thing. But seriously, please don't tell anyone else what you think, okay?"

We both turn back to stare at the crop circle again. The wind picks up, and the giant horses look like they're prancing through the whispering barley. For a while neither of us says anything.

I get out my phone and take some photos and a short video, trying to capture the complex beauty of the design, but I know from experience the photos won't do it justice. It's impossible to understand the scale of a circle unless you're close enough to see it or walk in it yourself.

"We should head home," Ma says eventually. "He's bound to be back."

Even as she's saying it, I hear the sound of a powerful engine in the distance. "Sounds like the combine's coming. We'd better step on it. Jaz and Clay are coming over soon. Jaz has made Clay a birthday cake."

We take our last lingering glances at the formation as we edge around Nine Acre to the gate. The crows lift off the ground and land again at the other side of the crop circle. My heart skips a beat at the sight of a girl standing in the field, close to where the crows have landed. I shiver despite the heat.

She's watching us.

She's a way off from where we are, by the bottom gate, but even at this distance I recognise her. It's the same girl, the one with the tattoos. I'm sure it's her. I can't make out her features, but her red hair and the way she dresses are so distinctive. I wonder how long she's been there. Is she following me? This feels like more than coincidence.

I don't say anything to Ma, but it's making me uneasy, the way the girl stands there, unmoving.

We climb back over the gate, careful to avoid the barbed wire. It's only on the way home I wonder if I should have called out a warning to the girl about Phelps coming with the combine. Even though she creeps me out, I wouldn't wish trouble with Phelps on anyone.

BACK IN THE cottage, Ma leans over the banister as she heads up the stairs to fetch her knitting. "Put the kettle on, could you, Arlo? I could do with a cup of tea."

Out in the kitchen, I'm about to fill the kettle when I suddenly freeze. The wooden stake and my surveyor's tape are lying in the centre of the kitchen table. My palms feel clammy and I nearly drop the kettle. How the hell did they get there? Has Phelps been in the house?

Then I rationalise. It can't have been Phelps. He'd have kept them as evidence. The tape's bound to have my fingerprints on it, and in any case, he wouldn't just walk into our cottage.

Clay must have come over while we were out. He probably grabbed the tape when he ran for it last night. Relieved, I go and fill the kettle, wondering if I've got time to drink a cup of tea before he comes back again with Jaz.

Chapter 5

We STAND BY the field gate, looking across to Wights Mound. The steep sides of the ancient monument shimmer in the July heat. Clay clutches a cider bottle to his chest.

"We could climb up there to drink it. Nice view..."

Jaz and I glance at each other. He has to be joking, right?

Jaz pushes her dark curls back from her forehead. "Clay, seriously? Do you want to get us all arrested?"

Clay looks at us blankly. He doesn't get it. "What do you mean? We go up there all the time!"

"Yeah, but only because we ignore all the signs telling us to keep off," I say. "Not to mention the fence we have to climb over."

"Exactly! Nothing has stopped us before. And we've never been arrested."

"But we weren't drinking cider," Jaz says. "And we're all underage. Why risk trouble on your birthday?"

Clay rolls his eyes. "Okay, I hear you. So how about we drink it by the spring?"

Jaz hesitates. "Would that be all right with you, Arlo?"

I don't like the idea, but the fact Jaz seems to care how I feel about it makes me glow inside.

I manage a smile. "Better than being on top of Wights Mound where everyone can see us, I guess."

Clay cheers up right away. "We haven't been near the spring for ages, have we? It'll be fun."

"Whatever. Let's not make too much noise, okay?"

He shrugs. "You worry too much, mate. Why don't you go ahead of us to check no one's around?"

By 'no one', he means Phelps, obviously. After what happened this morning, even Clay recognises it's a problem.

"I'll check instead if you like, Arlo?" Jaz says. "I can say I'm a friend of Hayden's, which gives me an excuse for being there."

"It's fine. I'll go."

I know the way like the back of my hand, so it won't take me a minute. Before we waste any more time debating, I hurry across the road and push my way through a gap under the hedge. It's the route I nearly always use to avoid being seen when I sneak back to the farm.

Once I'm in the woods, I scan the area carefully before heading towards the spring, treading as softly as I can across the dry leaf litter. There was a public footpath through here before, but Phelps got it closed. He convinced the authorities that people might contaminate the spring water.

I stop when I come to the grove. This was Dad's favourite part of the farm. I stand in the clearing in the middle of the ring of ancient trees, breathing in the smell of parched summer grass, swallowing my sadness. I listen out carefully for sounds of farm machinery or people nearby.

The only sound is the chatter of the rooks, high in the canopy above me. I duck cautiously under a low-hanging branch of the hollow oak and come out into the open. The spring glitters in the sunlight, bubbling up gently from the depths. A moorhen breaks cover noisily from the reeds, making me jump. There's no one anywhere in sight, but I suddenly feel uneasy, like I'm being watched. I turn back quickly to go and fetch the others.

JAZ SITS DOWN on the bank by the spring and stretches out her amazingly long legs. I try not to stare. She reaches into her rucksack and pulls out a Tupperware box.

Clay's eyes light up when she opens it. "You brought cake!"

"Birthday cake."

Clay looks stunned. "Did you make it?"

She nods.

"Wow, thanks, Jaz! No one's made me a birthday cake before."

I can believe it. Clay's mum's not really the cake-making type, though at least she remembered it was his birthday this year and got him the bottle of cider.

"I brought some plastic cups too. And a bottle of water."

"Water? Don't be stupid. Pass the cups over."

41

Clay opens the bottle, and the cider fizzes out noisily. He quickly gulps some from the bottle to save wasting it, then pours us all a cupful.

Jaz puts hers down on the grass and flips over to lie on her front. I watch as she reaches out over the bank and dips a slim hand into the water.

She looks up at me and wrinkles her nose. "Does something smell a bit weird around here?"

"Probably Arlo."

"Thanks, Clay."

"You're welcome."

I lean over and sniff the surface of the spring pool. The water is bubbling up from the bottom like it always does, yet it smells different.

"You're right, the water does stink a bit," I say.

Clay grins. "Just drink your cider. Then you won't notice it anymore."

Jaz sits up to take a swig. She pulls a face. "Bloody hell. Clay, this tastes disgusting!"

"Rubbish. It's proper scrumpy, so it's stronger, that's all. Probably had a couple of rats thrown in the brew to give it some kick." He raises an eyebrow at her. "You might find it tastes better with cake, of course."

Jaz takes the hint and cuts us all a slice. We sit in silence for a while, stuffing chocolate birthday cake into our mouths and gulping cider. I notice Clay is much keener than either Jaz or me on the lukewarm scrumpy. It tastes foul. I watch Jaz sneakily tip most of her cupful out on the grass and fill it up again with water. I'd do the same but don't want to offend Clay.

When he's finished his third cup of cider, Clay lies on his back and closes his eyes. Jaz smiles at me and my heart flips a little. I stare down at the spring to hide how I feel.

I breathe in sharply. There's someone else here. I can see a silhouette on the glimmering surface, the outline of someone standing by the pool. I look up quickly to see who it is.

Jaz is sitting in exactly the same position on the bank. Clay is lying on his back. There's no one else in sight.

I look back down at the water. The image is still there. My heart starts racing as I try to make sense of it. The reflection fractures in the ripples of green light, then becomes clearer for a second. The shadow figure flicks something in the air, something that sparkles, or maybe it's the sunlight on the water?

I scan the bank again. There's definitely no one else here. Just us.

Jaz catches my expression. "What's wrong?"

"Thought I saw something in the water."

Clay opens his eyes and turns to smirk at me. "Maybe it's a dead body? That would explain the smell."

Jaz chucks a big crumb of cake at him. "It doesn't smell *that* bad, you idiot!"

I force myself to smile and then look back at the spring. The reflection has gone. Down at the bottom, where the water wells up from the silt, I see something glittering.

"Hang on a minute." I turn my back on them to feel less self-conscious as I quickly pull off my trainers, T-shirt and jeans. I slide into the water in my boxers, trying not to disturb the silt at the bottom.

Clay stares at me, incredulous. "What the hell are you doing, Arlo? How much of my cider have you drunk?"

The water is up to my chest. Once you get over the shock of the cold, it feels okay in here.

I look down to where the water bubbles up from the bottom and spot the small, round shape, flashing gold in the light. I stick my head under and reach down to grab it.

Spluttering back on the surface, I open my hand. I'm holding a tiny coin. The edges are uneven and it looks old. There's a pattern on one side and a picture of a horse on the other. At least, I think it's a horse.

"What have you found?" asks Jaz.

"A coin of some kind."

Clay is suddenly interested. "Let's have a look, mate!"

I hand it to Jaz and take the opportunity to heave myself out of the spring while she and Clay gawp at the coin. I flop down next to them on the bank, wishing I wasn't wearing the stupid Superman boxers Ma bought me.

Jaz doesn't look up. "Arlo, this looks really old. Roman or something maybe!"

"Yes, I thought it looked old too, but surely it can't be. It's too shiny."

She holds the coin up to the light. "I think it's gold. Gold doesn't tarnish. Bring it over to my place next time you come and we can ask Mum what she reckons. She's good on local history stuff."

"Yeah okay, good idea…give it back a minute?"

I hold out my hand, and she places the coin in my palm so I can scrutinise it.

Considering how small it is, the pattern is intricate. A cross pattern of what looks like ears of wheat and two crescent moons, one waxing, one waning. I turn it over and study the horse. There's something about it. I shiver and close my hand quickly.

"Hey, you need to warm up a bit."

"Thanks, Jaz." I shift towards her slightly so I'm sitting in the full sun. I don't want to admit that I'm not really cold. I can't explain.

I open my hand to look at the coin again.

Jaz leans over to look at it with me. "Maybe it was an offering. I heard the Romans made offerings at springs."

"What a waste of money," grunts Clay. "Lucky find, though."

I can't stop staring at the horse. I feel like I've seen it before somewhere, but the memory stays out of reach.

"It doesn't look Roman, somehow."

Clay looks at me blankly. "Since when did you become such an expert?"

45

"I'm not. But I've seen Roman coins in the museum in St. Wylda. They always have some emperor on one side. This looks different, that's all." I hand it back to Jaz and stand up. "Just going to change a minute." I grab my jeans and T-shirt and duck back into the grove.

In the shade under the oak, I take off my wet boxers and pull my jeans and T-shirt back on. I glance over to the spot under the ash tree. I come here sometimes to talk to Dad. A shrivelled rose is still lying there from my last visit. I look away quickly. As I duck back towards the spring, I wonder whether to mention the reflection I saw to the others.

Back on the bank, Jaz looks up, smiles and hands me back the coin. "Take care of it, Arlo. I reckon it could be worth a bit."

The gold glints in the light. I stare at it again for a moment before stuffing it in my jeans pocket. I don't tell them about the shadow in the water. It was probably some kind of mirage, caused by the heat.

"Shall we go?" I suggest. "Don't want to risk being here longer than we have to."

Clay picks up his bottle and stares at the dregs left at the bottom. "Pity we can't go out and make a circle tonight, Arlo. I mean, it is still my birthday…"

"No way can I risk another run-in with Phelps. Besides, we'd never make one as good as the one he's accusing me of making already."

Jaz rolls her eyes. "Honestly, you two are such a pair of nerds. What is it with this crop circle making thing? Isn't it a bit retro?"

I stare at her like she's gone mad. "Jaz, how can you ask? Crop circles are one of the highest forms of art. Ask my mum!"

Clay butts in. "Though his mum still believes they're made by aliens, obviously."

I ignore him. "It takes great skill to create a good crop circle because they're very, very big. Practically field size, in fact."

Jaz grins. "You don't say."

"Clay and I are becoming experts. We're reviving a dying tradition."

"Why can't you go out and paint some graffiti like normal kids?"

Clay snorts in derision. "What, in Tytheford? Don't be stupid, Jaz. Everyone would know it was us! You're just jealous because your mum won't let you come with us."

"In the middle of the night with you two losers? I wonder why!"

I put my trainers back on while Jaz and Clay are bickering and take a last look at the spring, rubbing my arms to hide my uneasiness.

I can't shake the feeling that we're being watched.

Chapter 6

I KNOW I'M DREAMING, but I can't make myself wake up, however hard I try.

There's a fire burning close by me. Too close. I'm lying on the hard ground, on my back. The girl with the tattoos is next to me, dancing by the fire, twirling around faster and faster, her black dress billowing out as she spins. Smoke snakes up from the fire and coils around me as she dances, binding me to the earth. It flows up my nostrils, choking me. I want to call out to her to stop the dance, but I can't find my voice. My heart starts racing as I struggle to wake up, but I still can't pull out of the dream.

Suddenly the girl's not a girl anymore. She's turned into a huge black horse, woven from smoke and shadows.

"I'm your nightmare," she hisses.

I wake up coughing.

My head aches, and the stink of ash stays with me as I try to shake off the dream. Early morning sunlight glows gold through the curtains, and I hear Ma clattering about in the kitchen downstairs.

There actually is a smell of burning in the air, which probably accounts for the dream. At first, I think Ma must have burned the toast again, but it's too strong for that.

A quick glance at my phone tells me it's time to get up for work, but I lie back and stare at the ceiling for a moment. The nightmare was obviously all tied in with what happened yesterday. I'm worried about the seizure and how I stayed unconscious for so long. I think about the eyes staring at me out of the darkness before I passed out and the shadow image in the spring. Were they real—or more symptoms of having seizures? At least I know the coin is real. I pick it up from where I left it by my phone and turn it over in my hand. Then I check my phone again, panic about the time and run to the shower.

MA'S GOT A tray of seedlings on the table when I get downstairs. She's busy consulting her *Organic Guide to Planting by the Moon* and glancing at the calendar.

"Should be a good day for leaf vegetables," she says when she looks up. "Do you think that includes winter broccoli?"

I don't bother to answer and she probably doesn't expect me to. There's still a smell of burning everywhere.

"Smells like Phelps is burning stubble."

"Yes. He started before dawn."

"What on earth is he up to? He hasn't even harvested yet."

Ma shrugs. "Who can say. Law unto himself is Phelps. Still, guess it's better than the smell of pesticide."

I don't have time for breakfast, and anyway, it'll be easy to snag something to eat at work.

"Bye, Ma. Bit late, so best be off. See you later." I give her a quick hug and head out of the door.

UP THE ROAD, I see Ma's friend Mary, our old neighbour, waving at me from her gate at Spring Farm.

She calls out. "Hello, Arlo! Been waiting to catch you. Ronnie called to ask if you'd take more eggs into work with you. Liv wants an extra three dozen today."

Mary is so old she needs a stick to lean on when she walks. She turns and hobbles towards the chicken shed, so I run up to follow her. The hens are all outside, clucking contentedly in their wire pen.

It's cooler inside the shed and smells of straw and ammonia from the chicken dirt. A stack of filled egg trays stands on a shelf next to her record book.

Mary records three dozen eggs in the book and hands me the trays. "Would've brought these up to the gate to save you time, but Ronnie only called just before you came past."

I take the boxes. "That's okay, Mary. At least she'll understand if I'm a bit late for work."

Suddenly she grips my arm, and I nearly drop the eggs. "You take care, young Arlo. There's bad things happening. Your ma agrees with me—and I notice she's started her knitting again. And then this morning, I seen *her* about! Things must be bad when *she's* walking the land again. She looked older last time we seen her, mind. That would be back around the time we brought your poor father in from the grove..."

The way she's staring into my eyes, for a moment I wonder if she's getting dementia. I have absolutely no idea what she's on about, except the last bit about Dad.

"It was the barn, Mary. Not the grove."

She looks confused for a moment, then seems to realise what I've said. "Oh, yes, the barn. Getting forgetful in my old age!"

Her old eyes crease, and she smiles, and everything seems normal again. "You'd best be getting along, young man. No point standing there with your mouth open like a goldfish. Liv's waiting for them eggs."

I've known Mary all my life, and she often comes out with country tales and gossip, but today she's definitely weirder than usual. I make a mental note to ask Ma about her later, to see if she's noticed anything.

I wave goodbye as I head off to work with the eggs, my head now filled with memories of Dad I could do without.

CORN FLAKES CAFÉ peaks in crop circle season, which is now. People still come from all over the world to see the crop formations and visit Neolithic sites in the area, so the café gets packed out.

The season coincides with the summer break from college, so Ronnie and Liv, the couple who own the place, have taken me on full time for a few weeks. I'd probably be hanging out here anyway, along with the rest of my friends in the area, so it's good to get paid for being here. But it's hard work.

By coffee time, Corn Flakes is rammed. As I clear the tables, I keep catching snippets of gossip about some new circle and something about the farmer trying to destroy it by burning the crop. I wonder if it's another one that's appeared on the farm. Phelps can't pin it on me, if so.

I'm surprised to see Tracy Benger, a nosy neighbour of ours in Stanton, having a coffee with her husband. They're not the type that usually comes into Corn Flakes. Worse, they keep staring at me. I know Tracy doesn't like me, and it's making me uncomfortable. I wish they'd leave.

Clay saunters in at about eleven thirty. There's generally a bit of a lull after the coffee drinkers have gone before we start serving lunches, so that's when my friends tend to show up.

He plonks himself down at a table by the window and I go over for a quick catch-up.

"Heard the gossip yet?" he asks.

"Some farmer burnt his crop to destroy a circle? Yeah, everyone's been going on about it."

"Some farmer? It was Phelps, you idiot."

Suddenly I'm interested. "Phelps has set fire to a crop? He won't have much cereal left at this rate. Maybe he thinks it's easier than combining like he did to the one yesterday. Which reminds me, I'll come over later so we can take a closer look at the pics and footage I managed to get with Ma."

"Still can't believe you went with your mother and not me."

"There wasn't time, I told you. We nearly got caught as it was."

I take a pile of plates and cutlery out to the kitchen, where Liv is busy preparing massive bowls of salads ready for the lunchtime orders.

"Can you put them in the dishwasher for me, love?" she asks.

By the time I've stacked all the plates and come out again, Jaz has joined Clay at the table. As soon as Ronnie tells me to take a quick break, I go and join them.

Jaz smiles at me. "You feeling better today, Arlo?"

"Yes, thanks. Weird dreams, but I guess that's not surprising."

"Waking up with a gun in your face can probably trigger the odd nightmare," Clay says.

"There's talk about that circle you saw, by the way." Jaz looks uncomfortable and I wonder what's up. Without thinking, I reach for the tiny coin I put back in my pocket.

"What kind of gossip?"

"Gossip about you. Everyone thinks you made it. I had to put a few people straight in the shop this morning and tell them you didn't."

"Thanks, Jaz."

"Er, but that meant I had to mention the seizure. Hope you don't mind."

No wonder Jaz looks uncomfortable. She's told people I had a seizure and she knows I won't like it. That might also explain why Tracy Benger was in here earlier too. She probably came to see if she could get any gossip about me.

"Weird thing, though."

"What's weird?"

"Apparently, Phelps has burnt the crop, but the image of the galloping horses is still perfect. It shows up in the aerial photos even now it's burnt to the ground."

"No way! The same circle? How come? He'd already combined it! Why bother burning the stubble?"

Clay gets a glazed look in his eyes. "Arlo, we *have* to take a look when you finish work. We need to see this."

"But what if Phelps catches us back there again?"

"I'll come too," Jaz says, like that's going to make everything all right with Phelps or something.

I sigh. "Okay, I'll think about it. Right now I should get back to work."

"That's settled then, mate," Clay says. "We'll meet you back here at three thirty when you finish."

I've been roped in, whether I like it or not.

Back out in the kitchen, I'm loading the dishwasher when I notice a raven standing close to the open back door, looking at me. I'm surprised it's flown down this close. They usually avoid people. I search to find it some scraps, but when I look up again, it's flown off.

CLAY AND JAZ are waiting outside when I finish my shift. We make our way back towards the farm, taking all the back lanes.

After a while, Clay starts moaning. "Why are we walking the long way around?"

"I'm not getting caught again. It's all right for you two."

Jaz looks worried. "Did we push you into this, Arlo?"

I smile. "Just a bit. But got to admit, I'm curious."

We climb a gate and edge our way carefully around the borders of the fields. We cross Oak Field and Five Gates. There's not much cover here and we're far too exposed. I make a mental note of places in the hedge we could squeeze into if we have to.

There's a strong smell of burning in the air, a bit like a campfire put out by rain, yet when we reach the top gate at Nine Acre, all we can see is a crop that's been combined.

"I don't understand," mutters Clay. "I can definitely smell burning. Where's it coming from?"

"Let's get up nearer the viewpoint. Maybe we can see from there."

We walk over the stubble, not bothering to take care where we put our feet or stay in the tramlines anymore. He's destroyed his own crop so there's no point. A whole field of it. Dad would have been appalled at such waste.

We reach the top of the field and look down towards the mound. Clay stands with his mouth open.

Below us the horses are clearly visible. Someone must have set fire to the stubble but only within the circle. The effect of the careful burning is that the charred and blackened stalks of the design stand out starkly against the rest of the field. When I last saw them, the horses looked so alive, prancing and galloping in the wind. Now, with ash blowing over the stubble, they look like something from a horror film but somehow still eerily alive.

Jaz voices exactly what we're all thinking.

"Wow. How the hell did Phelps do that? It must have taken ages."

I can't believe it either. "More to the point, why? Seriously, it can't have been Phelps. The pattern stands out even more than before. Why would he be so stupid?"

Clay finally finds his voice. "People will come for miles to see this. It's AWESOME!"

We stand and stare in silence. A flock of crows flaps over our heads and down the field, circling for a while around the charred and blackened horses. I feel unsettled.

"We should go. We've been here too long."

Even as I'm saying it, we catch the distinctive sound of a Land Rover in the distance. It's heading our way.

We shift as fast as we can down the side of the field towards the gate, but it's too far. We can't get to the gate fast enough to avoid Phelps seeing us.

"In here, quick!" I point out a gap in the hedge where there's just enough cover for all of us to squeeze in.

"Are you serious? That gap's way too small and it's full of thorns."

"Shut up and get yourself in there, Clay." Sometimes he can be so irritating.

We squeeze our way in and peer out through the blackthorn in time to see the Land Rover arrive in the field and pull up, parking at about the spot where we'd been standing. Phelps jumps out, leaving the engine running, and stands looking down the field. Then he gets his mobile out. He shouts into the phone. We can't make out what he's saying above the noise of the engine, but he sounds angry.

"I'm getting cramp. Gotta stretch my leg out," moans Clay.

"You can't! He'll see you." I'm not prepared to risk getting caught in this field again because of Clay's stupid cramp.

Phelps finishes his call and takes another long look down at the burnt horses. Then he scans the field. He doesn't spot us as he climbs back in the Land Rover and turns the vehicle around. I breathe a sigh of relief as he grinds the gears angrily and drives off towards the farm.

Clay's out of the hedge hobbling on his cramped leg way before I reckon it's safe.

"You could have waited a bit. What if he comes back?"

"He won't. And don't be such a wuss."

"That's unfair!" Jaz pulls a few leaves out of her hair and scowls at Clay. "It's Arlo he's gunning for, not you. You can't blame him for being cautious."

"Whatever." Clay grins at us. "You know what, though? Watching Phelps shouting into his phone, I think you're right. I don't reckon he burnt the circle. He looked so angry."

"Yep. I don't think he'd even seen it until now. I was wondering how come he hadn't smelt it earlier, but I suppose the wind's blowing away from the farmhouse."

"Who do you think did it then? My guess would be whoever made it in the first place," Clay says.

"Dunno. But he's probably gone to hook up his plough. There's no way he'll let it stay like that."

Jaz stares at me. "Bet he thinks you did it, Arlo."

A shiver goes down my spine. I'm *sure* he does. I feel it in my bones.

Chapter 7

WHEN WE REACH the lanes, Clay turns towards his place.

"Need to get back. Mum's supposed to be coming home from her boyfriend's to see me and get some food in. Come over later, Arlo, if you can. We can look through the pics and vid you took before the circle was burnt."

"Okay," I say.

Clay looks at Jaz. "Are you coming with me?"

Jaz lives in Tytheford, same as Clay. It's about a mile away, so they usually walk back together, but she shakes her head.

"Think I'll go to Primrose Cottage with Arlo to see Melissa. I need to ask her something. Hope your mum does come back, Clay. You need food."

"Yeah, well. She'll probably give me money to get my own. Come over later with Arlo if you like. She won't be around for long, even if she shows up."

We stand and watch Clay until he turns a corner.

Jaz looks angry. "Poor Clay. I reckon she leaves him on his own way too much." She looks at me. "You don't mind me coming back with you, do you?"

I smile. "Of course not. Just allow for Ma being a bit more crazy than usual. She's started knitting black."

"Oh dear. Your poor mum. She must be worried."

We walk slowly back down to Stanton in the afternoon heat. Ma is out in the cottage front garden looking at the sunflowers again. Bees hum around the giant blooms, stopping every now and then to bury themselves in the pollen. She's standing with her gardening gloves on, watching the bees closely.

"Flowers look amazing, Melissa!" Jaz says.

Ma looks up. "Hello, Jazara love!"

Ma is one of the few people who calls Jaz by her real name and gets away with it. She gives Jaz a hug, then suddenly pauses and looks down the lane. "Quick, let's go inside. There's trouble coming."

"Trouble?" Jaz turns around curiously, as do I. There isn't anyone out in the lane. I'm not sure what Ma's heard, but I feel tense as we head indoors.

Ma and Jaz have just sat down in the front room when I hear the sound of a Land Rover through the open window. I look at Ma. Either her hearing is extraordinary or she's bloody psychic.

"Guess that'll be Phelps," I say.

"Reckon so." She instinctively reaches for her black knitting. I scowl at her, and she quickly hides it down the side of the chair.

"What's going on?" asks Jaz. "How do you know it's..."

She doesn't get to finish the sentence. The Land Rover pulls up outside and Phelps climbs out. Through the window, we watch him stride up the garden path, swatting bees away as he approaches the front door. The bell rings loudly. Even Jaz jumps.

We all look at each other for a second, not sure which one of us should go and answer the door. Then Ma and I both say "I'll go" at exactly the same moment. I'm quicker and get there first.

"You've got some explaining to do, you little git!"

"Good afternoon, Mr. Phelps." I smile ingratiatingly, but in my head I'm bricking it. "Would you like to come in?"

Even before I finish the question, he's pushed past me, straight into the front room. I hover by the door as he stands glaring at my mother and Jaz.

"I want an explanation for your son's behaviour, Melissa Fry. And don't think he'll get away with it. I'm getting you both out of here faster than you can say 'holiday rental.'"

Ma and Jaz stare at him, obviously mystified. I quickly move over to stand by Ma's chair, leaving the front door open in the hope he'll leave again soon.

"What on earth are you talking about?" asks Ma.

Phelps jabs a finger at me. "Ask him. He's responsible." He pushes his ugly face closer to mine. "Did you think you'd get away with setting fire to my field, sunshine? Arson is a criminal offence. I've called the police and told them to come straight over."

"Here?" Ma suddenly looks flustered. "But why?"

Before Phelps can answer, a police car pulls up behind the Land Rover. We can just about make out

and PC Chopra jumping out of the car,
obscured by the tangle of sunflowers by the
garden gate.

The front door's still open, but I go to ask them in.
I'm really glad they're here, which shows how wary I am
of Phelps.

"We got a call," says PC Colenutt. "Thought we'd
better come straight away to make sure everything is all
right?" She looks concerned.

"Come in," I say. I'm hoping Phelps isn't going to be
quite so rude, especially to Ma, now the police are here.

Phelps turns to them as they walk through to the
front room. "I've asked you here so you can arrest that
little bastard again!"

PC Colenutt flinches. "Mr. Phelps, I don't think
there's any need for bad language," she says. "Can you
tell us exactly what you think Arlo has done this time?"

"Ask him. He knows!"

Both police constables look at me expectantly.

"Sorry, I've no idea what he's talking about." It's a lie,
of course, but there's no way I'm admitting to something
I didn't do. It's easier to pretend I haven't a clue.

"He's only gone and burnt his precious crop circle
back in, hasn't he? I already had to combine my barley
too early thanks to his handiwork, but that's not enough
for him, is it?"

"Burnt it back in? What do you mean? How on earth
is that possible?" Officer Chopra sounds genuinely
interested, but probably not in a way Phelps appreciates.

"Who cares how he did it? The shape's back in there, clear as day. Bloody little vandal. I'll have to plough it now. More time and money wasted."

Jaz looks dangerously angry. "That burnt circle is the talk of the village. There's no way Arlo could have done it. He's been at work all day."

For a second, Phelps hesitates. "Of course it was him. Who else? He'll have done it in the dark."

"He was asleep," Ma says. "He couldn't have done. It's an omen, Phelps. It's nothing to do with my son."

Phelps steps up to Ma, and for a moment I think he's going to hit her. She must think so too, as she raises her arms defensively in front of her face.

"If I hear any of your omen talk around the village, there'll be trouble," breathes Phelps menacingly.

"Mr. Phelps, we understand you're angry about your crop, but you have no evidence to support your accusation. You can't go around threatening people like this." PC Colenutt sounds calm enough, but she looks annoyed.

"I can see whose side you're on," snaps Phelps. "This is all about the planning application for the test drilling, isn't it? I'm only trying to support the community here and bring more work to the area. I don't need this kind of protest vandalism stuff going on and neither does the rest of the local community. You should lock him up."

Glancing at Jaz, I see her eyes are blazing and she's clenched her fists. I'm worried she's actually going to hit Phelps.

"Your plans benefit nobody but yourself, and you know it." She spits the words at him. "You're planning to wreck the most beautiful countryside, a heritage site, purely for personal gain."

"Rubbish. And what's it to you, anyway? Maybe you should go back to Africa where you came from and leave us to run our countryside the way we want!"

PC Chopra breathes in sharply and I notice his eye twitch. But before either police officer can say anything, Ma finds her tongue.

"I'd thank you to get out of my house right now, Norman Phelps. You're not welcome here."

"Not your house for much longer, if I can help it," crows Phelps. He turns and stomps out through the front door without another word. As the door closes behind him, the tightness in my chest eases up a little.

The two police officers glance at each other briefly, then PC Chopra marches outside to catch up with Phelps before he drives off.

PC Colenutt looks apologetic. "We need to follow this up," she says, smiling at Ma. "If Mr. Phelps comes back here again, please ring us straight away, won't you?"

She hurries out after her colleague. We watch her through the window as she catches up with PC Chopra. Their conversation with Phelps looks increasingly animated. From the snatches of it we catch, it's clear they want Phelps to show them the damage. After their heated debate, Phelps gets back in his Land Rover and drives off, the police car following close behind.

Jaz looks worried. "He can't really get you out of the cottage, can he?"

"No," Ma answers. "That's one thing Michael made sure of before...well, you know."

Jaz just nods. Nobody ever says it out loud. Ma means before Dad hanged himself in the barn, when he realised he'd lost the farm forever.

Not for the first time, I'm angry with him for worrying more about the farm than about us. And then, as usual, I feel guilty about getting angry. He'd tried his best.

I sit down heavily on the sofa. "I hope you're right, Ma. I didn't make the circle, but I can't prove it. Is there anything in the legal documents Dad had made about what happens if we cause damage to the place? Would we still be entitled to live here?"

Just for a second, I see a shadow of doubt cross her face.

"You're innocent, Arlo. You didn't cause any damage. He can't prove anything." But without thinking, Ma's picked up the knitting again.

Jaz is determined to be upbeat. "Don't worry, Melissa. Phelps won't want any bad publicity right now. He needs planning permission for the test drilling to start. Trying to evict a widow from her home will bring him a lot of bad press. My mum would make sure of it!"

Jaz sounds so positive. I hope she's right.

But there's one thing I know for sure about Phelps. He doesn't give a damn what anyone else thinks.

Chapter 8

At Clay's, we go through all the photos I took of the horse circle before it was combined. Even Jaz is impressed. Seeing it again gives me goosebumps.

"Hang on, let's run it through my laptop," Clay says. "There's nothing else on the internet from before it was burnt, except that blurry picture up on the board in Corn Flakes."

"I know. Ma and I are probably the only ones who saw it."

On the bigger screen, I spot something I hadn't noticed before. I breathe in sharply. Is that her?

"Hang on a minute. Can you freeze frame, Clay? Go back a bit. I think I saw that girl from outside the café—the one with the tattoos. She was in the field. I was worried Phelps might catch her."

Clay goes back over the section in slow motion and freezes the film on the blurry figure.

"What are you talking about, you moron? It's a bird! Are you going blind or something?"

I look again. Clay zooms in. That's so weird. I would have sworn it was the girl, but Clay's right. It's a raven. The way it seems to be staring at the camera is creepy.

"Well, she was definitely there. The other side of the field from me and Ma."

"Yeah, right. Sure it wasn't just this bird on the film?"

I know Clay's only poking fun at me, but I feel uncomfortable. Did I mention the girl to Ma? She must have seen her too. I can't remember. I'll ask her later.

Jaz changes the subject. "Oh, Arlo, I keep meaning to tell you. Mum asked an archaeologist friend of hers about that coin you found. The woman reckoned it sounded like a Celtic coin, but she'd need to see it to be sure. So you were right. It's not Roman, it's even older."

"How old?" asks Clay.

"Not sure. But she said the Celts were around when the Romans arrived here, so must be more than two thousand years." She glances at me. "Which means it's also rare and probably valuable. Mum's friend suggested you take it into the museum, but if you did that, you'd have to say where you found it."

"No way. We were on Phelps's land."

She grins at me. "That's what I figured. You better hang on to it then."

"Thanks." I don't tell them it's still in my jeans pocket. "Let's take another look at the circle," I say.

JAZ'S MUM CALLS a bit later, and she has to leave. After she's gone, I stay and chat to Clay for a while until I notice it's nearly dusk. "I should go home too or Ma will start worrying. The days are getting shorter."

"That's good, Arlo. Shorter days mean longer nights, giving us more time to make a good circle."

I pull a face. "It's hard right now. For a start, we can't make one on Phelps's land. I don't want to give him any more grounds for getting us out of the cottage."

Clay doesn't say anything for a moment. We both know Phelps's farm covers our best fields. We like to make circles you can see from Wights Mound. It's like our signature trademark. The horse circle has kind of blown that for us.

I pick up my hoodie but don't put it on. It's still hot and sultry.

"You working tomorrow?" he asks.

I nod. "Yeah. Coming in?"

"Okay. Usual time. I'll see if Jaz is around too. I expect you'd like to see her."

"Don't start on the me and Jaz thing, okay?"

He grins at me.

As I leave, I'm still mulling it over.

OUT ON THE road, the dusk is gathering. A blackbird calls out in alarm as I pass and flits over a garden hedge. The scent of honeysuckle is heavy in the air. Suddenly I sense someone watching me, and I look around. My heart sinks.

It's that girl again. How come she keeps turning up wherever I go? She's standing by a field gate down the road from Clay's house. I can't avoid walking past her.

As I get closer, she keeps staring straight at me, same as last time. It's really disconcerting.

"Hello," I say, to break the tension.

She doesn't reply, just smiles. Even in this half-light, I can see how green her eyes are. Her black dress is low cut, and her tattoos are such an intense blue, I'm not sure if they're real or transfers. She looks too young to have that much tattoo work, whatever Clay said about her age.

The silence makes me cold, despite the heat. I try talking to her again.

"Seen you around a bit the last few days. Are you staying nearby?"

"I live here." Maybe I'm tired, but I hardly saw her lips move, and it feels like her voice came from somewhere in my head. She still doesn't take her eyes off me.

Although she's unnerved me, I feel drawn towards her and can't stop myself stepping closer. It's not a good feeling. More like a moth to a candle.

"But I've only seen you over the last few days." There's no way I wouldn't have noticed someone like her if she lives around here.

"I've been here all the time. You just didn't notice me before. I've seen you, though. Your name's Arlo. Am I right?"

She knows my name? I stare at her, startled. In the dusk, her eyes shimmer like iridescent beetle wings. Must be contact lenses, but I can't see the edges. They look so strange, I want to reach out and touch her to make sure she's real.

"Go on," she says.

I feel embarrassed. "What do you mean?"

She lets her hand drop from the top of the gate where it was resting and walks right up to me. She smells like the honeysuckle on the night air. A strong, heady scent.

Now she's closer, I'm transfixed by the pattern of her tattoos. They spiral up her arms and across her collarbone. Woven into the design are birds and animals, intricately drawn, almost alive in the detail. I realise I'm staring at her chest to follow the pattern. My face grows hot.

"Touch me," she says. "Make sure I'm real. That's what you want, isn't it?" A hint of mocking laughter resonates in her voice. A shiver runs down my spine. She's seriously weird.

"I didn't say that."

She moves in so close I nearly fall over. "I've seen you working in that café. Arms like yours, you should still be working the land, by rights."

She brushes my arm lightly with her fingers. So she *is* real. My skin feels like it's burning where she touched me.

"Did you find the tape?"

"Tape? Oh! On the kitchen table? Was that you?"

She smiles.

I'm dumbstruck. She's actually been in my house. That's off-the-scale creepy.

"But how...?" My voice trails off. I'm so confused, I don't know what to say. This whole encounter is surreal, and I get the feeling she's playing with me. Some game where I don't know the rules.

"Meet me tomorrow morning, Arlo. We need to talk. At the old yew tree in the graveyard."

My neck hairs prickle in alarm. "I can't tomorrow, early shift at work," I say, panicking. I don't want this girl to think I'm going on a date with her. Ever.

"Day after then. I'll be waiting for you. An hour before dawn."

She looks over my shoulder, and I turn to see what she's looking at. It's Jaz. Suddenly I'm really embarrassed and wonder how long she's been there.

"Oh, hi, Jaz. I didn't see you!"

"I noticed."

I feel myself blushing again. "I thought you'd gone home."

Hell. I've probably made it sound even worse. I turn to introduce the girl to her, but she's gone. Looking through the gate, I see she's almost halfway back across the field. I can't believe she moved so fast.

"So what's her name?" Jaz sounds upset. "I thought you said you didn't know her?"

"I don't! I don't even know her name. Didn't ask."

"You seemed to be getting on well. Weird tattoos. But she's kind of attractive, I guess. Fast mover."

I can't look at Jaz, and I don't know what to say. It's not what she thinks.

Neither of us speaks for a moment, then she breaks the silence. "I'm going back to Clay's. I left my book in his room by mistake."

I finally find my tongue. "I'll wait for you. Be good to walk you home before I head off. It's getting dark."

She holds my gaze for a moment before turning towards Clay's house.

"If you like," she says.

Chapter 9

I'M RUNNING LATE for work. I'm on the breakfast shift and Corn Flakes opens at eight. Not only that, Ronnie wants me to collect the eggs from Spring Farm again on the way in.

To help save time, Ma puts some bread into the toaster for me, and I blunder around the kitchen trying to find the butter and jam and grabbing a plate from the cupboard. It feels like a storm's brewing and the humidity is giving me a headache.

Suddenly, the cupboard starts to shake. For a second, I think I'm hallucinating, but then it feels like the whole house is vibrating and there's a deep rumbling sound far below our feet. I lose my balance and drop the plate. It smashes onto the flagstone floor under the juddering table.

Ma and I look at each other.

"Ma? What on earth was that?"

"Maybe Phelps has started test drilling already? Funny, I thought I felt something like this a few days ago, but not as strong."

"Test drilling? It felt like an earthquake!" I'm angry, not least because the plate I dropped is the one with poppies on, which always reminds me of Dad.

"Well that's Phelps's problem. The farm's not ours any more, Arlo."

"But he hasn't even got planning permission!"

"That wouldn't stop him. I'd better pop out and check the beehives are okay."

Ma opens the back door and takes her mug of tea out to the garden. She probably wants to hide how upset she is. Whatever she says, the farm still feels like it's ours. Phelps might own it, but my family worked it for generations, and it's part of us. It's in our blood.

I pick up the pieces of plate and wonder briefly if I could glue them back together, but there are too many fragments, so I put them in the bin along with the toast Ma made me. I don't feel like eating it now.

I lean out of the back door to say goodbye to Ma, who's standing at the bottom of the garden among the lavender bushes by the beehives. The bees are buzzing around her in distress, and I can hear her murmuring to them. I don't call out. Bees are sensitive. I don't want to disturb her efforts to calm them down.

WORK IS MENTAL. It amazes me how many people want cooked breakfasts when it's so hot outside, and the kitchen at Corn Flakes is like the inside of hell.

Clay comes in about ten thirty and manages to find a stool at the counter to sit on. He watches me making up an order of three mochas and a cappuccino without saying a word, but I can almost hear him thinking.

"Go on then. Spit it out. What's eating you?"

74

"Spoke to Jaz earlier. She'll be here soon."

"That's nice." I add a powdering of chocolate onto the mochas.

"Nice? What's going on with you? How come you were trying to get with some crazy old woman after you left mine last night?"

"I was *not* trying to get with her. And she's not old."

"What's her name, anyway?"

"Dunno. I told Jaz. Didn't even ask, okay?"

I'm upset about what happened, and I don't want to talk to Clay about it. I really wish I hadn't agreed to meet up with the girl again tomorrow.

"Too busy trying to feel her up?"

"I was not trying to feel her up! Is that what Jaz said?"

"No. But she said you were practically snogging. She made a joke of it, but I think she's upset, Arlo. What's with you?"

"It's not what you think, so leave it out! If you must know, right now, I'm much more worried about what's going to happen if Phelps tries to evict me and Ma from Primrose Cottage."

He looks at me for a moment without saying anything, then sighs. "Okay. Whatever. Will you get a break soon? I could kill for a coffee."

"Give me a minute. I'll just take this order over."

I walk off with the tray of drinks, thinking hard. Although part of me wishes the girl would go away, I have to admit I'm curious about her. Like, how come she knew the surveyor's tape was mine? The only explanation I can come up with is that she was out in the field that night. And if she was there, she must have made the horse circle—or at least know who did.

But I don't want to ruin any chance I have with Jaz by trying to find out. I know I should just stand the girl up tomorrow and make things easier for myself.

As soon as I offload the drinks, three men at the next table hold me up ordering cooked breakfasts. They're all wearing green boiler suits with yellow logos on the front that say 'EcoGas'. Not our usual type of customer. There's a van that matches their uniforms out in the car park. They must be passing through.

Jaz walks in and sits down with Clay. I attempt a smile in her direction. It probably looks more like I've strained a muscle.

Ronnie is delighted that she's got so many customers in, but when I make a joke about the men in the green boiler suits finding themselves in hippy central, she scowls.

"Reckon they're something to do with Phelps's mining application," she says.

"No way! Really? So what's EcoGas?" For a moment, I'm confused.

"He leafleted the whole of Tytheford yesterday, apparently. There's a copy on the board if you want to take a look. Shale gas extraction. That's what he wants permission to test drill for. Greedy git."

"Is that the same as fracking? Surely he won't get planning for that around here? I thought fracking was banned now!"

"Yes, it is, but if there's enough profit involved, the Government are bound to make exceptions. They always do. Look at that fancy high-speed rail track they're building through ancient forest. Don't underestimate Phelps either, Arlo, He's on the local council and he always gets what he wants, but we can talk about it later. Go and check how Liv's getting on with the breakfasts, could you? She probably needs a hand."

BY THE TIME I get a break, Clay and Jaz have managed to grab a window table, so I join them. I get the impression that Jaz is avoiding looking at me.

"Have you heard what Phelps is planning?" I ask.

"Of course. What do you think we've been talking about?" she snaps.

So Jaz is angry. I get it. A small part of me is secretly pleased that she cares, but mostly I don't know what to say.

"Jaz is starting a local protest movement with her mum. We want you to help run it," Clay says.

"Guess I can help behind the scenes. Can't afford any more trouble with Phelps right now, though."

"Arlo, Phelps isn't just destroying the farm but all the countryside around here! Did you feel that earth tremor everyone's talking about this morning? I bet that was Phelps starting up testing already. I mean, who are

77

those guys?" Jaz points to the men in the boiler suits. Fortunately, the loud trance music covers the fact she's practically shouting.

I try to say something sensible. "What kind of protest are you planning?"

"Something to rally the whole of Tytheford—and Stanton. It's not going to be easy, which is why we need you to help organise protests with us."

"So long as I don't have to talk in public."

Jaz's eyes flash with anger. "What's wrong with you? Don't you care about the mining?"

"Of course I care," I hiss.

"Well, you've got a funny way of showing it."

"That's not fair. I'm already in trouble with Phelps. He's threatening to chuck me and Ma out of the cottage."

"Which means you should be at the forefront of the protest movement, obviously!"

I stare at her. She's perfectly serious. Is this all because she's angry about last night? If so, I'm flattered, but she's still being unreasonable.

"It's my *home*, Jaz!"

"Exactly, and if he tries to evict you, it'll make national headlines. Bully landlord, forcing poor widow and son from their home over fracking protest—that kind of thing. Phelps won't want that kind of negative publicity, so it won't happen. This is the way to *keep* your home, idiot. And draw attention to his proposed mining operation at the same time."

Clay plays with his teaspoon. "She's got a point, Arlo."

Fortunately, Liv calls me back to the kitchen so I don't have to answer either of them.

It's not as if they're the ones who'd be thrown out of their homes. It'd be me and Ma. And Primrose Cottage isn't just any home.

It's the one Dad thought he'd secured for us to live in. They should know what that means to me.

Chapter 10

BY THE TIME I leave work, I'm hot and tired. I probably don't smell too good either. I need to go home to shower and change before going up to Tytheford.

Jaz made me agree to talk more about organising the protest movement. We're meeting at Clay's as usual because it's easier. His mum's never in, and things are chaotic at Jaz's, especially since Laurel, her baby sister, was born.

Back home, Ma's in the kitchen, making up ointments of some kind. She wipes her hands on her apron as soon as I come in.

"Guess you've heard the gossip about Phelps mining for shale gas?" she says.

"Yes. Jaz wants to organise a protest with her mum."

"Good for her! I hate to think what your father would have said about it all." She picks up another jar, then puts it down again. "Now you're back, I'll put the kettle on before I pot up any more comfrey balm."

She usually avoids mentioning Dad, so I know she's upset. As she reaches for the mugs, she's still going on about it.

"I was up at Spring Farm earlier. Mary thinks the same—all the signs point to trouble. There's a storm brewing, no mistake. We don't like it at all, Arlo."

When Ma and Mary talk about 'signs', they mean stuff like birds behaving oddly or bees being aggressive, not the obvious stuff like the minor earthquake this morning that was probably caused by Phelps starting test drilling without planning. Dad used to find it exasperating.

I'm about to ask Ma if she's noticed Mary being weirder than usual recently when she yells out in surprise and drops the kettle. The clattering echoes through the house.

"What on earth...? You okay, Ma?"

"A flame just came out of the tap!"

Crap. She's totally lost it. I go over to the sink.

Ma looks at me and turns the tap on again. For a fraction of a second, I think I see a thread of bright, green light flowing out with the water, but then it's gone. Ma keeps running the tap, and we stare at the water for a few moments.

"It's just water, Ma. You imagined it."

She turns the tap off. "I saw it, Arlo. Really I did! A green flame coming out of the tap!"

Green. The colour I glimpsed too. But I don't tell her. We must have imagined it.

I get her to sit down while I make the tea. As we sip our mugs at the kitchen table, Ma keeps staring at the tap.

"I'm off out to Clay's with Jaz in a bit. Will you be okay?"

"I haven't gone gaga, Arlo. I'll be fine. I've got to finish potting the comfrey, then I'm making a remedy for Mary's chest cough. Give Jazara my love, won't you?"

She gives me a meaningful look. She's as bad as Clay when it comes to Jaz and me.

But I can tell she's still worried. As I leave, I see her pick up her black knitting.

JAZ INSISTS WE sit and watch a film about the dangers of fracking, which is mostly documentary footage from America. I feel like she's pressuring me to get involved in her campaign. Fortunately, her mum is keen to front it for us, which is good news.

On the screen, a woman holds a lighter close to her tap and next thing, it's as if she's set fire to the water. Suddenly I'm interested.

"Can you play that bit back again, Jaz?"

"What bit?"

"The woman with flames coming out of her tap. Ma said she saw a flame earlier."

"*What*? And you hadn't thought of mentioning it until *now*?"

"I didn't think it was relevant."

"How could you possibly think it wasn't relevant? How stupid are you?"

Jaz is rarely that blunt. She must still be upset.

"Ma only saw one flame, and it was green. And she didn't set light to it like that woman in the film did."

Clay coughs. "To be fair, we're talking about Arlo's mum, Jaz. Arlo probably thought she was seeing fairy lights again or something."

I'm torn between being glad Clay's sticking up for me and irritated with him for poking fun at Ma.

Jaz pulls a face. "Sorry. I went a bit over the top, didn't I? But this is serious, Arlo. If she really did see flames, you need to do something! Hang on, there's more about it further on in the film. I'll show you—"

She's interrupted by the doorbell ringing downstairs. "Expect that's Hayden. I'll let him in." Jaz scurries out of the door.

I turn to Clay. "Did she say *Hayden*? Why has she invited him to your place?"

Clay shrugs.

I can't let it go. "She's never invited him here before. I didn't think they were that close."

Clay sighs. "Look, I'm not too happy about it either, but you can't blame her. Especially since she knows you're getting with that whacko woman."

"I'm not 'getting with that whacko woman'. We were talking, that's all."

"Are you sure that's all you were doing?"

Before I have time to answer, Jaz comes back in with Hayden. He blinks nervously at Clay and smiles at me. I'm confused. I'm also worried. Why on earth has Jaz invited *him*?

"Hayden wants to see the film too. Let's start at the beginning again, shall we?"

"Do we have to?" I say.

They all look at me like I'm a spoilt teenager.

Jaz purses her lips. "You're the one who told us your mum saw flames coming out of your taps."

"Seriously?" says Hayden, staring at me. He looks genuinely concerned. I feel bad. Hayden and I were good friends once, and I guess what happened probably wasn't his fault.

"Ma thought she saw a green flame coming out of the tap earlier. She could have been mistaken," I mumble. "I mean, I didn't see it."

I don't know why I'm lying. But what I saw wasn't the same. It reminded me more of the lights flickering over the ground in the field that night, and I'd rather forget the whole experience.

"Well, let's watch the film and we can talk about it afterwards," Jaz says.

When the film gets back to the bit with the woman setting fire to the water with her lighter, the flames are yellow. Jaz puts it on hold.

"Is that what happened, Arlo?"

"No, Ma didn't set fire to it like that. She said she saw the flame when she turned on the tap. And it was green."

I'm beginning to wish I hadn't said anything about it. It makes Ma sound crazy, and half the village thinks that about her already.

Hayden looks at me curiously through the thick lenses of his glasses. "Um, maybe try setting fire to it, Arlo, like in the film. Could be the gas has copper particles in it or something."

"Thanks," I say. It comes out sounding ungrateful and spiky, but I don't care. I still don't understand why Jaz has invited him.

Clay doesn't say anything. He probably wouldn't say anything about Ma in front of Hayden. Neither of us have seen much of him since his dad sent him to the posh school and told me to stay away from the farm. I was hurt, and Clay took my side. Jaz is the only one who made any effort to stay friends.

We watch the rest of the film, which is pretty grim viewing. People getting mystery illnesses and cancers they believe are caused by fracking poisoning the ground and the water; landscapes laid waste by the greed of the powerful mining companies.

None of us says anything for a minute when we reach the end. Hayden looks at me.

"Arlo, I know it's difficult after what happened the other day, and you're probably wondering why I'm here..."

"Yes, I am." I sound rude, even to me. Hayden goes deep red with embarrassment and Jaz glares at me.

Hayden stutters slightly when he answers. "Look, I'm not like my f-father, you know that. I actually care about the farm and the land. And I hate that Dad has

got involved with EcoGas. Anyway, I'd better be going."
He stands up and smiles at Jaz. She gives him a hug.

"Thanks for coming—see you soon," she says.

I feel a pang of envy and I'm not proud of myself.

"Sorry if I seem a bit off," I mumble. "Long day."

Hayden flashes me a smile of gratitude, and I feel
even worse. It's not his fault his father's a bully.
Or that Jaz likes him. Or that his dad bought the farm
and banned me from visiting.

As soon as he's gone, Jaz has a proper go at me.

"So it's all right for you to be all precious about
helping the protest movement because you're worried
about Phelps, but Hayden isn't allowed to hang out
with us? For goodness' sake, Arlo! Phelps is his *father*!
The least you could do is try and be nice to him."

"Okay, okay! I said I was sorry. Look, I've got to go
too now. I'm a bit worried about Ma."

Jaz scowls, then hugs me, if a little grudgingly. "See
you tomorrow then. We'll come up to the café on your
break. I want to see if those EcoGas people make a habit
of going there. Maybe we can find out more about what's
going on."

She's trying to be nice to make up for snapping at
me, and I feel bad that I haven't mentioned meeting the
tattooed girl again tomorrow. I replay what Clay said
about the girl being a whacko. If I'm lucky, she's so crazy,
she won't even show up.

Chapter 11

I CAN'T SLEEP. I lie in the dark staring at the window. The curtains are drawn, and there's a twig from the apple tree tapping on the glass like someone knocking to come in. The wind must have picked up.

I get out of bed in the dark and go to the window to see if I can break off the twig. I pull back the curtain and nearly jump out of my skin. A barn owl stares back at me from the other side of the glass, then lifts off the windowsill and glides into the night. The whole encounter only lasts a second, but my heart's pounding as I climb back into bed. I check my alarm again. I've set it for four in the morning. I should get to the old yew tree by four thirty; the sun doesn't rise until five.

As the night wears on, I can't stop thinking about everything that's happened. I must be stupid going to meet this girl. I'm having enough problems with Jaz as it is. There's no way I can sleep. I'm worrying too much.

The alarm starts beeping. It's four o'clock. Time to get up. I'm so tired, I wonder for the zillionth time if I can get away with not turning up. The whole arrangement was the girl's idea, and I'm sure she's more trouble than she's worth. But even as I'm thinking it, I'm pulling on my jeans.

THE LANES ARE quiet in the darkness. As I head towards the graveyard, I look up at the fading stars, Venus still sparkling brightly in the east. A barn owl flies ghost-like overhead, silently swooping over the hedge and across the fields, and I wonder if it's the same barn owl I saw earlier. As I reach the crumbling chapel building, the first glimmers of dawn are approaching.

I sit under the yew, staring into the mist that hangs over the fields, watching for any sign of the girl. Surreal shapes of trees loom above the mist around me, and I pull my jacket tighter as the chill touches my skin. It's still early August, but there's a taste of autumn in the air.

The sun is a good hour off rising, but the birds have already started calling. I hear a skylark lift out of the field, its song sharpening the morning sky.

After a while, I consider going back home. Clay is right. The girl is so off the planet, she makes my mother look normal. I close my eyes and rest my back against the rough bark of the yew tree.

A blackbird calls an alarm close by, and I snap my eyes open. The girl is there, kneeling in front of me, staring at me with those spring-green eyes.

"Oh, hi! I didn't hear you coming."

She doesn't say hi or anything back. She stands and reaches for my hand.

"Come with me, Arlo. I need you to understand what's happening here."

In the early morning air, she sounds strangely like she's talking in an echo chamber. I don't want to go anywhere with her and wish I hadn't come to meet her. I try stalling.

"Um, What's your name? Sorry, I forgot to ask before—"

She seems to think for a moment before she answers. "You can call me Andraste."

"Andraste? That's, um…unusual…" I sound like an idiot.

"It's an old name."

"I've never heard it before."

"No. You wouldn't have."

This girl is hard work. I'm going to tell her I need to get home. I stand up, and she immediately turns towards the mist.

"Follow me," she says. Then she starts running. I hesitate, thinking this is my opportunity to leave, but it would be incredibly rude not to say anything first. I run to catch up, but she's moving so fast, I'm lagging further and further behind. This is worse than going running with Jaz, and Jaz is a really good runner. It doesn't seem like it's any effort for Andraste, even wearing that long black dress and with her hair all flying loose behind her as she runs. Every so often, she turns her head to check I'm still following but doesn't slow down for a second.

"Wait a minute!" I shout. I'm hot and irritable. "I can't keep up with you! What's the hurry?"

She doesn't hear me, or maybe chooses not to, and keeps racing ahead at a relentless pace. All I can do is run after her, stumbling over the clods and dodging the sarsen stones around the borders of the fields with hardly enough time to draw breath.

It feels like we've been running forever, and I'm on the verge of leaving her to get on with it, when she stops short and turns to me. The sense of relief at a chance to breathe is overpowering.

The sun is only just rising, so we can't have been running as long as I thought, but I'm sweating horribly and wheeze in great lungfuls of air after all the exertion. She stands looking at me, seemingly unaffected by the effort, not a hair out of place in that mass of red curls that fall to her waist.

"We're here," she says, unsmiling. I look around. Ice knots form in my gut. There's something so different about this place, for a second I can't work out what it is. Then it hits me. The birdsong is deafening, a full-on spring dawn chorus. The May blossom's out on the thicket of hawthorn trees that surround us, yet it's August. The birds should be quieter now, and haw berries should be forming on the trees.

My mouth goes dry. There are no fields here, just wild woodland, no paths. Where the hell are we? Before I can ask, she moves towards me. Her green eyes flicker like pools of light in a stream. I really wish I was back home.

She moves suddenly, reaching out and pushing me hard on the shoulder. I stumble backwards and open my mouth in protest, but she puts her finger to her lips, gesturing silence.

"Be quiet and look. See where you are."

I turn away from her, closing my eyes to stop the feeling that I'm falling, but it makes it worse. I wobble so much I have to sit down to try and clear my head.

I open my eyes again. The woodland here is so thick, unmanaged, like no one's ever been here, and the flowers, the birdsong, the scents in the air—everything tells me it's spring when I *know* it's high summer. I blink. Nothing changes. There are no woods like this anywhere around Wights Mound. It all feels wrong, out of place, and I feel sick.

I take a few deep breaths, trying to take control of my fear. Glancing around, I get an uncomfortable sensation we're being watched. Scrutinising the space between the trees, I see shapes moving quickly, silently.

A huge dog pushes out from the undergrowth and paces slowly towards us, staring at me with amber eyes, teeth bared, panting. Then another appears. And another. They're not like any dogs I've seen before. My heart hammers faster as my mind struggles to come up with any breed of dog that looks that much like wolves. I can't think of one. I spring to my feet, ready to run.

I have no idea what's happening, but I'm frozen to the spot. Every instinct is telling me to run, but somehow I can't. Andraste whistles softly, and the wolf-dogs circle us.

Everything is going dark and sounds magnify to full volume in my head. I crouch, saliva filling my mouth. I'm going to throw up. Kneeling, I drop my head lower, but it's too late. The last thing I remember is a strong smell like dog breath as I fall to the ground.

I WAKE WITH a start. The sun is high. I try to make sense of what I'm looking at. A foot right by my face, tattoos spiralling all over it. Andraste.

I close my eyes against the explosion of pain in my head. After a few moments, I risk opening them again. I'm lying on the ground, and Andraste is standing next to me. I feel so weird, like I did when I woke with Phelps's gun in my face, as if I'm recovering from a seizure. I focus on the blue tattoos. They form an almost magical web over her skin.

She looks down at me. "It's late, Arlo. It's not good for you to stay here too long." She moves a hand, palm down, over the top of my head, as though she's trying to sense something without touching me. She frowns. "This visit has taken its toll. We need to talk, but it will have to be another time. You should go back now."

With difficulty, I get up off the ground but stay on hands and knees as I look around to get my bearings. I try to work out how long we must have run to get to wherever this is. There are no hedges or boundary walls to form the landscape. Just forest. And a slope. We're on a hill. I stand up quickly, head spinning, a cold sensation in my stomach.

"Where are we?"

"Think about it later, Arlo. Head back now, before it's too late."

Suddenly I remember work. What time is it, for goodness' sake? I look up at the sky again. Must be at least nine thirty by now—how long was I unconscious? My eyes ache in the light.

Nothing feels right. This place, Andraste, those wolves—*were* they wolves?—the weirdness of it all is overpowering.

Andraste stands close to me for a moment, and I catch the smell of honeysuckle. I stare at her, wondering who she really is. She looks wild, and close up, I've no idea how old she is either. On top of everything, I'm haunted by a sharp sadness, a feeling of intense loss, yet I've no idea what I've lost.

"It's time to run, Arlo. Head that way and don't look back!" Andraste points to a track in the dense woodland. I hesitate. I have no idea where I am.

"You'll have to trust me. Just run. If you keep running, soon you'll know where you are. Remember, don't look back. Things will be clearer next time."

Next time? Does she seriously expect me to meet her again? No way!

Everything feels so unreal, I'm worried I'm losing my mind. I'm trying hard not to freak out, and my stomach's knotted with fear.

I glance at Andraste, then turn and start walking slowly, like a sleepwalker, in the direction she pointed. I begin to feel a bit better as I walk, so I gradually pick up speed and break into a jog. The track widens, but I keep my eyes on the ground, focusing on putting one foot in front of the other, unthinking, remembering her words, *don't look back.*

I pick up my pace, and soon I'm running, racing as fast as I can, trying to blot all thought out and praying that when I stop, everything will be all right again. If I keep going, maybe I can stop thinking, constantly trying to work out what this place is, who Andraste is, how different she is.

At last, I look up.

I don't understand. In front of me, a few trees stand on the edges of a ditch close to a hedgerow. Only minutes ago, I'd swear on my life there was thick forest here. I slow to an easy jog while I try to make sense of it all. Then suddenly I see Wights Mound down the slope in front of me, and everything slots back into place. I know exactly where I am. I stop and stand still, chest heaving with the exertion of running. The sight of the Mound lifts my spirits, and my panic slowly subsides.

I turn back to look where I've come from, and for a second, I think I'm going to black out. I catch a glimpse of thick forest I know isn't there before my mind switches off like someone changed the TV channel and I'm scanning the familiar landscape in front of me. I try to figure out how I could possibly have felt so lost in an area I know so well. This land is so much a part of my life, it's wired into my DNA. I steel myself and turn to look behind me again.

This time, the fields and boundaries span out on the hills the way they always have. I see the outcrops of trees where the barrows lie on top of the hills, and the exposed chalk of the downs glinting white in the sunlight. There is no forest. There is nowhere here a forest could grow.

I'm sure my confusion is somehow tied in with Andraste telling me not to look back. She must have planted ideas in my head. Why else would I see a forest that isn't there?

I try to shake off the feeling and pull myself together, but the light's still wrong. My shift is supposed to start at ten today, and I haven't even called to say I might be late. I start running again, turning down towards Wights Mound, back to where I belong.

Chapter 12

I SEE MA OUT in the front garden as I hurry down the lane. Jaz is with her. I wonder why she's there.

Ma looks up and sees me, and her face lights up.

"Arlo! Oh, thank goodness!" As soon as I'm close enough, she grabs hold of me in a tight hug. Then she lets go and starts shouting at me.

"Where on earth have you been? I've been so worried about you!"

No pretence, she's seriously angry, which makes me anxious again. Is this about me?

"Sorry, Ma, don't know what happened to the time..."

She stares at me in confusion. "So where have you been? I even called the police to check you hadn't had an accident or something."

I'm getting annoyed now. Why has she involved the police? And why is Jaz looking so angry with me? "Seriously, Ma, I don't understand. What's the problem? I've only been gone a few hours. Why all the panic?"

Ma turns on me. "A few hours? What do you mean, a few hours? Ronnie called for you from the café this morning—up to that point, I thought you were at work. Where were you?"

"I went for a walk first thing because I couldn't sleep."

"A walk? What, you've been walking all day?"

All day? My whole body starts to shake as I take in what she's saying. The angle of the light… It's evening already?

"What time is it?" I ask.

"Nearly six. Why didn't you take your phone?"

"Six? It can't be…" I'm not just *a bit* late. I've lost a whole day.

Ma's shouting at me again. "I've been imagining you shot by Phelps, lying in a field, bleeding to death somewhere. You have to call me if you're going to disappear like that! It's not fair."

I'm only half listening because I'm trying to work out what's going on. Am I losing my mind? I can't have been with Andraste that long. It's not possible. I'm sure it was still only about nine when I left her in that place, and that can't have been more than an hour ago. But then I passed out when I saw those… huge dogs. How long was I unconscious for?

"Ma, I'm sorry. I had another seizure. I didn't realise I'd been out for that long."

MA HANDS ME a cup of camomile tea. I hate her herbal teas, but I drink it anyway. I'm still shaken up about losing a day, and I can't be bothered to argue.

Jaz is avoiding looking at me. I don't think she believes a word about the seizure. It's almost like she knows I spent the missing time with Andraste, and I can tell Ma isn't totally buying into the seizure idea either. She thinks there's more to it.

"You have to tell me exactly what happened, Arlo." She's using her special nice-and-slow voice, like she's talking to someone who doesn't speak English very well. "Jaz says you've been seeing some girl? Were you with her when you had the seizure?"

"Andraste. Her name's Andraste. I wasn't 'with her' exactly..."

"But she was there, right?" Jaz's voice is heavy with sarcasm, and I want the ground to swallow me. It's more than embarrassing having her around with Ma asking me personal questions like this. It's painful.

Ma's gone really pale. "Andraste. The old one," she mutters darkly. "Didn't you wonder how she came to have a name like that?"

"Of course I didn't! It's not the kind of thing you ask. I guess it's what her parents called her, like the way you're called Melissa. And how come everyone thinks she's old? She's not." I try unsuccessfully to keep the irritation out of my voice.

"Mary told me—" She breaks off before she shares whatever Mary said, but I think I already know. Mary's seen Andraste hanging around; that's who she was talking about yesterday when I thought she had dementia.

Ma is still staring at me intently, and I shrug.

"You don't understand, Arlo. Andraste is an *ancient* name. She's not...." She pauses and shakes her head. "So where exactly did you go with her?"

"I don't know. Honestly. It was sort of familiar, but I hadn't been there before. I can't explain." My lungs feel like the air is being forced out of them while in my mind, I'm screaming over and over, *where the hell was I?*

"That's not good. Sounds like *the other place*. You've been *chosen*, just like—" Ma breaks off again, and tears well up in her eyes.

"Like what?" I snap, but I know what already, and my panic is almost overpowering me. "Don't be so bloody stupid, Ma! And what do you mean, 'chosen'?"

Ma quickly wipes her eyes. "Calm down, Arlo. I'm trying to help. Was there anything unusual about the place she took you?"

"Such as?" I don't want to tell her anything, especially not in front of Jaz. And I don't want her to be right. It's too weird. I'd rather believe I had a seizure.

"I don't know, Arlo, but they say time is different there. The weather might not be the same, or the season…"

"The May blossom was out," I say without meaning to and hear Jaz's sharp intake of breath. "But that doesn't mean it was this *other place*! That's ridiculous. Look at the Glastonbury thorn. *They* say it always flowers at Christmas, but—"

"There's no need to shout," Ma interrupts. I hadn't realised I *was* shouting. "You didn't eat anything there, did you?" she asks. "That's never good."

"No."

"Or drink?"

"No!"

"What makes you think you had a seizure?"

"When I woke up, it all felt surreal and looked so different."

"You fell asleep in the other place?"

"We did a lot of running. Everything turned weird, and then there were these big dogs...really big, like wolves...it's hard to explain." I know what this sounds like, and my cheeks are burning with embarrassment. I catch Jaz looking at me, and I can tell exactly what she thinks. She tries to hide her expression, but I can read her like a book. She's upset.

"This is crazy, Ma. Only people like you believe all that *other place* crap."

No one says anything for a moment. Ma picks up her knitting. Great. Now I've hurt her too.

"I'd best be getting back home," Jaz says. "I'm supposed to be babysitting Laurel so Mum and Jake can go out."

She and Ma hug goodbye. I smile at Jaz, but she won't look at me.

"See you tomorrow?" I say. She doesn't answer or make eye contact as she leaves the cottage and walks back along the lane.

I feel all twisted up and out of my depth. I wish I'd never gone to meet Andraste this morning.

Chapter 13

RONNIE'S SURPRISINGLY OKAY about me going
AWOL and not turning up yesterday. She accepts
that I had a seizure and it wasn't my fault. In fact,
she starts fussing about whether I should be in work
after that.

"I'll be fine, Ronnie, honestly. I had a good night's
sleep, and look how busy it is already."

Ronnie sighs. I can tell she's torn. She's worried about
me, but at the same time she and Liv need my help.

"I really hope it doesn't happen again, Arlo. It's
a nightmare when someone doesn't show up. I had to
rope Clay in yesterday."

"Clay?" I try to imagine him helping in the café. He
can be so clumsy at times. "Did he break anything?"

She laughs and shakes her head. "No, but he spilt two
double-shot lattes and an orange juice over a table of
customers. Total nightmare."

It's the first time I've smiled since yesterday. "Were
they okay about it?"

"Yes, after Liv gave them free coffee and cake.
It was good of Clay to help out, but I'm glad to have
you back. Could you help her with the breakfast orders
this morning?"

Out in the kitchen, I'm surprised to see the raven's back, staring at me through the open door again.

"Liv, why does this raven keep coming so close to the café? Have you been feeding it?"

Liv glances up from buttering the mound of toast in front of her. "What raven?"

I look again. It's gone, and that uneasy feeling returns to my stomach.

Not surprisingly, I get the next two orders completely wrong and Liv has to redo them. I can't begin to tell her why I'm finding it so hard to concentrate; it's way too complicated.

I force myself to focus on the job, and gradually feel better as the day wears on. Around four, Jaz comes in with Hayden. She has her arm through his as they stand at the counter, and I wonder if this is her way of saying she's okay with everything, now she's hanging out with someone else. I feel like I've been stabbed in the heart.

Hayden smiles at me, and I try to smile back. My face nearly cracks with the effort. What really gets to me is how genuinely pleased he looks to see me, and I've got no real grounds to be jealous. I know he and Jaz are friends, but they didn't see so much of each other before... Andraste.

I get on with my work and try to ignore them sitting cosily together, laughing and chatting and enjoying each other's company. I'm relieved when Clay comes in and breaks up their little party.

When my shift finishes, I go and sit with them.

102

"Mum's booked the village hall for us, Arlo," Jaz says. "She's calling a public meeting next Friday. Hayden's going to print posters about it."

She sounds so excited, while I try not to think about how beautiful she looks when she gets all fired up about something. It's hard to focus on what she's saying, but soon I get the gist. Caroline's organising a public protest meeting about the mining application and we're helping her.

"Arlo, you have to be up on the platform with us," she says. "After all, the land Phelps is leasing to the mining company belonged to your family for so long. Maybe you can present the argument for why the mining is so destructive to farmland?"

I nod at Hayden. "That would make things even worse for me and Ma with your dad. I'm already worried I might have got us kicked out of the cottage. I can't do it."

"But we're relying on you!" Jaz says. She looks hurt and disappointed. "You'd make such a good speaker for this campaign. You genuinely care about what happens to the land...don't you?"

"Of course I do! I just don't want to be a focus point for it, that's all."

"You mean you don't want to stand up and be counted, more like. What about Hayden?"

"What about Hayden?" I try to keep the venom out of my voice, but Clay shoots me a glance that tells me I didn't succeed.

"Hayden is prepared to help, and it's his dad we're protesting against. What if his dad finds out?"

"At least he won't be thrown out of his home." Even as I say it, I think of Phelps cuffing Hayden around the head the other morning. He's a violent man. "But it's really good of you to help Jaz out, Hayden," I add grudgingly.

Hayden's been self-consciously cleaning his glasses the whole time Jaz has been having a go at me. He looks up and smiles, and suddenly I see why Jaz finds him attractive. Without his glasses, his eyes are enormous and an amazing blue. He looks nothing like his dad at all, and he still seems to like me, which is...annoying. I gave up on our friendship after I was banned from the farm. I want to enjoy disliking him.

"Look, I'll come to the meeting, Jaz, of course I will," I say, "but I'm crap at making speeches and stuff like that. You can talk and I'll back you up."

"I guess that's something," Jaz mutters, slightly mollified. "We need to meet up as much as we can before next Friday, so we can plan out what we're going to cover and make notes—if you're not too busy, of course, Arlo."

I catch her drift straight away and feel my face going red again. She means too busy with Andraste.

"I haven't any other plans," I mumble. "Apart from working here, obviously."

Clay looks at us both suspiciously, sensing there's some kind of undercurrent. "So you're definitely not dating that weird old goth, right?" he asks. "Did you ever find out her name?"

I shake my head. I don't want to talk about it.

"Her name's Andraste," Jaz says, trying to sound like she's not interested.

"Andraste? What kind of rubbish name is that?"

I can always rely on Clay to put an oar in. "An ancient one, apparently," I say.

Clay grins. "See? Told you she was old."

I cringe. I know Clay means well, but he's actually making it worse.

Hayden looks puzzled, but there's no way I'm telling him what's going on, and neither Clay nor Jaz seem likely to either.

Jaz quickly changes the subject. "We've got less than a week to sort ourselves out. When can we meet?"

"Can you all make tonight?" asks Clay. "Come to mine again. We can look at the film and pick out relevant bits for the presentation."

"Great," I say. As I stand up, ready to get back to the kitchen, I spot the raven again. This time, it's out the front, looking through the big window. I shiver. If I didn't know better, I'd swear it was watching me.

BACK HOME, MA is sitting hunched on the grass by the beehives, doing nothing. I suddenly feel exasperated with her. Guess I'm in for another round of signs and portents.

I try to be nice. "What's wrong, Ma? Do you want a cup of tea?"

She looks up at me, and for a moment, it's as though she doesn't recognise me, she's so wrapped up in her thoughts.

"Do you want some tea," I ask again, and this time she nods.

"Thanks. I'll come inside now." She gets up off the ground, and I notice she's brought her knitting out here, but she doesn't pick it up.

We go back into the house, where I make the tea and then join her at the kitchen table. Ma stares at her hands like she knows she's missing her knitting but hasn't figured it out yet.

"Okay, spit it out. What's upset you?"

She looks at me as though she's only just noticed I'm here. She takes a moment to answer.

"I'm so worried, Arlo. Everything's going wrong." Then, almost as an afterthought, she adds, "Maybe that's why *she's* back."

My hackles rise. I've had enough. "What are you talking about, Ma?" I'm shouting, and she's startled, but at least I've got her attention.

"I'm upset about the grove, Arlo," she says.

I try to calm down and talk at normal volume. "What about the grove?"

"I passed this EcoGas van on my way up to Mary's earlier, parked a little way up the lane. I overheard the men talking." Her eyes well up.

106

"What men?"

"Three men from EcoGas. They were standing looking in the direction of Spring Field, so busy they didn't see me." Her voice is shaky. "I think they're planning on cutting down the grove. I heard them saying something about the trees being in the way of a test drill."

And now I feel guilty. Ma has every reason to be upset. "No way! He can't cut down the grove, Ma. He'd never get planning."

"Would that stop a man like Norman Phelps? I don't think so."

"But those trees are ancient woodland! And there's St. Ann's Spring and the spring pool. There's no way..." I trail off. She's not listening. "Going to call Jaz," I say instead. "Don't worry, Ma. We'll do everything we can to stop him. I'll fetch your knitting in."

BACK DOWN BY the beehives, I call Jaz.

She doesn't even wait for me to say anything. "You're not ducking out, are you?"

I'm taken by surprise. "What do you mean?"

"You're meant to be coming to Clay's with me and Hayden. Thought you might be calling with some excuse." She sounds peevish, which puts my back up straight away.

"No, nothing like that. I was calling about Ma. It's not important. See you later." Before she can say anything else, I end the call.

LU HERSEY

I pick up Ma's knitting from where she left it and
stomp back inside. Cutting Jaz off like that was stupid.
I really wanted to tell her about the grove. Suppose I'll
have to do it later.

Whatever's going on with her and Hayden, I must
learn to deal with it. I need her help with this one.

108

Chapter 14

HAYDEN AND JAZ are already in Clay's room by the time I get to his place.

Jaz looks up at me from her chair by the computer. "Okay, Arlo? You're late! I was beginning to think you weren't coming."

I clear a few mugs off a stool so I can sit next to her. "I was worried about leaving Ma on her own. That's why I called earlier."

"Why? What's wrong? Is she okay?"

"No, she's really upset. She overheard some men from EcoGas saying Phelps is going to cut down the grove for a test drilling site."

Jaz gasps in shock.

Hayden goes pale. "Surely Dad can't do that?"

I turn on him. "Can you do anything to stop him? It's the most beautiful part of the farm, and it's bad enough he's banned public access!"

Jaz touches my arm. "Don't shout at Hayden. It's not his fault!"

"I know, sorry. But...it's a special place for me and Ma. My father's ashes are scattered there. She goes there to visit sometimes..." My voice cracks, and I feel like a total dick.

"No wonder your mum's upset," Clay says. "I would be too. Didn't know that's where you put the ashes."

I smile gratefully at him. It's rare he shows sympathy, but I can't trust myself to tell them why Dad's ashes are in the grove. When Ma and I scattered them, we didn't want anyone to know where he was. We'd been warned people can be weird about the graves of suicides, and Ma didn't need any more stress.

Hayden looks uncomfortable. "Arlo, I'm really sorry. I'll do anything I can to stop Dad clearing the grove if that's what he's planning. But he never listens to me. If the grove's in the way of what he wants, he'll chop it down."

"Unless we can prevent his plans from going ahead in the first place," Jaz says. "Which brings us back to the protest. Helping Mum organise it is the best thing we can do to prevent it happening. If we can't stop it that way, I'll tie myself to a tree if I have to."

When Jaz is on the case, she's the best. Even though we've fallen out over the whole Andraste thing, she's a good friend. I know she'll go out of her way to help me.

I smile at her, not sure what to say. Eventually, I find my tongue. "Thanks, Jaz, you're a star. Oh, and I've had a rethink about the protest. I'm with you all the way."

Jaz is so happy she jumps and gives me a hug. I'm annoyed with myself for blushing.

We settle down around Clay's desk to talk things through and watch more videos about fracking, but my mind's not really on it. I keep thinking about the grove.

The truth is I'm the one who goes there most, not Ma. Even though it creeps me out a bit being there these days, I take flowers to the spot where we put Dad's ashes, and if no one's around, I go out and sit by the spring for a while. It's the closest I can get to Dad.

I can't let Phelps cut it down. I feel more and more anxious thinking about it. In the end, I make an excuse and leave, hurrying back from Clay's along the lanes in the dusk.

WHEN I GET home, the place is in darkness. At first, I think Ma's gone out, but then I hear noises coming from the kitchen. I find her out there bottling some weird-looking brown liquid by candlelight. The room smells strongly of lavender and honey. She looks up, startled.

"Oh, is it that time already? Let me finish this and you can put the lights on."

I don't ask what she's been doing. This is unusual behaviour, even for my mother, and she seems embarrassed. At least, I think so, it's hard to tell in this light.

"Did you have a nice time with Jazara?"

"It was okay, thanks. But listen, Ma, we need to talk." I take a deep breath. "Thing is, I'm joining the anti-mining protest, and I'm going to help organise a village meeting. I know Phelps may use it as another lever to get us out, but I can't have him cut down the grove."

Ma turns and actually smiles at me. "I'm glad, Arlo. Everything's out of sorts because of this mining.

111

The land's been disturbed. Mary agrees with me. She suggested this remedy I'm making."

"You're not expecting me to drink that crap, are you?"

"No, silly. It's to settle the bees. And hopefully, *her*."

"Her? You mean Andraste? What are you supposed to do with it, chuck it at her or something?"

She pushes a cork into the last bottle. "No, pour it on the land."

"And this is Mary Suggeworth's idea? Great. Hope the bees like it."

"We need to try everything, Arlo. You don't realise how serious this is. I'm glad you've joined the protest. If you can stop the mining going any further, she might go back before..." Ma's voice wavers.

"Before what?"

"Things get worse."

I get the feeling she's avoiding telling me something, but I don't press it.

I change the subject. "Let's have some cocoa, Ma, then maybe we should get some sleep. Jaz is threatening to tie herself to a tree if they try and cut down the grove."

Ma turns the kitchen light on, and I'm relieved to see she's smiling. "She's feisty, that one. If anyone can stop them, she can."

"Yeah, so don't let it get to you like it has been. We're going to fight this all the way. But please stop going on about Andraste, okay? I'm trying to keep my distance."

She nods. "That's probably the best thing. Show respect, but don't get too close. And you stick with Jazara."

I don't say anything. What's the point? It's not worth upsetting Ma when she's just started looking a bit happier.

I CAN'T SLEEP. Standing at my bedroom window, I watch a barn owl swoop low, then up and over the cottage towards the grove. I think about Dad and wish I could remember more about what we did and what we talked about that day. Why didn't I notice there was something wrong? Maybe I could have stopped him.

The grove is the closest I can ever get to him now. Guess it wouldn't hurt to go out there for a while. I dress quietly and listen out in the darkness. There's no sound, so I reckon Ma's asleep. I creep down the stairs, open the front door and step outside.

Moving quickly and silently down the garden path, I head out into the lane. The quickest route to the grove from Primrose Cottage is through the gap in the hedgerow where we went on Clay's birthday. I squeeze my way in, catching the scent of badger as I go.

I try to make as little sound as possible, picking my way carefully through the woodland to the grove. A twig cracks under my foot, the sound ringing out like a pistol shot above the whispering of the trees.

The grove looks magical in the moonlight. Everything is silver, and the owl hoots from the branches above me.

I move into the glade at the centre, where the trees circle me like sentinels in the dark. A hedgehog snuffles under an ash tree, busily hunting for slugs.

Suddenly my senses tingle on high alert, and I scan my surroundings. Someone else is here, I'm sure of it. A shadow moves by the twisted hawthorn, and my heart practically jumps into my mouth.

It takes a second to realise it's her. Andraste. She walks towards me, silent as the barn owl in flight. She doesn't seem real, somehow. My pulse starts racing. Why is she here, out in the dark at this time of night? She has to be stalking me. But why?

My mind flits back to Ma, making potions by candlelight in the kitchen. I kind of wish I had the bottle with me in case it would actually make the bloody girl go away.

I focus on my breathing, and as she gets closer, I catch the smell of honeysuckle. She still hasn't said a word. My heart is thumping like I've run a marathon. This silence is scary.

She stands right in front of me, way too close for comfort, and stares at me, then reaches out and touches my arm.

"Be calm, Arlo. Come and sit with me awhile. We can talk a little more."

"Okay. But I can't go too far," I say warily. I don't want to go back to that place with her. I don't want to even think it's real.

She looks at me, and for a second, I see a flicker of green light in her eye. Maybe I imagined it? Then she turns and walks slowly under the overhanging branches and out towards the spring. I follow her.

She sits down on the grass, close to where we had the picnic on Clay's birthday. I try to decide how much distance I can keep without seeming rude and sit a couple of metres away from her. She turns to face me, the moon reflecting silvery white on her skin.

"You are right to come out to defend this place, Arlo. Your father would have wanted you to. You must protect it from further damage at all costs. The harm done here will bring untold suffering to the village."

I shiver. I want to ask her how she could possibly know anything about my father, but there's something so surreal about this meeting, I wonder if I'm dreaming. Maybe I can force myself awake? I put my hand into the clear, cool, moon-silvered water. Andraste leans closer and reaches under the surface, catching hold of my hand. I have to fight the instinct to pull away from her grasp, but now I know for sure she's real. I can feel her cold touch.

"You have the power to save this place when the time comes. I'll help you all I can."

"Save it? You mean with the protest?"

"It's a forfeit." Her eyes glitter in the moonlight. "The payment for the damage done here must be in blood. I can't prevent that. It's always been the agreement."

I nod as if I understand, but I don't at all. Does she mean the protest will get violent? I think of Dad's ashes scattered in the grove and look over my shoulder, back towards the glade.

"I'll do anything to protect this place," I say.

"Then we are agreed."

A cloud passes over the moon, and the glade goes dark. I turn back to look at her.

She's not there.

I leap to my feet in shock. How could she disappear like that? I stay where I am, searching the darkness for any sign of her. The owl flies past me, so close I feel the waft of air current from its wings and practically jump out of my skin. It swoops and lands on the old hollow oak.

I leave the grove and make my way back towards home, totally spooked. A forfeit paid in blood?

What on earth have I agreed to?

Chapter 15

I T'S EASIER TO shake off the sense of foreboding in the light of the early morning sun. As I'm getting ready to go to work, a car pulls up in the lane outside the cottage. Ma's standing by the window.

"Looks like Caroline."

"What, Jaz's mum?"

"How many Carolines do we know? Of course Jazara's mum. Oh, look, she's getting Laurel out of the baby seat! I wonder what they want." Ma gets all excited about seeing the baby and goes to the door to greet them.

A few minutes later, Caroline comes in carrying Laurel, followed by Jaz, who's holding a collection of baby toys to keep her little sister occupied.

Jaz grins at me. "You're probably wondering what the heck's going on, right?"

"Kind of. Obviously, it's nice to see you. Got to get to work in ten, though. Ronnie's asked me to cover as many shifts as I can until we start back at college."

"Mum wanted to ask you about the grove."

I'm slightly puzzled. "Okay..."

Caroline waves a purple spotty velvet dinosaur in front of Laurel and looks up. "Yes, I want to talk to you and Melissa both, if you're not too busy."

I hesitate and look at my phone. I've still got a few minutes. "How long will it take?"

Laurel starts squawking and batting the dinosaur away. Caroline smiles. "Not long, don't worry, Arlo. I don't want to make you late for work. Jaz, please can you get some water for Laurel? Might keep her quiet for a second." She hands a baby cup to Jaz, who goes out to the kitchen and fills it for her. Meanwhile, Laurel tries to eat Ma's bunch of keys.

I smile. "Ew, Laurel, I wouldn't eat them. Have you seen the inside of my mum's bag?"

I try to take the keys off Laurel gently, but she immediately starts yelling. Jaz rushes back with the baby cup and a glass of water for herself. Jaz takes a big gulp of water and offers Laurel the cup. It works like a charm. Watching her big sister drinking from the glass, Laurel stops yelling, grabs her cup and drinks noisily.

I'm worried I'm going to be late and try to get Caroline's attention. "So what do you want to ask us?"

Caroline lowers her voice to a conspiratorial whisper, almost as if she expects Phelps to be listening at the window. "I want to put in an application to make the grove and St. Ann's Spring an SSSI—before Phelps can do any more damage."

"Fantastic idea!" Ma says.

I nod, feeling a bit stupid. "Er, what's an SSSI?"

"Site of Special Scientific Interest, which means it has rare plants or animals and gets proper legal protection. And that's where you both come in." She nods at me and Ma. "I was hoping you might be able to think of rare plants or insects or anything at all that live in or near the grove?"

Caroline scrabbles in her bag and fishes out a notebook and pen. I look at Ma. She frowns.

"I can think of a few things," Ma says, "but Arlo will need to check they're still there. I'm not sure how much damage Phelps has done already with all the chemicals he uses."

"There are quite a few owls," I say, thinking of last night. "The oak is at least a thousand years old and might be a lot older. That's what Dad told me."

Caroline scribbles as she talks. "What about St. Ann's Spring?"

"It's pure," Ma says. "You can drink it without filtering of any kind. It supplies us here in Stanton. We used to have it pumped up to the farm too, but I think Phelps has had the place connected to the mains. Not enough water for the piggery."

"Does it have any water species in it? Rare marsh plants, that kind of thing?"

"There used to be lots of butterwort and marsh marigolds, but I don't think they're that rare. There were always a lot of different dragonfly species, though."

"Yes, there are still loads of them about," I say. "And newts."

Laurel starts squawking and chucks her drinking cup on the floor. Caroline picks it up.

"That's great, Arlo. Look, I'd better take Laurel out of here so you can get off to work. But maybe you and Jaz could go to the grove later? If you point stuff out, she can take photos with my camera and collect samples to support the application. We can't have that idiot polluting one of the most beautiful parts of the countryside like this. He has to be stopped."

"Be careful, though, both of you," Ma says. "If Phelps gets wind of what you're up to, he'll probably fell the trees without even applying for planning."

"Good point," says Caroline. "But they're both very resourceful. And we need the information."

Ma and Caroline walk out to the car together, chatting about plants in the grove and the possibility of getting the SSSI application in before Phelps's planning for the test drilling goes through.

Jaz hangs back a moment. She looks at me seriously. "Have you got time to go there with me later?"

"Yes, of course. I finish at four today—shall I meet you somewhere?"

"May as well see you at the café later. Hayden's meeting me there. In fact, we could all go."

"To the grove? With Hayden?" I can't keep the irritation out of my voice. I was hoping this would be a chance to spend time with Jaz on her own.

"Don't worry, Arlo. There's no way Hayden will tell his dad what we're doing. You need to trust him again."

Trusting Hayden isn't really the problem, but I can't tell her that.

"Okay," I say. "Let's talk later."

HAYDEN COMES INTO the café to meet Jaz, and I watch them, heads together, totally at ease in each other's company. I'm not at all happy about Hayden coming with us to the grove, but for all the wrong reasons. Even I can see the big advantage. If Phelps shows up, we can make out we're just hanging out with Hayden. Phelps might not be overjoyed with his son's choice of friends, but it's a convincing excuse.

As soon as I get a chance, I go over to find out what they're planning. Hayden flashes a friendly smile; I manage to resist the urge to squash a chair in between him and Jaz and instead sit down opposite them.

"Hayden's keen to come with us, Arlo. He thinks there may be other species apart from those you mentioned."

I want to say *what the hell does Hayden know?* but bite my tongue. I force myself to smile and change the subject to one close to my heart.

"Hayden, does your dad work much at night?"

"Sometimes he goes to make sure the security lights are working on the pig unit. And sometimes deliveries of farm stuff arrive late. Why?"

"It's been playing on my mind. If he finds out what we're planning, do you think it's possible he'd go out and chainsaw the trees down in the dark, when no one's around to see what he's doing?"

"Wouldn't put it past him. He'll do anything to get his own way. And I mean anything. He's not a nice man. You know that." There's an edge of bitterness in his tone.

"I wish I could persuade my mother to leave him, but she won't. She's too afraid."

I suddenly remember the pale face at the window the morning Phelps called the police on me. It must have been Emily Phelps.

"I don't see your mum much these days," I say. "Weird really, being as how you live so close by."

Hayden's face flushes red, and for a moment I think he's angry with me for asking. But he's not. He's upset.

"She mostly stays at home," he says quietly. I don't push it. I guess his home life can't be much fun.

I get back to the point. "Look, I know it's a lot to ask, but if you see your dad go out at night, please can you message me? The cottage is so close to the grove, I can easily slip over there and check he's not doing any damage."

"Of course. I'll get your number off Jaz, shall I?"

How come he doesn't ask *me* for my number? I try not to feel irritated by that. I have to do whatever it takes to protect the grove.

"Sure!" I say.

I GET MA to put her knitting away the moment Hayden and Jaz walk up the garden path. We've arranged to set out from my place because it's closest to the grove. I know Ma's eager to meet Hayden again, so hopefully she'll try to be normal.

Hayden looks nervous as he shakes Ma's hand. "It's so nice to get a chance to meet up again, Mrs. Fry."

"Lovely to see you, Hayden," Ma says. "And don't be formal. You always called me Melissa, remember?"

I was worried how Ma would react to having Hayden here after all that happened, but they seem pleased to see each other again. Jaz keeps giving me *told you so* looks. I can't decide if I'm more annoyed or relieved.

Jaz is getting fidgety. "We should make a start, you guys. It's already five."

I pick up her bag to hand it to her, then almost drop it again, it's so heavy. "What on earth have you got in here? It weighs a ton!"

"A few jars for water plant samples, some bags for specimens, a trowel to dig things up with—oh, and Mum's camera."

"A few jars? Feels more like a recycling centre in there!"

"Nothing we don't need. In fact, since you haven't got anything much together, you can carry it." She grins as she goes to open the door.

Hayden hesitates a moment and looks at Ma. "Would you like to come with us, Melissa?"

I glare at her behind his back. Hayden's politeness is doing my head in.

She gets the message. "No, I won't come, Hayden, but thanks for asking." She smiles at him, then gives me an *as if I would* look.

123

Jaz is a bit on edge and keeps reminding us to keep quiet. "Where's that gap under the hedge, Arlo? I thought we'd be there by now."

"We are, don't worry." I point it out to her, but her nervousness is catching. Instinctively, I look around to check if anyone else is nearby.

"Let's go in one at a time. I'll go last. Wait for me on the other side."

"I'll go first," says Hayden. "If by any chance Dad's there…" He doesn't need to finish the sentence. If Phelps is around, obviously Jaz and I won't follow him.

Hayden ducks under the hawthorn and pushes his way through the gap. There's total silence back in the lane except for the buzzing of bees and the rustling of blackbirds hunting insects in the hedgerow. Jaz and I keep as still and quiet as we can.

"It's okay, there's no one about!" Hayden's voice comes through the hedge.

Jaz squeezes herself through, and I pass her bag to her. I check the lane again before I follow. I don't want anyone passing by to see us.

We head towards the grove, not saying a word until we reach the clearing in the centre. There's no sound of traffic, just the faint bubbling of the spring from the other side of the grove and the hum of insects. I can smell the bark of the old oak tree, mingling with the scent of dry earth in high summer.

A dragonfly zooms past Jaz towards the spring, and she steps back in alarm.

"Don't worry. It won't hurt you."

"I know that! It made me jump, that's all."

"It's amazing here, isn't it?" Hayden stops and gazes around like it's the first time he's seen it.

"Yeah, I guess, but it might be best not to spend too much time here in case we draw your dad's attention to it."

I'm more worried he and Jaz might start hanging out here together. In my mind, it's the one part of the farm that still belongs to Dad.

Suddenly, I'm aware of another sound above the bubbling water. Someone crying. I touch Jaz's arm and signal to both of them to be quiet. I scan around desperately for somewhere to hide and beckon them to follow me over to the hollow oak, hoping we can all squeeze in there.

Too late. A woman walks into the grove, appearing right in front of us. Emily Phelps. She sees us and gasps in surprise. She quickly shades her eyes with her hand, but not before I've seen her face. She's not shielding her eyes from the sun. She's trying to hide the livid bruising.

"Mum? What are you doing here?" Hayden looks as startled as she does.

"Came out for a walk. I'll be going back now." Her voice catches a little but otherwise shows no sign she was so upset.

Hayden nods. I can tell from his expression he's seen the bruising too.

"We won't be here for long if you want to stay?" he says gently.

"No, it's time I was getting back. I need to start cooking for this evening." She smiles at her son but doesn't take her hand away from her eyes.

"Okay. But Mum, please don't tell Dad you saw us here. You know what he thinks of Arlo."

His mother doesn't say anything for a moment. I think she's watching me through her fingers, but I can't be sure. I try to look friendly, but she's making me anxious.

"So why risk bringing him here, Hayden? You're asking for trouble." She sounds frightened, and my hatred of Phelps intensifies. No prizes for guessing how she got the bruising.

"His dad's ashes are scattered here."

Normally, I'd be furious with anyone, let alone Hayden, for sharing that. But not now. His mum goes completely still for a moment.

"I...I didn't know. I'm so sorry, Arlo." Her voice wavers. "And it's nice to see you again. But don't spend too long here, okay?"

"We won't. So..." Hayden hesitates. "You won't tell Dad?"

"No. It's okay. I haven't seen you." With that, she turns and walks back out of the grove, past St. Ann's Spring, and off towards the farm.

I exchange glances with Jaz. Her eyes flash with anger. I guess she saw the bruising too. Neither of us mention it.

Hayden breaks the awkward silence. "Don't worry, she won't say anything. She won't want to get me in trouble."

I noticed he didn't tell his mother what we were really doing there, and I'm glad, even at the expense of Hayden telling her about Dad's ashes. It's better than Phelps catching wind of what we're trying to achieve and cutting down the grove.

"We'd better get on with it," Jaz says, trying to sound efficient and businesslike, but I can hear the emotion in her voice. Seeing Hayden's mum like that has upset us all.

Chapter 16

EVERYONE'S STILL IN a sombre mood when we leave, despite the number of rare plant samples we've collected and all the photos Jaz has taken. Hayden's hardly said a word for the last hour.

Out in the lane, he glances at Jaz and me, then stares at the ground and mumbles something about having to get back home.

"Are you sure you don't want to come back to mine with us?" asks Jaz. "We can look up all this stuff to see what we've got and check out whether it's rare or not."

"Thanks, but I want to make sure Mum's...well, y'know..."

"Oh, um, yeah. Of course." Jaz looks like she's itching to say more, but she holds back and smiles and gives him a hug. For the first time since they bought the farm, I almost feel like hugging him myself.

"Thanks for your help, Hayden." It's the best I can manage, and at least it doesn't sound totally insincere.

He looks up and attempts a smile, but I see he's close to tears. He turns away quickly and sets off towards the farm. Jaz and I stare at each other.

"Poor Hayden," I say.

Jaz sighs. "I've got to talk to him about this, Arlo. I couldn't while you were with us. But I'll definitely try when I next see him."

A rising bubble of jealousy immediately overpowers my sympathy for Hayden. I try to squash it, but I can't.

BACK AT JAZ'S, Caroline is delighted with all the samples and photos we've got.

"Reckon this is more than enough to help us with the SSSI application," she says. "And I've been looking into the history of the place while you were out, too. Turns out it's a very old site, which also might help our case along. Hang on a minute, I'll show you."

Caroline picks up a musty old book lying on the coffee table. As she flips through the pages to find what she's looking for, I see the title on the Spine. *Tales of Old Stanton and its Surrounds* by The Rev'd Dexter Parrish.

She finds the page. "Listen to this," she says, and starts reading out loud.

> In the vicinity of the Stanton Stones and Wights Mound is a spring of surprising antiquity. Now called St. Ann's Spring, it was reputed to have held healing properties during the years of the Great Plague. However, it is quite probable the place was considered a sacred site long before Christianity even reached these shores. Local legend has it that in ancient times,

St. Ann's Spring may have been a place of worship to the old British goddess, Andred, a goddess who is often compared to the Morrigan in Irish mythology. Ancient Britons held natural springs and groves of trees as pastoral temples to their heathen gods, so this old folktale may well hark back to our dim and distant past.

Caroline looks up at us. "That's great, don't you think? It shows St. Ann's Spring, and possibly the grove, are very interesting historically, as well as potential SSSIs."

"That could be a clincher at the protest meeting," Jaz says. "People love history. Are there any pictures?"

"Only an old engraving. This book predates photos." Caroline turns the book around to show us the illustration.

Jaz peers at it. "Suppose it might be worth scanning to use as part of the presentation."

"Can I see?" I ask.

A sudden wailing from upstairs tells us Laurel has woken up. Caroline hands the book to me. "Be careful with it, won't you, Arlo? I think it's quite rare. Have a look while I check on Laurel a minute."

As she disappears upstairs, Jaz yawns. "Got time for a hot chocolate before you go, Arlo?"

"Yeah, thanks, that would be great."

While she clatters about making the drinks, I read through the passage again and study the old engraving of

St. Ann's Spring. There's a drawing of a woman in a long dress standing by the pool with a couple of buckets of water swinging from a yoke over her shoulder.

The text continues under the picture, so I start reading the next bit.

> As far as we may judge, Andred was considered by our forebears to be a goddess of battle and death, yet perversely also a goddess of fertility and the land. Our only written record of Andred was made by the Romans, who referred to her as Andraste. As the goddess favoured by Queen Boudicca when entering battle, Andraste was a name to bring fear to the Roman heart!

I swallow hard to fight off a wave of nausea.

Jaz puts a mug of chocolate down in front of me. "What's up?"

"Nothing. Just reading the book," I say. "Could be useful background, I guess."

She looks at me like she suspects it was more than that, but I just smile and take a swig of chocolate, trying not to gag. The last thing I want to do is discuss the subject of Andraste with Jaz. In any case, it would be hard to explain how weird the book has made me feel.

I LEAVE JAZ's filled with anxious thoughts about almost everything: Jaz, Ma, the cottage, Andraste, Phelps and even the grove. But as dusk falls and I'm nearly home, I realise the grove is the one thing I can do something about. If I sleep out there for the next few nights, I can make sure nothing bad happens before the application to make the site an SSSI is in place.

As I go to open the garden gate at the cottage, I nearly jump out of my skin. There's a raven sitting on the gatepost. We look at each other for a moment. I'm waiting for the bird to take flight, but it doesn't move. Is it the same one that was outside Corn Flakes?

I talk softly to the bird. "What's up with you? Are you injured? Hungry?"

The raven stares at me for a moment, then hops off the gatepost onto the wall.

I edge slowly towards it, looking for signs of wing damage. As I get close enough to touch it, it croaks loudly and lifts effortlessly off the wall, calling as it flies away in the direction of the grove.

Ma opens the door for me. She must have been waiting. "Arlo? Glad you're back. With that raven about, I was worried."

I roll my eyes at her before plonking down on the sofa.

She sits next to me. "You think I'm crazy, don't you?"

"Yes, I think you're crazy." I grin…and twist to avoid Ma's slap to my arm.

I take a deep breath. Ma's really not going to like my idea. "I've decided to go and camp out in the grove tonight," I say.

"You can't! What if Phelps finds you?"

"He won't. It's a fine night. I'll take a sheet of plastic and a sleeping bag. I'll come back first thing."

I run upstairs to find my sleeping bag, trying not to think too much about what would happen if Phelps does find me.

"Do you want me to come with you?" Ma appears at my bedroom door, still clutching her knitting.

"No, Ma. That would be weird." I try to keep my voice light.

"I couldn't bear it if anything happened to you as well, Arlo. Please don't sleep out in the grove. You know how dangerous Phelps can be."

I grin at her. "Nothing's going to happen, okay?"

Back downstairs, I make her put her knitting on the sofa so I can give her another hug without getting speared by a knitting needle.

"Bye, Ma. See you in the morning. Look, it's not that far. If I think there's going to be trouble, I'll be straight back. Stop wringing your hands like that, it's making me nervous."

She smiles. "I'll make you a nice breakfast as soon as you're back."

As I step out into the dark lane in front of the house, I see Ma in the brightly lit front room, picking up her knitting again. We could both be in for a long night.

THE AIR IS filled with the pungent smell of sap and sliced-up plants from the hedgerow. Phelps must have been out with the hedge cutter this afternoon. I walk quickly up the lane and around the corner to the entrance under the hedge.

Even though I know this place well, it looks different now it's been hacked back, and it takes a while of searching to find the right spot in the dark. By the time I do, sweat is prickling down my back. I take a moment to breathe and calm down before pushing my way through. I make every effort to be as quiet as possible, but I'm about as subtle as a bulldozer in this silence.

I don't want to use the small flashlight I've brought with me unless I have to. No point in drawing attention to myself unnecessarily. I make my way carefully to the centre of the grove and stand in the moonlight, wondering whether to set up my sleeping area under the trees and risk being covered in falling twigs and branches, or stay here under the light of the moon where I'm much more visible. Either way, I want to make sure I'm not sleeping too close to Dad's ashes.

After about five minutes of waiting, listening to the rustling sounds of the nocturnal animals and the chafing of the crickets in the long grass, I decide to stay where I am. The grass and bracken are long enough to give me some degree of cover. At least this way I get a clear view of anyone approaching, and I can make a quick getaway if I have to.

I lay out the groundsheet and put my sleeping bag on top, bundling my rucksack up to make a pillow. I keep all my clothes on, except my shoes, and climb into the bag, then lie on my back, gazing up at the stars.

I can't sleep. The passage in Caroline's book is playing on my mind. Anything to do with Andraste touches a raw nerve. I try to think of something else and start worrying about Jaz getting together with Hayden instead. And then about Phelps trying to get us out of the cottage. And then what if I find out I'm epileptic at my appointment with the doctor next week.

The sleeping bag is too tight, so I unzip it. Then I get cold so I zip it up again. Eventually, I relax and close my eyes.

I sleep fitfully, drifting in and out of dreams.

I WAKE UP in a sweat, my heart pounding after a nightmare about the village hall meeting. In the dream, Tracy Benger, our annoying neighbour, breathed in a cloud of poisonous gas, and I watched her die in agony before dissolving like a vampire in a horror movie.

The sky is filled with the faint light of daybreak. I climb out of the sleeping bag immediately and stand up, trying to get rid of the nightmare image. I hate dreams like that, and they're always the ones that stay with me for a while after I've woken up.

Gradually, I calm down. The grove is so beautiful in the soft light of dawn. As the birdsong gets louder with the increasing light, I start to feel better. I sit on my sleeping bag for a few moments, breathing in the fresh morning air. Everything looks so magical here,

I don't understand where the nightmare came from. The melodic song of the blackbird chases the shadows away.

I rub my arms thoughtfully. I probably should be heading back home to check Ma's okay.

I'm rolling up my sleeping bag to put it back in my rucksack when I hear the distant sound of a Land Rover engine. I keep still and listen. It's getting louder. It's coming this way. Panic rising, I shove my sleeping bag into my rucksack. The last thing I need is a confrontation with Phelps right now. Not here.

I make a quick decision: I squeeze myself inside the hollow trunk of the oak and push right up against the inside of the ancient tree, staying in the deep shadow. Unless Phelps joins me in here, he won't see me. I shove my rucksack behind my legs where the hollow trunk widens out a bit.

Very soon, I'm made aware of the number of creatures making their home in the oak. Something crawls down my back, under my T-shirt. It's scratchy. Probably a beetle. I try not to move or squash it as I wait.

The Land Rover pulls up somewhere to the left of St. Ann's Spring. I hear both doors opening. Phelps is not alone.

"We'd strongly advise against damaging any of these trees for the next drill site, Mr. Phelps. It's unnecessary, and you'll potentially alienate a lot of local people you want to keep on board."

"I don't care about bloody tree-hugging neighbours. This is more important. If it's the best site, I want you to use it. I'll deal with the eco mob."

There's a bit of mumbling I don't quite catch, then I hear who I assume is the EcoGas man again. "That flat patch in the field is close enough, and hopefully no one will object if we test drill there. Believe me, it's not worth making things more difficult for yourself when you don't have to, and those trees will help screen the drill from the road."

"Show me which bit of the field you mean."

The voices move away, still talking, but I can't hear exactly what they're saying. The rooks have woken up somewhere in the branches above my head, and they're making enough noise to blot out most of the conversation. Even so, I catch odd words.

"Grove better...don't care what they bloody think..." That's Phelps talking. He's shouting, so I can hear him more clearly than the replies from the EcoGas man.

The rooks settle down, still chattering and bickering with each other, but not as loudly, and I can hear Phelps and the EcoGas man a bit better.

"What time are you detonating the shaft in Dingle Hollow?"

"Six thirty. We'd better get back up there and make sure the land's clear. Don't want any accidents."

"Should be fine. Ploughed it after the crop circle incident. That should keep the riffraff out of it."

"Even so, Mr. Phelps, safety is paramount. If you kill someone by mistake, you won't be having any more drilling on this land, believe me. We're risking far too much already."

I hear them get back into the Land Rover and drive off. I wait until I can't hear anything except the noisy rooks above me and a wood pigeon calling from somewhere in the grove. Then I step cautiously out of my hiding place and walk out to the field next to the spring. Phelps drove right up to the marshy border. There are tyre tracks in the soft ground, and a cigarette butt still smoulders where he chucked it.

My heart aches for Dad suddenly. I wonder if he knows what's happening to his land. I sit next to the spring for a while, watching it bubble in the dawn light. The sun rises and sparkles diamonds on the water. I listen to the rooks settling into their daily routine.

As I'm about to leave and go back home for breakfast, there's a loud booming sound, like underground thunder. The ground shakes. The rooks lift from the trees and circle in alarm, croaking their panic to each other. St. Ann's Spring ripples with the aftershock, water lapping over the marshy edges. A cloud covers the sun and the water goes dark.

I stand staring at the water until the sun comes back out. The rooks are unsettled and fly off towards the cottage. There's something different about the spring, but it takes me a while to realise what it is. It's no longer bubbling.

MA IS WAITING anxiously by the gate. She looks relieved to see me.

"Thank goodness you're okay, Arlo, I was so worried when I heard the explosion. It sounded close."

She looks like she hasn't slept much.

"I think the explosion was in Dingle Hollow," I say. "I overheard Phelps talking this morning."

"Phelps? He didn't see you, did he?"

"No, it's okay. I was hiding inside the oak. It was close, though. He came at dawn with someone from EcoGas looking for a potential drill site."

"You're lucky he didn't find you! Come in and eat some breakfast."

We go through to the kitchen, and Ma puts some bread in the toaster.

"So, did you sleep all right, out in the open?" she asks.

"Not great. Had such weird dreams."

"What kind of dreams?" She hands me a plate and puts the butter on the table.

"Tracy Benger from the bakery breathed in a cloud of poisonous gas and died."

She smiles. "You've never liked Tracy. Probably your subconscious trying to kill her off."

I smile. "Maybe. But I don't dislike her *that* much."

"Where were you in the dream?"

"She's not dead, Ma! But it was at the meeting in the village hall in Tytheford if you must know."

The toast pops; Ma butters a slice and hands it to me. "Hope it's not another omen."

"For goodness' sake, you and your bloody omens!
I'm sure Tracy's fine."

"I was thinking more of the poisonous gas, what with
Phelps disturbing things the way he is."

I hesitate, wondering how much to tell her.

"What is it?"

"Weird thing happened after the explosion.
The spring stopped bubbling for a while."

Ma goes pale. "Stopped? How long for?"

"Not sure. I had to leave it and come home. Thought
you'd be worried about me."

She stares at me. "You mean it didn't start up again?"

"Probably has by now. Don't worry about it," I say,
but my toast is like rubber in my mouth.

Ma knits a short, tight row of black.

140

Chapter 17

AFTER SPENDING TWO sleepless nights in the grove, I'm really hanging at work. I wanted to see Jaz last night to talk everything through with her, but she was busy. Worse, she was busy because she had Hayden over at her place. She said she wanted to see him on his own.

I couldn't get to see Clay either because he'd gone to the cinema in St. Wylda with a mate, so I haven't told either of them about what happened at the spring yet.

Corn Flakes is packed. I'm so busy, by the time Clay arrives for coffee, it's a while before I get a quick break and a chance to chat.

"Wow. You look rough."

"Thanks, Clay."

"No probs. Hey, you haven't been seeing that old goth again, have you?"

"She's not old. And no, I haven't. Been sleeping out in the grove, that's all."

"Eh? How come?"

"Worried about what Phelps might do if he got wind of the SSSI application."

"Yeah, Jaz told me about that. Said you went there with Hayden to get samples and stuff. Do you reckon her and Hayden are an item now?"

"Not sure. Why do you ask?" I try to sound like I don't care, but my heart feels like it might have slightly frozen. It's exactly what I spent half last night worrying about.

"Seems like she's been seeing a lot more of him than before. Could just be she feels sorry for him, I guess. She said his dad beats his mum up."

"Either that or his mum's walked into a lot of doors recently."

Clay looks at me thoughtfully. "But do you reckon we can trust Hayden? I'm really not sure about him."

"Yeah, I think so. Felt bad for him when we ran into his mum, to be honest. He looked so upset seeing her like that. It made me think."

"Jaz wasn't too happy either. She wants to report Phelps to the police. So what's wrong? Obviously something's up or you would have got more sleep."

Clay is surprisingly observant sometimes.

"Keep having nightmares, waking up and not being able to get back to sleep. And I can't stop worrying about everything."

"Like if Jaz is going out with Hayden?"

"Don't be stupid!"

Clay stares at me without saying anything.

"Okay, maybe a bit," I admit, "but I'm more worried about the grove. And Phelps."

"Not surprised. Last time he caught you, he shoved a gun in your face. That kind of thing would keep anyone awake."

"What would keep anyone awake?" Jaz sits in the chair next to me. She's already got a coffee and I didn't even see her come in. I hope she didn't hear what we were talking about.

"Arlo slept out in the grove the last couple of nights. Or rather, didn't sleep. Worried about Phelps instead."

"God, I'm not surprised! Heroic thing to do. Or possibly amazingly stupid..." Jaz pushes a mass of beaded plaits behind her ear and grins at me. She looks stunning, as usual. And she smells sort of citrusy today, which is nice. Unlike me. I probably smell like a full English breakfast, since I've been serving them up to customers all morning.

"Yeah, well, nearly got caught yesterday. Fortunately, I was already awake, but Phelps turned up with some guy from EcoGas at daybreak."

"Was that anything to do with the explosion everyone's been talking about?"

"No, I think that was in Dingle Hollow. I could hear them talking about it before they left to set the charge."

Jaz's eyes widen in alarm. "No way! Where were you?"

"Hiding in the oak tree."

"Bloody hell! Bet you were crapping yourself," Clay says.

I attempt a smile. "Yeah, I was. But what I'm more worried about is the spring. It stopped bubbling almost immediately after the explosion, and it still hasn't recovered."

There's a silence where Jaz and Clay both stare at me. In the background, I become aware of a gap in Ronnie's trance music over the sound system and the hubbub of people talking and laughing.

"Probably temporary," Clay says, but he doesn't look convinced.

"I'd better get back to work. Maybe we can we talk about it later?"

"I think we should," Jaz says. "And maybe we should organise a rota for staying out in the grove?"

"Nice idea, but I can't see your mum wanting you out in Phelps's territory by yourself all night."

She hesitates. "Well, we'll think of something."

Clay doesn't say anything, just shuffles his feet a bit and looks at the floor. I know he'd probably stay out there with me if I asked him, but he won't want to do it alone. He watches too many horror movies.

THE MINUTE I get home, I know something serious has happened. Ma's slamming pots around in the kitchen, making such a din she doesn't even hear me come in.

"I could bloody KILL HIM!" she shouts as another pan slams down on a work surface. She's talking to herself. It's not a good sign.

I walk in. "What's wrong?"

"Oh, Arlo! Sorry, I didn't hear you. It's that bloody Norman Phelps. Read this."

She picks up an envelope from the kitchen table and hands it to me. I can see her anger is subsiding and she's close to tears.

My heart sinks. I pull an official-looking letter out of the envelope. It's an eviction notice from his solicitor. I read it through a couple of times to make sure I'm understanding it right.

> Due to your unsuitability as tenants and the ongoing criminal proceedings against you, Mr. Phelps hereby issues a notice to quit.

According to the letter, we've got three months to get out.

"He can't do this."

"He already has." Ma's tone is flat.

"I'm so sorry, Ma. This is all my fault, isn't it?"

She sighs and attempts a smile. "No, Arlo. He's always wanted us out. Right from the beginning. I just wish we could afford a good lawyer."

"Do you have a copy of the tenancy agreement?"

"I think so, somewhere. It says we can live here 'in perpetuity'. But without backup, it's probably not worth the paper it's written on."

She looks so upset, I struggle to find words to make her feel better. "We're going to fight this, Ma. There's no way I'm letting this happen. He hasn't even given us a proper reason. Not a proven one. I'll take it to Jaz's and show Caroline later. Maybe she can help?"

Ma doesn't object. She doesn't say anything. I think she's forgotten I'm here, as she starts putting the pans away again. I stuff the letter in my pocket and take it up to my room, where I call Jaz and tell her.

"He can't do that!"

"That's what I said. Jaz, I feel so guilty. If Phelps hadn't caught me in the field, this wouldn't have happened."

"But you're supposed to be able to live there forever. I remember you telling me."

"Do you think your mum would mind looking at our tenancy agreement to see what she thinks?"

"I'm sure she wouldn't mind. You know how much she cares about you and your mum."

"Would it be okay if I bring the documents to yours?"

"Of course. Do you want to come over now?"

"Give me an hour. Thanks, Jaz."

"No problem. Have you told Clay?"

"Haven't had time."

"We can go over to his after you've shown the legal stuff to Mum. We need space to talk about this."

"In other words, you'd like to get out of the house?"

I can hear that she's smiling. "Got to admit, Arlo, Laurel is driving me mental at the moment. And her bedtimes are like torture!"

HAYDEN OPENS THE door when I get to Jaz's. My heart sinks. Jaz didn't tell me he'd be here. I'm so busy trying to squash my jealousy, it takes me a second to notice how worried he looks.

"I'm so sorry, Arlo. Dad's just...the worst."

My annoyance fades a little. Hayden looks like he's having a really bad day. Even so, I wish he wasn't here. The fact he opened the door shows how close he's got with Jaz, which is hard for me to swallow.

I follow him into the house. Caroline and Jaz are sitting at the table, looking through some papers. Caroline looks up and takes her glasses off.

"Hi, Arlo! Jaz told me what happened. Have you brought the eviction notice with you?"

"Yes, and the tenancy agreement." I pull them out of my pocket and hand them to her. Caroline puts her glasses back on and reads silently. Then she slams the papers down on the table in annoyance.

"I'm not surprised Melissa is upset! But I honestly think, reading this agreement—which I see is signed by the solicitors who dealt with your father's estate— Phelps doesn't have a leg to stand on."

"Try telling him that," I say.

"I intend to. According to this, you and your mum are effectively tenants of Primrose Cottage for as long as you want to stay there."

"But what about the crop circle business? He's determined to prosecute, and I can't prove I didn't make it. Worse, I was trespassing on his land at the time."

"I don't think it makes any difference," says Caroline. "Tell you what, can I make a copy of these and take them to show my solicitor friend?"

"Would you? That would be amazing! Ma seems to have given up already, and I'm worried she won't put up a fight. Which means Phelps would win."

"Leave it with me and I'll get on to it this evening."

I smile for the first time since I got back from work earlier.

As soon as Caroline has scanned the documents, Jaz suggests we leave to go to Clay's.

CLAY LETS US in. He glares at Hayden and mouths *what's he doing here?* to me behind his back. I shrug.

Once we're all perched around the table in Clay's incredibly messy kitchen, Jaz brings us all up to date on the plans for the village hall meeting. Apparently, her mum is chairing and presenting the meeting, and we just need to get all the backup pictures and information together to help her. We discuss the kind of pictures we think would work.

I notice Clay glowering at Hayden from time to time and wonder what's up with him. It's all feeling a bit awkward, and I'm too knackered to deal with it. I can't stop worrying about the eviction notice.

I stand up. "Sorry, guys, I need to go. I'm too tired to concentrate, and I want to make sure Ma's okay."

I reach down to get my rucksack and suddenly feel faint. I try to stand up again, but I can't. The room starts to go dark, and I stagger, unable to stop myself falling. I catch the look of horror on Clay's face, the shock and concern on Jaz's as I try to grab a chair. Then my head hits the floor hard and the chair crashes next to me, loud as thunder.

WHEN I OPEN my eyes, everything is different. I know instantly where I am. I'm back somewhere in the place Andraste took me to before. The air is filled with the myriad scents of dense woodland. I must be dreaming. I pinch my arm, but I can't wake up.

The darkness echoes with the sound of someone wailing, a heart-wrenching sound that goes right through me. I can't stop shivering.

A wolf howls. Another joins it. Within seconds, a whole pack is howling all around me. I'm frozen to the spot, my heart beating so fast I can hardly breathe.

There's a moment of silence when all I hear is my ragged breath. I try pinching my arm again, as hard as I can. It's no good. I'm stuck here.

The terrible wailing starts again. I don't want to move, but I have to find out what's happening. Inching forward as silently as possible, I pick my way over the thick leaf litter of the forest floor. The darkness and the trees make it hard to see. I'm so intent on trying to feel where I'm putting my feet, I walk straight into the low branch of a tree and practically spike my eye out. I grunt in surprise, then crouch low, worried I'm making too much noise.

From here, I can see through into a forest clearing. I make out the silhouette of someone moving on the far side.

I breathe in sharply. It's Andraste.

I watch her bend down to lift a dark shape off the ground, something so heavy she needs both arms to hold it up. At first, I can't make out what it is, but as she turns, I see the massive head and paws hanging limp and lifeless from her arms. It's a wolf. Her wailing fills the air again, and I feel her anguish in my heart.

Shadows slip around her in the dark, and I see eyes glinting. A wolf sniffs the air and looks in my direction. Can it see me? My heart skips several beats, and I try not to make a sound. If only I could get out of this nightmare and wake up back on the floor in Clay's room, where I should be.

Andraste lowers the dead animal gently back to the ground, then she crouches and puts her hand inside the creature's mouth.

She brings her hand out and lets out a high-pitched keening sound, which makes me jump. It feels like it's right inside my head. A couple of the wolves circle her, whining. I think they're upset too.

She stands up and looks straight towards where I'm crouching. She points at me. She can see me. She knows I'm here. I start to fall backwards.

CLAY'S FACE IS inches from mine. "Bloody hell, mate, are you alive?"

I rub my head. "I think so. What happened?"

Jaz pushes Clay out of the way. "You should probably lie there a minute, Arlo. You gave us such a shock! Would you like a glass of water?"

I nod. "Thanks. How long was I out for?"

"Only a few seconds. I was worried we were going to get the whole frothing, twitching thing, but it looks like you just fainted."

"Clay, for goodness' sake! You can't say stuff like that!" Jaz snaps, but she's smiling, probably with relief.

I carefully lever myself off the floor, and Hayden gives me a hand to get back onto a chair.

"Don't tell Ma about this, will you, Jaz?"

She hesitates. "Okay... but you should definitely see a doctor. Something's not right if you keep having these blackouts."

"I don't think it was a seizure, though. It's probably because I'm tired. And Ma's made me an appointment for next week."

"Look, I'm tired too, mate. You don't have to be so melodramatic about it."

"Clay!" Jaz scowls at him, but I can see she's trying not to laugh.

Fortunately, everyone seems to agree with me that I blacked out because I'm so tired. I say nothing about what I saw. I must have been here the whole time. I'm seriously worried I might be going insane. It all felt so real.

Jaz goes to get me some water, and after I've drunk it, I make a second attempt at leaving.

"I'll come with you," says Hayden. "If that's okay. I'm going your way anyway."

"Sure!" I'm surprised. It's not like I particularly want to walk back with Hayden right now, but it means he's not staying here cosying up with Jaz and saves me thinking too much about what just happened.

HAYDEN AND I head out of Tytheford towards Stanton. He starts asking me stuff about Jaz, which probably means he's been thinking about her. I tense.

"Do you know why Jaz's parents split up, Arlo?"

"Why don't you ask her?"

"Thought it might be something she didn't like talking about. I remember when she came to Tytheford Primary, of course. But we didn't think of asking questions like that back then."

"Just didn't work out, I guess. Very different cultures," Jaz says. She's okay with it. Remember, she was still very young when Caroline brought her back."

"Does she ever see her dad?"

"They've been out to Ethiopia a couple of times. It's expensive, though, and now Caroline's with Jake and has Laurel…"

"Jaz is very beautiful, isn't she?"

"Yeah, she's okay." Pretending I've never noticed how beautiful Jaz is makes me sound bitter and defensive again.

Neither of us says anything for a while.

By the time we get to the part of the lane that passes closest to the grove, the silence is getting awkward. I'm about to say something when I see the shadow of someone standing close to the hedge, and my breath catches. I recognise Andraste immediately, even in this light.

"Oh, that's weird," says Hayden.

I turn to him quickly. "What?"

"For a second, I thought I saw her there, but it was a raven."

I look again. She's not there anymore. A raven flies up from the lane to the top of the hedge.

"I think it's the same one that's been hanging out in the farmyard a fair bit. I keep worrying Dad will shoot it or something."

"Ravens are way too clever to get themselves shot. I've seen farmers try it around lambing time. Very rare they actually kill one. Strange behaviour getting so close to humans, though. I've seen that one around the café too."

"Maybe it was hand-reared or something."

"Yeah, maybe." I'm only half listening to him. I feel an increasing sense of dread and try to crush the urge to walk faster.

We get to Primrose Cottage and I'm pleased to see the light is on.

"Hope your mum's okay. Tell her I'm very sorry about Dad and the eviction thing, won't you?" Hayden says.

"Thanks. Will do." I suddenly think of Hayden's mother shading her face to hide the bruises. "And I hope your mum's okay too."

Hayden freezes. The subject of his mother is obviously taboo. I open the garden gate and walk towards the front door.

"See you tomorrow maybe," says Hayden.

"Yeah, maybe." I guess if he's going to start seeing Jaz, I'll have to learn to like him again. I can't let anything ruin my friendship with her, even her getting a boyfriend that isn't me.

As I watch him walking on down the lane towards the farm, I come to a decision. Once I've checked in with Ma, I'm going to head to the grove for the night again, even though it's the last thing I want to do.

Andraste will be there; I feel it in my bones. It's time I asked her some questions. I need to know what's happening to me, and I think she's the only one with the answers.

Chapter 18

I SLIP OUT OF the cottage into the twilight. Ma seems a lot calmer now she knows that Caroline's getting in touch with a solicitor friend about the eviction notice, so I'm not so worried about leaving her.

Apart from the occasional screech of an owl, the night is silent, and the garden is heavy with the fragrance of roses. Before I walk out into the deep shadow of the lane, on impulse I pick a rosebud for Dad from the nearest bush, carefully avoiding the thorns. Dad loved roses.

A light breeze blows through the trees bordering Phelps's land, and they rustle like they're talking to each other in the dark. My pulse quickens as I approach the hidden entrance to the wood.

The grove feels different. I listen out, but there's still no sound from the spring. I hide my rucksack in the hollow oak, then walk out to look at the water, still holding the rose I've brought for Dad.

As I reach the spring, a faint scent of decay hangs in the air. The full moon is reflected perfectly in the water. There's no movement. Any hope I had that it might be bubbling dissipates.

"He's killed it."

I jump at the sound of Andraste's voice. I didn't hear her approaching at all, even though I was listening out for her. She stands next to me as I look into the spring, and I catch the heady scent of honeysuckle.

"Do you think it will recover?"

"Things will only get worse until the forfeit is paid."

A chill goes down my spine.

"How do you know they'll get worse?"

She doesn't answer.

"Is the rose for me?"

I don't like to tell her it was for Dad, so I offer it to her.

"Thank you." She takes the rose and places it on the ground before untying a pendant from around her neck. She hands it to me. "I made this for you."

Even in this light, I know instantly what it is. A wolf fang. She's threaded it onto a leather thong. My legs feel like jelly. It's her way of telling me she saw me in the other place.

"It's a talisman to help you."

Help me do what? I can't bring myself to ask, so I just tie it around my neck. I don't want to offend her. I'm actually shaking as I mumble my thanks.

She picks up the rose and puts it in her hair. Her eyes glitter in the dark. "Come, Arlo. We need to make it clear to him things can't go on like this. You can help me tonight. It's time to unleash the wolves."

"You're not seriously going to confront Phelps with them, are you?"

"It will be a warning. Come with me. You'll see."

She grasps my hand and pulls me with her as she starts to run across Spring Field, I find it hard to keep up. and want to pull my hand away so I can run at my own pace, but her grip is like iron.

As the ground slopes up towards the boundary hedge, she suddenly stops and turns to look at me. She lets go of my hand.

"We'll start here."

I look back down the slope we've climbed. We're on the shadow side of Wights Mound. It towers up from the land below, dark and silent under the silver moonlight.

"Start what?"

She's wearing a plain black dress tonight, with no sleeves. The tattoos weaving up her arms seem almost to move and spiral in the moonlight. She stares at me, and I'm hypnotised by the reflection of the moon in her eyes. I can't remember ever seeing the moon reflected like that in someone's eyes before. It's eerily beautiful.

She reaches out and taps me sharply on the forehead. I gasp in surprise and close my eyes to stop the intense feeling that everything is moving.

"Open your eyes, Arlo. It's time to start the circle."

I open them. Somehow, nothing looks how it usually does. I gaze around me in amazement. Everything seems to be alive. Literally everything. The land we're standing on, every tree and rock and feature. Alive and breathing. I must be dreaming.

"Now start running," she says.

Instead of racing ahead, Andraste keeps pace with me until we fall into the same rhythm, moving together, not holding hands, keeping about a couple of metres apart. She leans forward and makes the weirdest noise ever, a shrieking sound—the same sound I heard out in the field the night I had the seizure.

"When you see the earthlight, start to follow the pattern," she says.

At the edges of my vision, I see faint threads of green light, like the ones we saw in the barley field that night and, I realise, like the flash of green I saw in the water pouring from the kitchen tap. Gradually, the strands become clearer, stretching in front of us, as if the land itself is guiding our path. Andraste follows a thread and crosses in front of me, not slowing down for even an instant.

"Your turn," she cries.

I get it. Following a separate strand, I cross in front of her, then she crosses back in front of me again. We keep up the pace, following the earthlight, weaving in front of each other in sequence, as though we're taking part in some weird and intricate dance.

The crop is flattened by our feet as we go, gradually creating a pattern as complex as the tattoos that spiral Andraste's skin. We move faster and faster, until we're running, constantly crisscrossing each other, following the streams of light.

We keep up the momentum for what feels like hours, never stopping. I'm exhausted, but I have to follow the strand that stretches and bends ahead, guiding me, informing the direction I run.

At last, we start to slow down, completing the final spirals. As the pattern we've created weaves back in on itself, the earthlight fades away, and I drop to the ground, exhausted.

I lie on my back between two rows of barley, chest heaving, trying to catch my breath, staring up at the stars. I've never seen them so clearly before, a million pinpoint lights sweeping together to form the diamond river of the Milky Way over our heads. One galaxy in the ocean of the universe. The beauty and enormity of it are overwhelming.

Andraste leans over me. I see the whirling stars and planets reflected deep in her eyes. She reaches towards me, and for a moment I think she's going to pull me into her arms, but instead she taps me sharply on the forehead.

Again.

Why didn't I see it coming this time? Falling into the warm earth, I wrap my arms around my body and curl up like a seed. Embracing the weight of darkness that cocoons me, I sleep.

I OPEN MY eyes. I heard something. Voices, some way off. Directly in my line of vision is a single red rose, the one I picked for Dad but gave to Andraste. At least, I think I did.

My head feels like a lump of lead, and I wonder if I've had yet another seizure. I'm seriously worried.

I try to sit up but can't and start to panic, then realise I'm trapped in my sleeping bag. I almost laugh out loud at my own stupidity and quickly unzip the bag and climb out. I don't remember getting the sleeping bag out last night, or even getting back to the grove. I must have been completely zonked. It looks like I fell asleep right in front of the oak. Looking around, I find my rucksack still inside the hollow trunk. Was the whole thing a dream?

Listening out for anyone approaching, I carefully roll up the sleeping bag. Then I step inside the oak and crouch down, making a fumbled attempt to stuff it back in the rucksack.

I hear the voices again. I think they're getting closer. One of them is Phelps. I can't hear what he's saying, but it's definitely him. I recognise the sharpness of his tone.

Heart thumping, I look out across the grove, wondering whether to make a dash for it. I turn to peer out through a narrow split in the trunk where I get a view towards St. Ann's Spring. The Land Rover is parked really close by. My chest tightens. I must have been so visible sleeping out in the open in a bright-blue sleeping bag. Phelps obviously didn't look into the clearing, or I'd be in deep trouble right now.

As he gets closer, I can hear him more distinctly.

"Revenge...I'll bet you. We'll go there now and catch him sleeping."

"Are you sure that's a good idea, Mr. Phelps?" I don't recognise the other voice.

"Just because I'm evicting them doesn't give him the right to break the law. Come on, jump in."

He's talking about me. I'm not certain what he thinks I've done, but I'm guessing there must be another circle. I blink and images from last night come flooding back to me. Andraste. Running. Chasing strands of green light. My blood chills.

No time to look now, the minute the Land Rover drives off, I scramble out of the tree and race back across the grove. I have to get back to Primrose Cottage and warn Ma before Phelps gets there.

Chapter 19

I RUN IN THROUGH the front door and go straight upstairs to dump my bag, shouting out to Ma as I go.

"Ma? Quick, Phelps is coming. I overheard him saying so when I woke up in the grove. Get ready to call the police."

There's no answer. As I put the bag down, I see her from my bedroom window down by the bees. I thunder back down the stairs and out into the garden.

"Ma? Are you okay?"

She turns to look at me and smiles.

"Hello, love! I'm fine. I had a lovely dream about wolves last night and was wondering what it means. I must look it up in my dream book."

Sometimes I could shake her for being so flaky. "Ma, listen. Phelps is going to be here any second. Tell him I've been in the house all night, okay? I only just got up."

"Okay." She sounds dubious. "What's wrong this time?"

"I reckon someone must have made another circle on his land last night. He thinks it's me."

"Wasn't it?"

"No." It's easier to lie to Ma than explain anything about what happened last night. There's no time.

162

We both hear the loud banging on the front door. "Call the police, Ma. I'll deal with him."

We hurry back up to the house. Ma picks up her phone in the kitchen, and I go to the front door and open it.

"Well if it isn't Arlo Fry. Surprised to see me?"

"What do you want?" I glare at Phelps standing at the door, his rifle slung over his shoulder. The stocky little man with him looks familiar. I think he works at the piggery.

"Don't pretend you don't know. You obviously haven't learnt your lesson."

I hesitate. Has he come here to fight? I can hear Ma talking quietly on the phone out in the kitchen. I hope the police step on it.

I look Phelps in the eye. "I've no idea what you're talking about, but you can't come around here and threaten us like this. It's harassment."

Phelps grabs the front of my T-shirt and pulls me out of the front door. I see his fist a second too late. He punches the side of my head so hard I stagger and fall back against the door. For a moment, I can see nothing but stars in front of my eyes.

Then I focus. I can't believe he hit me like that. I'm so angry I don't even think about it. I lurch forward and punch him as hard as I can in the solar plexus. His grunt of pain is kind of satisfying, but my pleasure at hurting him doesn't last. He grabs his rifle from his shoulder and swings it around. He cracks my shins with the rifle butt and knocks me off my feet.

When I try to stand up, it's so painful, I nearly throw up.

Then out of nowhere I'm suddenly showered with cold water, and I gasp in surprise. Ma stands in the doorway holding a bucket in one hand, glaring at Phelps. He's completely soaked. In fact, it looks like he got most of the bucket load.

"How dare you come here and attack my son, Norman Phelps! I've called the police. They're on their way."

Phelps smirks. "You didn't see what happened. He attacked me. It's his word against mine, and I've got a witness."

I look up at the farm worker. He looks very uncomfortable and avoids my eye, but I can guess whose side he's on. He'd lose his job otherwise.

Ma stands right in front of Phelps and yells at him. "Why? Why are you doing this? What's wrong with you?" I've never seen her so angry.

"No one gets away with destroying my crops. He should have learnt the first time." He turns to the man with him. "Come on. Let's leave them to it. They won't be living here much longer."

Somehow, I manage to stop myself spitting in his face. After all, things are bad enough already. I don't want to end up hospitalised.

As soon as he's in his Land Rover, I hobble back inside with Ma. At least my leg's not broken.

PC COLENUTT SITS on the sofa and looks at me sympathetically. "Are you sure you don't want to press charges, Arlo? There's not much we can do otherwise."

I grimace. "There's no point, to be honest. Phelps had a witness with him, and I'm pretty sure he'd say I started it."

"And you didn't see anything, Mrs. Fry?"

"No, sorry. I heard the commotion, but I was busy filling the bucket."

Neither PC Colenutt nor I comment on that. Ma's behaviour can defy logic at the best of times.

PC Colenutt changes the subject abruptly. "So sorry to hear about your eviction notice, by the way. I hope you manage to contest it successfully."

I'm guessing this is all off the record, but it's nice to know she's on our side.

"Thank you," Ma says. "Arlo has managed to get us some legal help, and we're trying to stay optimistic."

Ma starts smothering my head and leg in some weird-smelling ointment from her herbal remedy selection in the kitchen cupboard. I realise she's actually smiling. Maybe covering Phelps in cold water earlier has made her feel better. I'm glad one of us is happy.

"Well, I must be off now," PC Colenutt says. "Duty calls. Apparently, someone's made another crop circle on Mr. Phelps's land. Which you know nothing about, I'm sure." She stares at me, unblinking, as she says this. I hold her gaze.

"A new circle? I'd like to see it too." I'm not lying. Even if I actually helped Andraste make it, I've no idea what it looks like.

"Remember it's private land, Arlo," PC Colenutt says sharply.

I grin at her. "Yeah, I know. Don't worry, I've no intention of running into Mr. Phelps twice in a day if I can help it."

She smiles. "I'll leave it at that then. If you're sure about not pressing charges?"

"I'm sure."

"We'll record the incident anyway, in case he tries it again."

The minute the police car drives off, I reach for the phone.

"Clay? You busy? There's a new circle on Phelps's land. I happen to know he's going to be caught up with the police for a bit. You coming?"

WE PUSH THROUGH the gap in the hedge and head towards the spring. I figure the trees will give us good cover to suss out what's going on before we step into the open.

We stand in the grove for a moment, listening to the chittering of the swallows as they dip and skim over the spring. There's no sound of farm machinery or people anywhere close by.

"What's that around your neck?"

I instinctively reach up and touch the wolf fang.

"It's an animal tooth. I think it's a talisman."

"A what? You're not seeing that old freak again, are you?"

"Not in the sense you mean."

"But she was here, right?"

"I saw her, yeah."

"What did she want with you?"

"To talk about the spring dying, since you're being nosy."

Clay looks at me hard for a moment, then sniffs. "So where do you think the circle might be?"

Clay always assumes I'll know what's happening on this farm, as if I still live here, which is kind of nice, even though I don't.

"No idea. Let's get to the top of Spring Field and take a look around."

We trudge up the hill. The day is getting hotter, and it feels like a thunderstorm's brewing. When we get to the hedge boundary with Nine Acre, we stop and turn to take a look at Wights Mound. That's when we see the circle. We just walked up past it.

Clay's jaw practically hits the floor. "Bloody hell! Who do you think made that one? It's awesome!"

I'm dumbstruck. My heart starts racing and my mind whirrs in panic, remembering what happened last night, the pattern we made running together, flattening the barley with our feet as we wove through it. Surely it's not possible? Yet it's in the right place.

Absentmindedly, I touch the pendant hanging from my neck and feel a tingling sensation in my fingers. I stare at the wolf fang for a moment. Is the tingling connected to the circle? I can't be sure.

"Look at the wolves, man. It's almost creepy the way they seem to move. I love it." Clay is awestruck.

"It's a warning."

"Eh? What are you talking about?"

"Just think it could be some kind of warning about the mining."

"So you reckon it's been done by a bunch of eco warriors?"

"Maybe."

I can't tell him. He's one of my oldest friends, but I just can't. How do I begin to explain that I think I helped to make it? Instead, I tell him to get his phone out to film it.

"We'd better not take too long out here. Phelps'll be out combining it as soon as the police leave."

Clay films the circle for a few minutes, giving me a chance to stand and stare at it, watching the wolves snarling, racing, chasing each other as the breeze sings through the surrounding barley. The beautiful Celtic knot pattern of the circle is breathtaking, weaving around and between the three wolves, holding the pack together. Just like one of Andraste's tattoos.

Whatever's happening to me, it's off the scale weird. I'm so out of my depths right now. The power Andraste holds over me is really scary, yet at the same time I'm increasingly fascinated by her.

"Okay, so what are we waiting for?" Clay asks. "Keep your mouth open like that, and you'll catch flies."

"I was thinking—"

"No time to think, Arlo. I hear someone coming."

I listen. He's right. A vehicle's coming our way.

We run as fast as we can back down the hill, past the spring and under the branches of the oak, into the grove. We only stop to catch our breath when we're hidden by the trees again. I can hear an engine ticking over in the distance. Maybe Phelps is showing the circle to the police.

"I think they've stopped up the field. Let's get out of here."

There's no time to stop and pay my respects to Dad. It feels wrong to be running away from his resting place like I'm a criminal, but I really don't want another encounter with Phelps anytime soon.

We scrabble through the hedgerow and back out onto the lane.

"That bruise by your ear is coming up a treat, Arlo. You should go and put some steak on it or something."

"Steak? In my house? That'll be the day. Ma'll be weaving some crappy yoghurt poultice to stick on my head if I'm lucky. Do you want to come back with me?"

"Nah, think Mum might be home, and I want to catch her before she swans off back to her boyfriend's again.

I need to talk to her about money for food. You not working?"

"Not today. Was going to prepare some more stuff for the town hall meeting. By the way, I meant to ask, what was your problem with Hayden yesterday? You were being so hostile!"

"Oh, that. He made me angry. Saw him out in Tytheford with Phelps. I was about to say hi, but he ignored me and stared straight ahead like he didn't know me. I was left standing, grinning at no one like an idiot. And I *know* he saw me. I can understand why he wouldn't want his dad to know who he hangs out with, but he could've said hi."

"Maybe he was trying to save you getting punched in the head? This is a small place. Phelps knows you're a friend of mine, and most people don't make crop circles by themselves."

Clay sighs. "Yeah, maybe. Since he's getting close with Jaz, suppose I should try to be nice."

The pain in my head suddenly feels much worse.

Chapter 20

I WAKE UP IN a cold sweat, the stink of the stagnant spring in the air. The grove is starting to smell of dead things.

I was dreaming about Dad again. The dreams always start the same way. Dad's body, noose around his neck, swinging to and fro in the wind. Last night, the body tried to whisper something to me. Something important.

As I climb out of the sleeping bag, I remember what it was. *Phelps is already fracking on the farm.* The dream was probably my subconscious coming up with answers to my questions, but I bet I'm right.

That's why he gets so angry about people making crop formations, and why he's so determined to keep people off his land. He's desperate to keep his mining operation in Dingle Hollow a secret because he doesn't have planning permission.

Snippets of conversations I've overheard come back to me. *We're risking a lot as it is.*

If I'm right, it would explain everything. But what I really need before the public meeting is some photographic evidence to prove it. I can't wait to catch up with Jaz and Clay to tell them. The meeting's the day after tomorrow. Hopefully, that'll give us enough time.

I quickly pack away my sleeping bag and head out of the wood.

BACK HOME, AFTER a shower, I stare at my face in the bathroom mirror. My hair is dark like Ma's was before she started getting all the grey streaks, but my eyes are like Dad's. At least, I think they are, from what I remember. It's funny how you live with someone all your life but you forget the colour of their eyes. I think his were grey, like mine. Too late to check now. I could ask Ma, but it would only upset her to talk about him. I know she still misses him so much.

I turn my face to look at the bruise by my ear. It's not that noticeable, but there's a bit of puffiness around my left eye still. I shout down the stairs.

"Ma?"

"Yes, love?"

"Have you got any kind of remedy I can put on my face before I go to work? Think I might be getting a black eye."

I hear Ma muttering under her breath and the sound of her moving jars and bottles in the kitchen cupboards. I take the opportunity to call Clay while she's busy.

He doesn't pick up. Probably still asleep. I take a deep breath and call Jaz. I haven't spoken to her since the fight with Phelps.

"Hi, Arlo, how's your head?"

"You heard about the fight?"

"Yeah, Clay said. Can't believe Phelps would do that. How come you didn't call me about it?"

She sounds a bit hurt. I think fast.

"Sorry. Was worried you'd say something to Hayden if he was there. Must be so difficult for him, y'know, having a father like that."

"You're telling me. I wonder how his mum is. I haven't found a tactful way to ask him yet." She sounds slightly appeased, but I can tell from her voice how much she really cares about Hayden. Great. I feel like I've been stabbed in the heart. Again.

"I need to talk to you, Jaz. I've worked out why Phelps gets so angry about the crop circles. Only thought of it when I woke up in the wood this morning."

"You're still sleeping out there? That's a bit risky, isn't it? Phelps is gunning for you! We should ask Clay to take a turn or at least stay there with you."

"It's okay. Let's be honest, I'm the one who cares most about whether Phelps cuts the grove down. You know that."

Jaz hesitates. "Yeah, I guess you're right."

"The point is, I think he's already started fracking. He gets uptight about anything that draws attention to the farm."

There's a brief silence.

"Actually, that would explain a lot!" Jaz sounds excited. "Like why he wants you out of the cottage. You're too close. And why he was so angry that he risked starting a fight with you. I can't believe he did that. I'd have called, by the way, but Hayden came over."

Ouch.

I try to sound indifferent. "Are you seeing him tonight? I wanted to run something past him."

"Sure. He's coming over later. You should come too."

"I don't want to get in your way…"

She laughs. "Arlo, you're being ridiculous. Make it after seven when Laurel's gone to bed."

"Okay. I'll try and get hold of Clay as well." I don't mention that I tried to call Clay first.

"Good idea. We need to talk about the public meeting. Mum's arranged for a speaker to come from the national protest group in London."

I breathe a sigh of relief. At this rate, I might be able to duck out of talking on stage. "Brilliant! Tell me more about it later."

Downstairs, Ma gives me a pack of frozen organic sweetcorn to hold above my ear, and I sit out in the sun for a while, trying not to think too much about Jaz and Hayden. I call Clay again, but there's still no answer, so I leave a message.

Now I'm running late, and as I leave the house, I remember I have to pick up the eggs again on the way to work. Wish I'd remembered earlier.

Mary's already out by the gate when I get to Spring Farm, the boxes of eggs next to her on the ground. I say hello, and she stares at me blankly for a moment. Then she focuses and pushes a wisp of white hair back from her face. She attempts a smile.

"You're late again, Arlo! Got you the eggs ready. Thought I'd save you coming in."

"Thanks. You're very kind!" But the way she's looking distractedly at the hedge behind me, I can tell she's not really listening. I touch her arm. "Are you okay, Mary? You seem a bit worried."

She stares at me, eyes suddenly dark with fear. "There's trouble coming, young Arlo. Seen lych light in the water this morning. Death is stalking us."

"Lych light? What's lych light?"

"You know, corpse candles—Hob's lantern, some call it. The light that leads you to your doom. I seen it in the water. Green, it was. Reckon time's up for me or my Harry."

I pick up the egg boxes from the ground where she's stacked them, mostly to hide what I'm thinking. Green light. Like what me and Ma saw. Like the earthlight. My stomach twists with anxiety.

"Don't worry, Mary. Ma saw a light in the water the other day too. Reckon it might have more to do with Phelps and his gas mining than any corpse light."

"Dunno 'bout that. But I reckons someone will be paying the forfeit before this all stops."

I nearly drop the eggs. Mary steadies the boxes in my arms to prevent any falling.

"What do you mean, 'paying the forfeit'?"

"Blood on the ground. The forfeit needed to restore the balance, so they say. Something from the old ways. You'll be going to the meeting in Tytheford Hall, I'm guessing? Your ma says you're opposing the mining."

I glance into her crinkly old eyes. "Yeah, I'll be there." I try to sound normal, even though my hands are shaking. "Are you and Harry going?"

"I'll go. Bit far for Harry, what with his leg and all. But that fancy-pants Norman Phelps needs stopping, that's for sure. There's bad trouble coming, make no mistake."

I can tell she wants to talk, and if I wasn't in a rush, I'd stay longer. "See you at the meeting then, Mary, if I don't see you before. Ronnie can sort out the payment for these, okay?"

"Don't you worry about that. You get off to work now."

As I walk on towards Corn Flakes, I feel really on edge. Even the breeze through the poplars sounds like Andraste whispering *forfeit, forfeit, forfeit*...

BY THE TIME I leave work, my head's aching and I'm exhausted from lack of sleep.

It's already quarter past six as I'm locking up the café, too late to bother going home, so I head straight to Jaz's place, hoping Hayden and Clay won't have arrived yet.

Hayden answers the door. I try to hide my disappointment by smiling. I'm getting better at this.

"Clay said it would be you! Come on in," he says.

So Clay's here too. I feel a bit like I'm late for my own party. I follow Hayden through to the kitchen, where Jaz and Clay are transfixed by her laptop screen.

"Can I get a look-in?" I say.

"Sit down, Arlo. I'll get you a Coke." Jaz tries to be hospitable as always, but it's obvious she's excited. I nick her chair and sit in front of the computer.

"Start again, Clay. I want to see the whole thing!" Hopefully, I sound enthusiastic. Truth is, I feel like I'm falling down a mineshaft every time I think about the wolf circle.

We watch the clip in silence: the only sound on the film is the wind blowing.

Seeing it again, my heart starts racing. I feel sick. Without thinking, I rub the talisman Andraste gave me between my fingers. I only stop when I notice Jaz staring at it curiously.

When the clip ends, Clay looks up at me. "Never thought I'd say this, but I don't see how it's humanly possible to make a circle that good in one night."

"You're starting to sound like my mother!" I tease him to cover how weird I'm feeling.

"Let's watch it again." Jaz clicks play before anyone has time to disagree with her, but I notice her eyes are drawn to the wolf fang again while the clip is playing.

Suddenly Hayden reaches over and pauses the film. "Look, Arlo! Isn't that the raven we were talking about?"

I hadn't noticed the raven while Clay and I were out filming, but now Hayden's pointing it out, I can see it, staring up at us from the edge of the circle. I get a feeling like ice running through my veins.

"Hasn't anyone ever told you that one raven looks a lot like another, Hayden?" Clay says.

His sarcasm makes him sound mean. I feel uncomfortable.

Jaz quickly changes the subject. "Arlo's come up with a theory about why Hayden's dad doesn't want people coming to see the crop circles, even though it would make him money."

"Yeah, he's stupid," Clay says.

Jaz ignores him. "Arlo reckons he's already started fracking operations at Home Farm."

"Slimy toerag!"

"Clay, you're really not helping." Jaz glares at him.

"What do you think, Hayden?" I ask. "Is it possible?"

Hayden looks at the floor. "Maybe. I honestly don't know. He doesn't allow anyone near Dingle Hollow, where the planned drilling site is."

"Not even you? But you live there..." Jaz sounds incredulous before her voice trails off. She glances at me. I reckon we're both thinking how Hayden's mum looked when we saw her. Guess no one argues with Phelps.

"Dad's employed a security company to stop anyone getting close," says Hayden. "Been there a while already. He says it's a health and safety issue, but Arlo could be right. It could easily be an excuse to hide what he's doing. I wouldn't put it past him."

"Pity. I was hoping to get some photos. They could be useful for the public meeting," I say.

Jaz looks worried. "Well, don't risk it, Arlo. You'd be nuts to go there."

"Yeah, I know. Thought it might help if we knew the scale of things. It's not that important."

"Yes, it is. We need all the evidence we can get. He'll probably have a whole PR team on his side." Clay glares at Hayden like it's somehow his fault.

I try to get him to focus on the problem. "Yeah, but Clay, it's not worth getting arrested over."

Jaz smiles at me, but the atmosphere here has put me even more on edge. There must be something else going on between Clay and Hayden I don't know about, and it's making everything hard work.

I decide to leave and make my excuses.

"Okay, you guys. I'm on yet another long shift tomorrow, so I'm heading off home."

Jaz gets up to show me out. "We've got one more day to sort out what we're doing at the public meeting. Shall we hook up again tomorrow and run through it all?"

I nod, and Clay grunts in agreement. Hayden just looks anxious. I'm not sure if he's worried about the meeting or if Clay's attitude is getting to him.

Chapter 21

As I'm heading out of the door, Hayden grabs his jacket. "Can I come with you, Arlo?"

"Yeah, sure." I'm not exactly overjoyed he's coming with me, but I'm not surprised either. Clay's difficult when he's that spiky.

As we make our way out of Tytheford along the Stanton road in the dusk, Hayden suddenly ducks into someone's front garden and hides behind a hedge. At first, I wonder what on earth's going on, then I hear the Land Rover. I look around in time to see Phelps glaring at me as he drives past.

Hayden can't afford to be seen with any of us, especially me. He jumps back out of the garden, brushing leaves from his hair. I don't blame him for hiding, but I'm curious.

"Will you actually be able to come to the public meeting, Hayden? Like Clay said, your dad is bound to be there."

"I know. I'm going to have to give it a miss. I tried to explain to Jaz and Clay earlier, but I don't think Clay got it. He doesn't like me much at the best of times. But I can help you all set up, so long as I leave before Dad arrives." He looks at me carefully. "You understand, don't you?"

I nod. "Yeah, I get it." Despite my jealousy about him and Jaz, I actually feel sorry for him.

We don't talk much on the way back, but it's not an uncomfortable silence. More like it used to be before, when we were close friends.

"You know," he says after a while, "I could take photos of Dingle Hollow."

"Don't take any risks with your dad, Hayden. It's not worth it."

"It would be easier for me. I'm less likely to attract attention."

"Too dangerous. I don't want to cause you any trouble. It's not that important."

"I think it is. I can probably get away with it if I plan carefully. But if I get the photos, I don't want anyone to know it was me who took them, okay?"

"Except me and Jaz and Clay?"

"No, just you. The fewer people who know, the better. Honestly."

I'm dubious. "Sounds like you're sticking your neck out too much. I mean, you have to *live* there."

He smiles. "Not for much longer if I can help it. I'm waiting to see if I can get Mum to come with me before she has the baby."

"She's pregnant?"

"Yes, but it's early days. Dad doesn't know. I think it might help her to leave."

"All the more reason to be extra careful. If he catches you..."

"He won't. I'll try and get the photos for tomorrow."

I hesitate. "Thanks, Hayden. But not at the expense of anyone getting hurt, okay?"

He doesn't say anything, but I know he understands what I mean. A few moments of awkward silence later, we reach my house.

"See you tomorrow, then!" he says and continues on his way.

"Yeah. See you tomorrow."

Back in the cottage, I feel exhausted. I need to catch up on some sleep. I decide to take a chance that Phelps won't cut down any trees in the night so I can sleep in my own bed for once. Ma will probably rest easier having me at home too. I've noticed the circles around her eyes are getting darker recently.

I fall into a deep, dreamless sleep the moment my head hits the pillow.

HAYDEN ARRIVES INCREDIBLY early the next day—before I set off to work. I take him through to the kitchen, and he hands me his phone. He looks excited.

"Sorry I couldn't get closer. Even at six in the morning, I'm pretty sure the night watchman was there. This is the best I could manage. I've messaged them to you already."

"Thanks for risking it. You're a star!"

Hayden goes red and fiddles with his glasses.

I start scanning through the photos and nearly drop his phone in surprise. It's obvious that the mining operation has been going for much longer than anyone realised. Must be several months, at least.

"What the heck? Look at that crane! It's massive! I don't get it, Hayden. There must have been so much traffic going in and out of the farm when this arrived. I can't believe I didn't notice all the lorries passing by the cottage."

"Look, I live on the farm and I didn't realise either. But Dad's had loads of construction work done, with the piggery and everything, and we get a lot of deliveries either late evening or very early in the morning. That's how Dad operates."

Hayden's right. I've seen Phelps up and talking to the EcoGas men way before normal work hours, which means he's trying to avoid anyone knowing his business.

"Do you think…maybe I'm wrong here, but it's just crossing my mind…" I hesitate, trying to decide if it's okay to talk to Hayden about this.

"Go on." He looks at me expectantly.

"Well, I wonder if building the piggery and that massive ugly new barn in Elm Field was a blinder for this mining operation. I mean, your dad isn't much of a farmer if you don't mind me saying so."

"It's okay. I know he's not. It's all about the money for him. That's why he married Mum. Her family's really wealthy and he's a gold digger." I can see from Hayden's expression that talking about his mum is hard for him.

Ma always wondered how Phelps managed to find the money to buy the farm. That would explain it. It wasn't his.

Hayden shifts uncomfortably. "I reckon Dad stands to make a fortune from the gas if he strikes lucky. He's always doing shady deals with finances, you know that. And like I say, making money is all he's interested in."

We're interrupted by Ma coming in from the garden with a bunch of freshly cut herbs. The clean, pungent smell of thyme fills the air. If she's surprised to see Hayden, she doesn't show it.

"Nice to see you, Hayden. Fancy a cup of tea?" She quickly places the thyme in a muslin drying bag and picks up the kettle.

"Thanks, but I must be getting back." He sighs. "Dad wants me in the piggery. One of his workers is off sick."

"Never mind," Ma says. She opens a cake tin on the countertop. "Here, take a piece of flapjack to eat on the way. Sounds like you need it."

"Thanks so much, Mrs. Fry. It's very kind of you." Hayden blushes as he takes a chunk from the tin and pushes his fringe off his forehead with his free hand.

"My name's Melissa," Ma says. "You've known me practically all your life. There's no need to be formal."

I'm proud of Ma. She managed not to ask any awkward questions.

And I bet she's really curious.

I'M RIGHT. SHE IS.

"Whatever did he want, so early in the morning?" she asks the minute Hayden's left.

"He managed to sneak some photos of Dingle Hollow for the village hall meeting tomorrow."

"Must have been difficult for him."

"Yes, but he said it was less risky for him than for me. The thing is..." I stop short. I've already told her too much.

"What?"

"Nothing."

"You were going to say something."

Guess I'll have to tell her. "Look, I said I wouldn't tell anyone, but I'm worried it might affect you too."

"Go on..."

"Hayden doesn't want anyone to know it was him who took the photos."

"He expects you to take the rap?"

"No, it's not that. Though I guess I'll have to make out to Jaz and Clay that I took them."

"I don't get it."

"Me neither, really. And to be honest, I'm not too happy about it."

"So why did you agree?"

"Probably sounds crazy, but I don't want him or his mum getting hurt. Phelps can't really fight me again in public, but he could hit out at Hayden, same way he does with Hayden's mum."

Ma absentmindedly picks up her knitting and sits at the kitchen table. "Then I think you've done the right thing," she says.

I watch her knit a row of black while I make a coffee. The rows are definitely getting shorter and tighter.

I take my coffee upstairs to find my phone and check for Hayden's message. I'll have to download the photos before I forward them to Jaz, so she doesn't know they came from Hayden. It all feels very underhand, but I have no choice.

I wish he'd told Jaz, though. I'm still not entirely sure why he hasn't. I think about the way he ducked into a hedge to hide from his dad yesterday and ignored Clay in the street. How is he going to manage a relationship with Jaz if he can't even be seen with us?

JAZ WAITS UNTIL my break before she shares the photos with the others. She wants us to look at them together. I still feel bad about getting the credit for taking them when it was actually Hayden.

"Here you go—have a look." Jaz hands her phone to Clay and Hayden.

As Clay flicks from one view to another, Hayden does a good job of being amazed, as if he's never seen them before.

Clay's eyes are practically popping out of his head. "Look at all that wire fencing! It's like some secret MOD site or something. And the mine's so big! It takes so much land!"

Jaz gets all enthusiastic. "But when people at the meeting see these, a whole mining outfit on farmland, with no planning permission..." She grabs her phone back and flicks through the photos again. "Whatever, I think we can add these into our presentation. We'll just be vague about where they came from. Don't want you getting into any more trouble, Arlo."

"Well done for getting them, mate. Can't have been easy," Clay says.

I feel really uncomfortable, but when I glance at Hayden, he stares at me meaningfully, shaking his head almost imperceptibly to make it clear he doesn't want them to know it was him, so I don't say anything.

"Hey, more good news by the way," Jaz says. "Mum got a notice back from Natural England to say they want to look further into preserving the grove and spring as SSSIs, which means in theory Phelps can't legally damage any of the trees while they investigate."

"Too late for the spring, though," I say.

"You're such a pessimist, Arlo. I'm sure it will run clear again soon." But Jaz stops smiling. Even she isn't really convinced.

We chat a bit more about plans and arrangements for the village hall meeting tomorrow, then my break ends and I have to get back to work.

Over the rest of my shift, I see the raven by the front window a few times. I don't want to end up thinking like Ma and Mary, but I feel in my bones there's a lot more trouble brewing.

Chapter 22

THE VILLAGE HALL smells of dust and floor polish. I already feel nervous as hell, and there's still a couple of hours to go before the doors open. I catch myself twisting the wolf fang in my fingers and try to focus on helping Jaz.

There's no sign of Hayden. I'm surprised. I thought he'd be keen to help her get things ready, even if he can't stay for the meeting. I still can't work out their relationship.

Jaz is staring at me expectantly, and I realise I've been daydreaming and not helping her look for a socket so Clay can charge his laptop. A quick hunt around the room and we find one behind the stage.

Caroline calls everyone over to discuss a last-minute problem that's cropped up. A leaflet was distributed to every household in Tytheford and Stanton last night, although unsurprisingly we didn't get one at Primrose Cottage. Phelps probably delivered them himself.

"The bottom line is he's now trying to *bribe* everyone into supporting him," says Caroline, handing me a copy to look at.

I glance through quickly. Along with the 'bringing jobs to the area' stuff, there's a paragraph about 'a substantial lump sum' to be given to everyone living in the parish once full-scale operations start.

"It's just a cheap trick," Jaz says.

Caroline reads the paragraph again. "I don't think we need to worry too much. No one around here is going to fall for some bribe he can't substantiate."

I catch myself twisting the wolf fang again and quickly stuff my hands in my jeans pockets.

We have a last run-through of the presentation. The plan is that Caroline will do most of the talking, but the guest speaker from the national protest campaign will give a speech too. All Clay and I have to do is sit at the side of the stage and make sure the screen changes to show the right photos at the right times. Clay's in charge of that. I don't want to mess up and draw attention to myself.

When we've been through it all for the third time, everyone seems happy with the running order. Hayden hasn't shown up at all, so I figure he's not coming. I feel secretly pleased.

"Where did your boyfriend get to?" Clay asks Jaz. "Too busy out leafleting with his dad, maybe?"

She looks stunned. "You mean Hayden? He wanted to be here, but Phelps has had him working in the piggery all day. You know he can't risk being seen with us. We talked about it earlier."

Well, that's told me all I need to know. Hayden is officially her boyfriend. My heart sinks. Now I feel depressed as well as anxious.

We spend the next half hour arranging the seats while Caroline drives off to St. Wylda to pick up the speaker coming from London. The chairs are heavy and need dragging out from under the stage, so by the time we've finished, I feel like I need a shower. No time for that, though; Jaz goes out to unlock the doors.

Clay elbows me, grinning with excitement. "What are you looking so jumpy about?"

"Can't explain. Feel a bit anxious, I guess. Not sure how people will react to this bribe Phelps is offering."

"You okay, though?" He looks at me more seriously.

"Hope so."

"Just keep out of the discussion if you can. Leave it to Jaz's mum and the guy coming from London."

"Okay."

He smiles. "None of that falling on the floor, making a spectacle of yourself stuff, okay?"

I have to laugh. "I'll try not to."

"Good. Now stick a bloody smile on your face and come and sit down."

WE HANG OUT at the side of the stage while the hall fills up. After a while, I'm lulled into a false sense of security by the background hubbub. I try not to look out at the audience.

Jaz comes up onto the stage to talk to us.

"Okay, so Mum's back with the London guy, thank goodness. I was beginning to think we'd have to do it without them. Is your mum coming, by the way?"

"I hope not, to be honest. I don't want her getting upset."

"That's a shame," Clay says. "She's just walked in."

I look up and see Ma. Damn. I wave at her, but she doesn't see me because she's too busy trying to find somewhere to sit. The woman walking in behind her sees me though. It's Tracy Benger from the bakery. She scowls. A shiver runs down my spine. It's ridiculous. Of course she's going to turn up at the public meeting. This is a small community. She looks fine, and it was a stupid dream. But why's she scowling at me?

Ma finds a seat at the end of a row, sitting next to PC Chopra. I watch them chatting for a bit before she finally looks up and sees me and smiles. I glance around to see where Tracy Benger is sitting. I spot her at the back. She's put her bag and cardigan on the free seat next to her and keeps looking at the door. Probably waiting for her husband who works in the petrol station in St. Wylda.

I start to feel better about her. I know she's never liked me, but she doesn't look like she's about to dissolve like a vampire or anything. Ma thinks I'm looking at her and waves at me. I raise a few fingers like I might be going to scratch my nose and hope it passes for a wave back. I don't want to draw any attention to myself now the hall is nearly full.

The door opens and Phelps comes in. Hayden's with him, staring at the floor like he wants to tunnel straight back out again, which is probably close to the truth. And there's a man wearing a green EcoGas boiler suit.

He goes over to sit next to Tracy Benger, and I realise with a shock that it's her husband. I elbow Clay.

"Check out David Benger. When did he leave the petrol station?"

"Where?"

"Back row on the right. Don't stare at him."

Clay stares anyway. "Bloody hell, he works for EcoGas? That could be trouble. No prizes for guessing whose side they're going to be on."

I watch Phelps persuade Ronnie and Liv to shift back a row, so he and Hayden can sit next to each other right at the front. Ronnie doesn't look happy about it, but Phelps is all smiles and pleasantries. Hayden's face is a picture of misery.

"See Phelps has left his wife behind. Probably didn't want anyone seeing the bruises." Clay makes no reference to Hayden, so I bring it up.

"Hayden doesn't look too happy."

"He shouldn't have come if he was going to sit with his dad. Still don't trust him, even now he's with Jaz."

I feel cold inside but try not to react.

"And remember what happened when they bought the farm, and Hayden said you weren't allowed to visit him anymore?"

I sigh. "Yeah, I know. But maybe with a father as violent as Phelps, he had no choice."

Something makes me look up, and my heart nearly stops. Andraste is standing in the shadow at the back of the hall. I think she's looking at me, but I can't be sure. Somehow her tattoos seem to act almost like camouflage.

I look around to see if there are any seats left for her, but I don't think there are. Already there are people leaning against the wall down one side of the hall, and a few people I know from school are perching on a precarious-looking trestle table on the other side.

I start to feel panicky. There are so many people here. I look for Andraste again, but she's disappeared. Maybe she's gone outside? I scan the room but stop looking when I meet Tracy Benger's gaze. She narrows her eyes as she stares back at me. I feel the sweat prickling my forehead and look away quickly. What's her problem?

Caroline comes up onto the stage with Dougie, the man she's picked up from London, and introduces us. He's probably in his early twenties and seems nice. He's got spiky blonde dreads and a load of face piercings, and his T-shirt reads NO FRACKING WAY in great big letters.

As soon as they move away to discuss the running order, Clay groans.

"Holy crap. No one's going to take *him* seriously for a start."

I wish he wasn't right, but I know he is. People here in Tytheford tend to think like Tracy Benger. They'd have far more respect for someone who turned up wearing a suit and a shirt and tie. My mouth feels really dry.

"Maybe this whole meeting thing was a bad idea?"

Clay glances at me. "Too late to duck out now, Arlo. Just take a deep breath. It'll be fine. All I meant was it's a shame the London bloke looks like someone most of this crowd would enjoy lynching."

I can't help smiling even if it's true.

Caroline knocks the table in front of her with a little hammer to silence the crowd. The hubbub dies down. She smiles around the room.

"Lovely to see so many of you tonight. As you all know, we're here to discuss the issue of shale gas extraction, or fracking as it's generally known, and how it might adversely affect Stanton, Wights Mound and the rest of this area of outstanding natural beauty."

"And bring money and jobs to the area!" shouts someone from the room. It's Tracy Benger. Her eyes blaze with triumph at her own remark. Her husband puts his arm around her, and a few people around them clap in appreciation.

"Not such a great start," Clay whispers in my ear.

Ronnie stands up and turns to Tracy. "Tracy, you might be feeling smug about your husband's new job, but it's not all about you, you know. You're in a minority here! Most of us love this bit of countryside."

"Yay! Go Ronnie," mutters Clay under his breath.

Tracy's about to shout back at her, but Caroline gets in first.

"So how many local people in the room have got jobs with EcoGas or have been part of the construction team at the massive mining operation already in place on Home Farm?"

The room falls silent.

"Just Mr. Benger then, by the looks. The rest of us have to put up with the eyesore that is now on farming land, without any planning permission that I know of, in Dingle Hollow. Clay, could you bring up the photos, please?"

Clay's amazing at stuff like this, He immediately finds the images Hayden took and projects them onto the screen behind Caroline, one after the other. There's a brief ripple of exclamations through the crowd.

"Bloody disgusting. You should be ashamed of what you've done, Norman Phelps!"

I recognise Mary Suggeworth at the back. I didn't see her come in. Ronnie whistles loudly in approval, and a smattering of others applaud Mary's remark. But not as many people react as I'd expect, considering the scale of Phelps's operation. I'm starting to wonder if they're taking Phelps's money bribe seriously.

I glance at Phelps and find he's staring at me. I feel clammy and my skin prickles.

Caroline points to the last picture as it comes up on the screen. "The problem for the village with this operation taking place on Mr. Phelps's land is manifold. Not only does it create something as ugly as what we see here, but the explosions from recent exploratory testing could affect both Wights Mound and Stanton Stones— ancient sites of historic importance—not to mention St. Ann's Spring and nearby woodland."

She gets all animated and talks for several minutes about the dangers of mining. Then it's the London bloke's turn, and he brings up horrific examples of land pollution and suspected fracking-related cancer deaths from America. Clay manages to keep up with it all and find the relevant images to flash up on the screen.

It seems to be going okay, and nobody shouts Caroline down, but I don't like the way this crowd is being so placid. Apart from the occasional gasp of dismay at the pictures, they're not as supportive as I thought they'd be. I get the impression they're all holding back, and I'm not sure why.

I whisper to Clay. "What's with the audience? They're too quiet. It's weird."

"Don't worry. They're saving the bloodbath until the Q and As at the end."

"Great. I can't wait." I feel a rising sense of dread. Something's up, and I've a hunch Phelps is behind it.

Caroline finishes the presentation. Her parting shot is to tell the crowd that she's heard rumours the spring has stopped bubbling since the mining started and therefore she's put in an application to have the site preserved as an SSSI.

I look briefly over at Phelps. He's staring at me again.

"Phelps doesn't look too friendly," hisses Clay in my ear.

"I noticed. Reckon the trouble's about to kick off."

"Get ready for a sharp exit maybe."

But of course, being up on the stage, even sitting at the side, makes escape impossible.

"And now it's time to open up the debate to the floor. I'm sure you're all dying to ask questions!" Caroline sounds bright and breezy, but she looks nervous.

Phelps stands up and turns to face the crowd. He's smiling, even though a few people, including Ronnie and Liv, are booing him. "Thank you, Caroline.

I'm sure you'll all agree with me, that was a very one-sided presentation—and from someone from outside our community, only having recently returned from Ethiopia."

"I've been back for nine years, actually!" Caroline's face is flushed with anger. "And unlike you, I was born here!"

Phelps smiles smugly. "Whatever. I've spent most of the day talking to people here in Tytheford and the surrounding area about the EcoGas operation, trying to gauge public opinion. I'd like to put forward a more practical side to this debate, if that's all right with everyone? Let's start with the key issue here—money. Once the extraction gets underway, I am going to personally guarantee a one-off payment to everyone living in Tytheford and Stanton of £10,000. Because make no mistake, this business is lucrative for *all* of us."

There's a low murmuring through the crowd. Some people look shocked, but most of them don't seem surprised at all. Phelps must have been busy spreading the news of exactly how much he was proposing to give everyone, which explains a lot.

Ronnie stands up. "So you think you can bribe us into destroying our countryside, Phelps? We all know all about your history of dodgy dealings. I don't think so!"

Liv and a few other people applaud her, but when someone at the back tells Ronnie to shut up and speak for herself, there's far too much clapping and cheering coming from all around the room. Tracy Benger is particularly loud with the whistling and whooping. Cow. Phelps has a triumphant smirk on his face.

"Is he serious about giving away that much money?" hisses Clay in my ear. "If so, we're totally stuffed."

Phelps makes his way up onto the stage, glaring as he passes Clay and me—close enough that I can smell his deodorant—but I notice he's all smiles as he looks at his audience.

"Good evening, everyone. It gladdens my heart to see such a good turnout, and I'm delighted so many of you are here tonight." He pauses a moment. It's infuriating how many people are smiling back at him. Seems like practically everyone can be bought for £10,000.

He coughs. "So, we've heard the views of the Nimbies here on the stage—in case some of you don't know, nimby stands for 'Not In My Back Yard', a term used to describe people opposed to any forward thinking and change—but I'd like to share my more practical, down-to-earth farmer's point of view with you now if I may. I welcome this chance to tell you all about the benefits of the extraction operation with EcoGas and the great lengths we've gone to on the farm to ensure none of you are affected by the operation except in a beneficial way... with jobs... and increased spend in the local shops and so on." His smile widens like a crocodile. "And of course the substantial payment you stand to gain if operations go ahead!"

I can't believe how quickly the crowd have come around to his point of view. From the atmosphere in the room, it seems that instead of caring that Phelps is destroying the land, most people have now switched to thinking he's a good man, helping to boost the economy, all because they think he's going to line their pockets.

There's only a handful of villagers, including Ma, Ronnie and Liv, Mary, maybe PC Chopra and a few others, who seem at all dismayed at this turn of events. And there must be over a hundred people here.

Sensing the crowd are now with him, Phelps warms to his subject. "I know there's some bad feeling in the village about the mining taking place on the farm, particularly amongst some of the younger members of the community." Phelps turns and waves a hand to indicate me and Clay, sitting at the side of the stage with the laptop. "My son has been hanging out with these guys and keeps me up to date with all their pranks."

Pranks? What the hell's he talking about? I shoot a quick glance at Hayden. He's flushed crimson and looks angry as hell.

"So I know all about young Arlo up on stage here, who as many of you know, is often up to no good on my land, making crop circles and the like...but with his tragic history, what happened to his father and so on, it's only to be expected."

I hear Clay's sharp intake of breath. I feel sick. Clay clutches my forearm.

"You okay?" he whispers.

I nod, and glance into the hall at Hayden. There are tears of anger glistening in his eyes, and his dad hasn't finished sticking the knife in yet.

"And of course Hayden told me about Arlo taking photos of the operation going on in Dingle Hollow. He was worried I'd be upset, but I understand where this young man is coming from. He's just misguided."

"So that's why you're evicting him from Primrose cottage, then?" Clay says, his voice heavy with sarcasm, but no one picks up on it. The audience's attention has suddenly turned to Hayden, who's got up and is walking quickly towards the exit, looking really distressed. There's a low murmur of people speculating about what's going on.

Jaz is standing by the door at the back of the room, arms folded, tight-lipped and angry. She opens it as Hayden approaches and lets him out. Neither of them say anything to each other, and part of me wonders why Jaz doesn't follow him outside.

My eye is drawn to Ma, who's fidgeting in her seat. She's pulling her black knitting out of her bag. Normally, I'd die of embarrassment seeing her do that in public, but right now I don't blame her. Phelps bribing everyone to get them onside and pretending to be the nice guy? I want to get up, walk across the stage and push him right off it. That might wipe the stupid, hypocritical smile off his ugly face. I rub my head. It still feels tender. The bastard can't wait to get us out of our home. Pity no one was listening to Clay when he mentioned that.

I'm so angry, I realise I've missed a big chunk of what Phelps was saying, but that's probably a good thing. I start listening again. It sounds like he's finally reaching the end.

"So to help tell you more about the potential benefits of introducing EcoGas to our part of the world, I'd like to invite Dave and Tracy Benger up to the stage. You'll all be familiar with this lovely, hard-working couple, both born and bred in nearby Stanton, and I'm hoping they can tell us how it's changed their lives for the better."

The audience clap, and heads turn to look at the Bengers. Dave Benger is already standing. I watch as Tracy tries to stand up, but then she suddenly makes a choking sound and I can't see her anymore. I can't work out what's going on for a second, until I hear Dave Benger shouting for a doctor. Tracy's collapsed on the floor.

The room seems to be spinning, and I start to panic. For a split second, I think I see Andraste standing in the shadows close to the Bengers, but when I look again, I can't see her. I must have been mistaken.

This is too much like my dream. Different, but too close for comfort. My hand instinctively goes to the wolf fang pendant Andraste gave me. I feel the smoothness of the tooth enamel with my fingers and try to breathe calmly.

"What the hell's going on?" asks Clay. Without waiting for an answer, he jumps off the stage and runs up the centre aisle to get to the row where the Bengers were sitting. Phelps goes over too, not even glancing at me as he jumps down from the front of the stage. He looks furious.

I'm unable to move. I sit frozen to my chair, staring out at the people crowding around Tracy, trying to help her. Doctor Bill from the local surgery pushes through the throng and tells people to stand back so he can check Tracy's pulse and breathing, but it looks like she isn't getting up again. I don't even think she's conscious.

I hear Phelps telling people it's all fine, Tracy's okay and is still breathing, but no one is listening to him anymore. Caroline is already on her phone calling for an ambulance.

Time stands still. I manage to prise myself off my chair and get off the stage. I lurk at the edge of the room, not knowing what else to do. The ambulance seems to take forever coming from St. Wylda, but it's probably not that long. It's only a few miles away. At last, I hear the faint sound of an approaching siren and watch Jaz run outside.

She comes back in with a couple of paramedics. They clear people out of the way, talk to Doctor Bill briefly, and after a quick examination of Tracy, one of them goes back outside. He comes back in with a stretcher, and they lift Tracy onto it and carry her out. Doctor Bill goes out to the ambulance with them, and Dave Benger follows close behind, looking shocked and haggard. His bright-green EcoGas boiler suit seems incongruously cheerful. I think back to the night the ambulance came after they brought Dad back in from the barn, and shudder.

The meeting is obviously at an end. No one cares about mining or EcoGas anymore. As soon as the ambulance goes, everyone starts talking about what's happened, worrying about Tracy, talking about her family history and speculating on what might be wrong with her. Heart attack? Stroke? People start leaving the hall in dribs and drabs, huddled together as if company can protect them from anything contagious. Liv comes over to check I'm okay, which is nice of her, then hurries off with Ronnie to give Mary a lift home to Spring Farm.

I've scanned the room several times and still can't see Andraste anywhere. Did I imagine she was here? Ma and PC Chopra are standing next to each other, talking in low voices. Ma seems to have forgotten she's still holding her knitting. I walk over to join them.

"Are you all right, Arlo?" she asks, looking at me in a concerned way. "Strange this happening after that dream you had!"

"I'm fine, Ma, don't worry. I'm bloody angry with Phelps, though."

PC Chopra studies me curiously. "What was your dream about?" he asks.

He looks very different dressed in jeans and a T-shirt. He's older than I first thought too, probably about Ma's age. He's got a really kind face, which seems surprising for a policeman.

"It was just a stupid dream."

"I'm interested. Honestly."

I guess it can't do any harm, so I tell him.

"It was here in this hall, like this evening. Tracy was dying and nobody noticed. She breathed in a cloud of poison, but only I could see her. She wanted me to help her, but there was nothing I could do."

"Is she a close friend of your family?" asks PC Chopra.

"No, not really. The opposite, in fact. I'm pretty sure she doesn't like me any more than Phelps does."

He shakes his head thoughtfully. "My mother back in India would say your dream was an omen," he says. He smiles at me. "But then, she's a very superstitious woman."

I attempt to smile back. I don't tell him my mother is too, mainly because she's standing next to us.

We don't say anything much for a while as people make their way out of the building. Then PC Chopra offers Ma and me a lift home.

"That's very kind of you, thank you, Constable Chopra," Ma says, finally realising she's still holding her knitting and stuffing it hastily into her bag.

"Please, not so formal! Call me Sanj," he says. "It's short for Sanjiv."

Ma smiles at him. "Thank you, Sanj," she says. "Call me Melissa."

"That's a lovely name," he says. Ma blushes. I feel a bit awkward.

"You get a lift with PC Chopra, Ma. I'll stay and help clear up for a bit if that's okay," I say. "I won't be long."

IT TAKES A while for the hall to clear, but eventually, I get a chance to catch up with Jaz and Clay while we stack the chairs away.

"How are you feeling, Arlo?" Jaz's dark-brown eyes are filled with concern. "I can't believe what Phelps did this evening. If it hadn't been for Tracy getting ill like that, I was going to give him a real piece of my mind. How dare he bring up the subject of your father like that!"

"More to the point, how come that little scumbag Hayden grassed you up to his dad?" Clay's really angry.

"We don't know the whole story, Clay, give him a chance," Jaz says, but she looks upset about it too.

I should say something. I should tell them Phelps was lying. Hayden wouldn't have said anything, especially since he was the one who took the photos, and I saw how upset he was.

But I don't. I don't say a word. For the time being, it feels good to have the comfort of friends without any complications. I hope that's all it is. I'll definitely tell them later. For now, I want the attention and sympathy. I need it.

As we go over what happened this evening, we all agree that it feels like we lost the battle. It doesn't matter that the Bengers never got to tell everyone their side of the argument about the advantages of shale gas extraction.

"Everyone was against us, right from the moment he mentioned the amount of money he's giving them." Jaz looks so miserable, I want to put my arm around her.

I don't, of course. It wouldn't be right. Even if she's angry with Hayden right now, he hasn't done anything wrong and I don't want to take advantage. Well, not *that much* advantage.

"I don't get it," Clay says. "How come everyone is so easily bribed? Doesn't anyone in the village care about the way he's destroying the place?"

"No. They care about money. End of," I say. "They're prepared to take a gamble that fracking won't do any harm."

"But they're wrong!" Jaz is so annoyed I half expect her to stamp her foot.

"Yeah, well, tonight it felt like we were in a minority."

Jaz puts her hands on her hips and glares at us. "Hey, welcome to my world!"

Clay and I laugh, and Jaz smiles.

She's so attractive when she smiles like that. I think about Hayden again and wonder whether to say anything. Maybe later.

"I should be getting back," I say. "Ma will be sending out a search party if I'm not careful. Let's meet up tomorrow."

Chapter 23

Walking back by myself in the twilight, I mull over all the weird things that have happened to me recently. Everything was okay up to the point when I had that seizure in Phelps's field. Now it's all changed, and I've no idea how to make it right again.

I turn a corner, wondering if the public meeting could possibly have gone any worse this evening, and notice a Land Rover parked up in a gateway by the side of the lane. It's Phelps's Land Rover. What on earth's he stopped there for? Probably some of his livestock has escaped. If it was anyone else, I'd go over and offer to help. As it is, I stick my hands in my jeans pockets and try and make myself invisible as I walk past.

The driver door opens. "Is that you, Arlo?"

With a sudden shock, I realise he's been waiting for me. Now what?

"What do you want?" I wish my voice didn't sound so shaky, but he's caught me off guard.

"I think it's time we had a chat. About the cottage."

"What about it?"

"Your imminent eviction."

"Yeah? Well, we intend to fight the eviction order all the way."

"Shut up and listen. I want you to stop coming on my land and interfering. It could be very dangerous for you. I could mistake you for an animal after my crops, or poachers—there are any number of reasons I might have my gun with me." I can see him smirking, even in the darkness.

"Is that it?"

"No. I'm feeling generous, and I reckon you might need some incentive. If you agree to this, keep away from Hayden and leave the protest movement well alone, I might—I say *might*—forget about the eviction notice and drop the criminal damage charges I'm pressing against you. Depends on you."

I can't think of anything to say. I really wasn't expecting that. This evening has shown most of the village is on his side, so why worry about me?

The silence stretches, and I can see he's getting impatient.

"I'll think about it," I say.

It's the best I can manage. I'm too stunned to think properly. I'd like to tell him to stick his offer where it hurts, but I've seen how upset Ma is about the idea of leaving Primrose Cottage.

"Don't think too long. You've got a couple of days, tops." He gets back in his Land Rover and starts the engine.

I stand in the lane for several minutes after he's gone, trying to calm down. For the first time in a while, I allow myself to think back over everything that happened the night Dad died. The sound of Ma sobbing, dragging Dad's body in through the front door with Mary helping her. The ugly mark around his neck. His lips, blue. It's the image that still haunts me whenever I think about him.

I don't know why Mary was there, or why they didn't wait for the police or the ambulance to come before they cut him down and brought him in. I blacked out before I got a chance to ask. I guess it's not important. It wouldn't have made any difference to Dad.

BACK HOME, PC Chopra is still drinking cocoa with Ma. She looks surprisingly upbeat considering everything that's happened this evening.

PC Chopra puts his mug down as I come in the door. "I should be leaving," he says. "Thank you so much for the cocoa, Melissa. I've really enjoyed our chat."

"Me too, Sanj," Ma says.

I try to be invisible but fail. On his way to the door, PC Chopra stops in front of me.

"I'm sorry about the way things went tonight, Arlo. Unfortunately, the prospect of money often persuades good people against doing the right thing. Try not to get downhearted." He smiles.

I smile back. Even with the criminal damage charges pending against me, it sounds strangely like he's on my side.

"Thanks. That means a lot," I say.

When he's gone, Ma and I talk about what happened to Tracy Benger.

"Sanj tells me there have been a few cases here in Stanton. He thinks we should watch out in case it's something catching, a new virus of some kind."

"A few cases?"

"Yes, one of the Henderson kids is in hospital, proper poorly. And old Mr. Braithwaite down in Peppercorn Cottage has died. They're not sure it was the same thing, but it came on as sudden as Tracy's illness did. He collapsed in the butcher's yesterday. Dead within hours, apparently."

I can tell Ma is worried about it, and I'm not surprised.

I try to reassure her. "Old people don't have such good immune systems. You know that. Even so, I'm glad you weren't sitting too close to the Bengers this evening!"

"In more ways than one," Ma says darkly. "That Tracy Benger's always had a thing for Phelps. Or so I hear."

"What, you mean—"

"Just gossip. But she's always loved a man with money."

"Hayden told me that all the money to buy the farm came from his mum."

"Really? Poor Emily. She made such a mistake marrying that awful man. I heard a rumour she's leaving him, though. Not before time."

Thinking about Hayden, I feel guilty again about not telling Clay and Jaz that he took the photos. I sigh.

"Ma, do you mind if I sleep out by the spring again tonight?"

"Why? Phelps isn't likely to cut the grove down now, is he? The whole village knows about the SSSI application."

"I need to think things out a bit. I feel closer to Dad there."

For a moment, her eyes darken, almost as if she's afraid, and I'm not sure why. But she doesn't object.

"Don't take any risks, will you? Especially now Phelps thinks you took those photos."

"I won't. I'll be back first thing. Please don't worry about me. I'm sure we can sort everything, but I'd like to sleep under the stars while this weather holds."

I give her a hug. She's still not happy about it, but she doesn't stop me going.

I SIT FOR a while with my back against the old oak. The Perseid meteor shower is only a day or so away, and I see a few shooting stars falling through the night sky. The earth is getting parched in this heatwave, and the air smells mostly of dry grass. A barn owl swoops overhead, ghostly pale. I watch the gibbous moon as it rises, tinged blood red by the dust in the air.

Gradually, I silence my buzzing thoughts and settle down to try to get some sleep. I'll have to be up early to make sure I avoid seeing Phelps. I can't be stupid enough to let him find me just because I oversleep. I climb into the sleeping bag and stare up at the night sky for a while longer. At some point, I drift off.

DAD IS TRYING to tell me something. His voice is so quiet, it's like a whisper in the trees.

"It's in the water. Don't drink the water."

"Dad?"

I look around, and there he is, face distorted, swinging from the ash tree. Instantly, I wake up, heart pounding, staring into the dark. He's not there, of course. It's just the usual nightmare.

But now I'm wide awake again. I gaze up into the trees to try and regain some calm. It's probably about four a.m., so dawn isn't too far off. I unzip the sleeping bag and stand up. A faint smell of rotten egg reaches me on the breeze, coming from the direction of St. Ann's Spring.

I think about Dad's warning in the dream. St. Ann's Spring supplies all the houses in Stanton. What if the water has become toxic in some way? Is that what happened to Tracy Benger and the others? Maybe it's something in the water.

I quickly roll up my sleeping bag and set off for home. I have to get back before Ma wakes up, so I can warn her. Just in case.

Chapter 24

By the time I get back to Primrose Cottage, the first faint light of dawn is in the sky. I open the front door and find Ma is at the bottom of the stairs in her dressing gown, heading for the kitchen. She's holding an empty glass.

"You're up early," I say, trying to quash the panic rising in my chest at the sight of the glass.

"So thirsty, Arlo. Worried I might be coming down with something. Drank loads of water in the night."

I'm too late. I try to act normal.

"Boil the water before you drink it, Ma. I was thinking about what PC Chopra said last night—"

"Sanj? He didn't say anything about water!"

"No. But he said something about other cases in Stanton. Last night, I dreamt about Dad, and in the dream, he told me the trouble was in the water. You know how everyone in Stanton gets it piped from St. Ann's Spring."

I leave out the bit about Dad's body swinging from the ash tree, but Ma's already gone white as a sheet. She attempts a smile. "I hope you're wrong, Arlo, or I'm done for."

I realise too late how tactless I've been. "Well, boil it from now on. Can't be too careful. And I'll buy some bottled water in Tytheford after work today."

"What about the plants? I can't water them with bottled water. It'll cost a fortune."

"I'm sure the plants will be fine. But St. Ann's Spring is stagnant, and the water might be bad for us to drink."

I don't say anything about the stink of gas coming up from it. There's no point. I hope I'm wrong about this. I try to think when I last had a drink of water from the tap. It was probably several days ago. I mostly make myself hot drinks or have orange juice from the fridge when I'm at home, and I've been at Jaz's or Clay's every night up until the meeting last night.

It's only Stanton that's supplied by the spring. Even Corn Flakes, only half a mile away, is connected to the mains.

I'm not sure what to do next. I put the kettle on for Ma while I think about it. I watch her as she sits on a chair by the table, rubbing her forehead. Ma doesn't get headaches. Something is wrong.

"What time do you start today, Arlo?"

"Early shift. I'll have a quick shower and get ready now." For once, I've got plenty of time to collect the eggs from Mary on the way.

Ma looks out of the kitchen window onto the back garden. Dawn has broken, and the sky is fired purple and red. "I'll go and check on the bees. You go and have your shower."

WHEN I'M READY to leave, Ma is out in the garden. I boil the kettle twice before I make her a cup of tea and leave it on the table for her to drink when she comes back in. I wave at her through the window and she waves back. I hope she's okay. She looks more or less the same as she always does. But so did Tracy Benger before she collapsed.

I'd like to take the day off to make sure she's all right, but at the same time I don't want to worry her unnecessarily. I decide to call Jaz and ask her to check in on Ma later. I grab my rucksack and head out.

The sun is up, but the morning is still fresh and cool as I walk up to collect the eggs. There's no sign of Mary at the farm this morning, and she hasn't left the eggs out. I go to the farmhouse and ring the bell. Maybe she's forgotten or the hens are off lay or something. It's strangely quiet in the yard. I wait a bit, then ring again. No one comes to the door.

I head around to the back door. That's when I realise why it's so quiet. The hens aren't out. They're still shut in the chicken shed. I feel uneasy. I look through the kitchen window at the back of the farm but can't see anyone. I try the back door, but it's locked, so I decide to go and look in the chicken shed.

When I open the shed door and the space fills with light, the chickens all wake up and start clucking and jumping down off their perches. No one has been in to check them yet this morning. That's not like Mary at all, and I'm increasingly worried something has happened to her, or maybe Harry, in the night.

I lift the wooden flap that lets the chickens out into the hen run and look around the shed. There are a couple of egg boxes filled with eggs by the record book, and I find a stack of empty boxes by the door. I need more eggs than have been collected already, so I go around picking up eggs laid this morning, the smell of dusty straw making me want to sneeze. Some of the hens follow me and peck around by my feet. They're hungry.

I find the chicken feed in a big plastic dustbin and fill up the chicken feeders, then make sure they've got fresh water, which I get from the water butt outside. All the time I'm doing it, I half expect Mary to turn up and apologise for being out earlier, but there's no sign of her. I find her record book and leave a note to let her know I've taken three dozen eggs for Corn Flakes.

It's noisier outside now the chickens are out in the run, scratching about and clucking, but it doesn't feel right. I'll tell Jaz when I call her. I want to make sure the Suggeworths are okay.

AT FIRST, RONNIE is annoyed that I'm late, until I explain about Ma and how weird it was that Spring Farm was deserted and I had to collect the eggs myself.

"That's very strange. Not like Mary at all, is it?" she says. "And Harry's always in. Wonder where they've gone?"

"I don't know, but I'm going back after work, Ronnie. Something didn't feel right."

"And after what happened last night with poor Tracy Benger…"

"Doubt it's anything like that," I say quickly, but it's already crossed my mind.

While Ronnie opens up, I take the chance to call Jaz quickly out in the kitchen area.

"Arlo? It's a bit early, isn't it? What's up?"

"Jaz, I think it's in the water. Whatever's happening to people, I think the water is contaminated. Any house that's supplied from St. Ann's Spring—"

"Are you at work?"

"Yes. But I'm worried about Ma. She didn't seem right this morning. Look, I have to go. I was already late because the Suggeworths weren't around and I had to collect the eggs myself. Ronnie's getting angsty because Liv's at the market this morning, so it's just me and her. Customers will start arriving any minute."

"I'll call by the café later. And I'll pop in to check up on your mum first."

I sigh with relief. Jaz is amazing.

"Thanks, Jaz. You're the best. Can you check Spring Farm again too if you've time? See you later."

She hangs up.

"Arlo? I thought you were supposed to be grinding the coffee!" Ronnie flicks a tea towel at me and then becomes serious. "Is everything okay, love?"

"Yeah, I guess. I asked Jaz to check things for me."

"That's good. It'll stop you worrying. Now about that coffee…"

"Sorry, Ronnie. I'm right on it."

THE NEXT COUPLE of hours are filled with making up orders for all the customers wanting breakfasts and coffees. At the back of my mind, I can't shake the image of Ma holding the empty glass. The way she was absentmindedly rubbing her forehead. Every time the door opens, I look up, hoping to see Jaz come in.

I'm clearing some plates when I glance over to see PC Chopra standing in the doorway, in uniform. Everyone turns to look at him curiously. He beckons for me to come over, then steps outside to wait for me.

The hubbub in the café seems to crescendo in my ears as I walk to the door. The smell of coffee tastes bitter in the air, and my heart's really thumping. Outside, the sunlight is stark after the shade of the café.

"What's up?"

"I'm sorry to disturb you at work, Arlo." He stares at me, his dark eyes clouded with concern. "There's no easy way to say this. You need to come with me. It's about your mother."

I feel sick. "Is she—"

"She's been taken ill. She's in the hospital in St. Wylda. Your friend Jazara has gone with her and asked if I could come and collect you."

"I'll just tell Ronnie. I'll be right with you."

I run back inside, tears of shock stinging in my eyes. I can hardly get the words out to explain why I'm leaving. Ronnie hugs me and tells me to hurry. There's nothing else she can say. We were both there last night. We saw what happened to Tracy.

218

Chapter 25

P C CHOPRA STARTS the car and we set off towards St. Wylda.

"What happened to her, exactly?" I ask.

"Jazara called an ambulance from Primrose Cottage. She found your mother unconscious down by the beehives. She tried to get hold of you, but she couldn't get through. Is your phone off?"

I pull my phone out of my pocket. I must have turned the sound off after I'd called Jaz. There are six missed calls from Jaz, two from Clay and one from Hayden, and several voice messages.

"Do you mind if I listen to my messages?"

"Of course not!"

I listen. The ones from Jaz are heartrending. I have to bite my lip hard to stop myself crying. She sounds beside herself with worry—the last call was from the ambulance on the way to the hospital. I call her straight back, but it goes to voicemail. I leave a message anyway.

"Jaz? Thanks for going with Ma to the hospital. I should be there soon. Constable Chopra is giving me a lift. Sorry my phone was off." My voice cracks with emotion, and I end the message abruptly.

The two messages from Clay are updates on last night. He says he wants to talk to me later. He obviously hasn't heard about Ma, and I can't face calling him.

Hayden hasn't left a message. He must have hung up the minute the phone went to voicemail. He must think everyone hates him after last night. I'm still the only person who knows it was him who took the photos of Dingle Hollow.

I realise I haven't said anything for several minutes while I've been checking my phone.

"Are there any other new cases of this illness besides Ma?"

PC Chopra hesitates. He's probably wondering whether he should tell me or not.

"There have been a couple more today. It seems to be spreading."

"Was it the Suggeworths?"

"Your friend mentioned them, but I don't think so."

"They live at Spring Farm. They weren't there this morning when I went to collect the eggs for work."

"Hold on a minute." PC Chopra gets on the police radio, and I hear him ask if PC Colenutt can go out and check on the Suggeworths.

"So the other cases?" I ask when he's finished.

"Sorry, I can't remember their names, and I probably shouldn't be telling you."

"I bet they both came from Stanton, didn't they?"

"What makes you say that?"

"I think it's something in the water. I thought about it last night and told Ma this morning, but she'd been drinking it for days already. Everyone in Stanton is supplied by St. Ann's Spring, and since the mining started, the spring has gone stagnant. Worse, I think it's poisoned."

He doesn't ask me how I know. "Are you sure? All the houses are supplied by the spring?"

"Primrose Cottage is for sure. Home Farm used to be too, but Phelps had to get a mains supply when he built the pig farm."

"Thanks, Arlo. That could be very helpful. I'll let the medical staff know when we get there."

"Too late for Ma, though, isn't it?"

"I'm sure the hospital is doing everything they can."

I can't talk anymore. I don't trust my voice.

THE HOSPITAL DOESN'T know yet if the illness is catching, so all the affected people are isolated from other patients and are being looked after on the same ward. A nurse tells me to put on a face mask and rub antibacterial cleanser over my hands before she lets me in.

Jaz is sitting on a chair by Ma's bed, holding Ma's hand. She's wearing a face mask too. She jumps up when she sees me and comes over to give me a hug.

"Your mum's still breathing okay, but they can't get her temperature down."

221

I can tell Jaz is trying to keep her voice calm while she tells me what's going on. I wonder if she realises she has tears dripping down her face into the mask.

"Thanks so much for coming in with her, Jaz. How was she when you found her?"

"I got the feeling she'd been unconscious for a while. But it was weird, Arlo. The bees were circling her. Loads of them. Like they knew she needed help or something."

I look around the ward quickly. There are five other people in here, and I recognise them all. I can't see Tracy Benger or the Suggeworths.

"Where's Tracy Benger?"

More tears spill down Jaz's face. Her mask is damp with them.

"What? What's wrong?"

"Dave Benger has paid to have her moved to a private room. But she's still unconscious and doesn't seem to be getting any better."

I sit down on Ma's bed and stare at Jaz. "So no one has recovered from this thing?"

"Not yet."

"Not even slightly?" I hear myself clutching at straws.

For a minute, Jaz and I just look at each other. I try to imagine a world without Ma. It's unthinkable. I bite my lip again, but my eyes still well up.

It's almost as if Jaz has read my mind. "Your mum is a strong woman, Arlo. I'm sure she'll pull through this."

"No one else has yet."

"But they're alive."

"Except Mr. Braithwaite."

"He was old. They're not sure he had the same thing."

A nurse comes in. "Hello, you two. Just came to let you know PC Chopra is waiting for you both outside the ward. He says he'll give you a lift home."

"It's okay, I want to stay here with Ma. Jaz, you take a lift while you've got the opportunity."

"No, I'll stay with you, Arlo. Mum can pick us up later."

The nurse shakes her head. "To be honest, we're actively discouraging families from staying until we find out what this illness is. We can't risk spreading it any further. I'm very sorry. It would be better if you both leave now."

I want to argue that if it's contagious, I've probably already got it, but I don't. I squeeze Ma's hand. There's no response, but her hand's still warm. She's so pale, though.

I can't help wondering if this is the last time I'll see her alive. I try to push the thought away, but my heart is heavy as we leave the ward to find PC Chopra.

He looks at me steadily. "Arlo, I've told them what you said about all the people affected so far being supplied with water from St. Ann's Spring. They're going to investigate straight away. Hopefully, it will help to narrow down the search to find the right treatment."

"Thanks. But it could still take them ages. It could be too late for Ma." I dig my nails into my hand so hard, I draw blood.

PC Chopra doesn't contradict me, and I'm grateful in a way. There's no point in him lying to make me feel better.

"Come on, let's go. I'll drive you both back home."

I sit in the front next to PC Chopra and Jaz climbs in the back. I think about when I got home the other night and he was talking to Ma, and how he chose to sit next to her at the meeting in the Village Hall. Maybe he likes her?

"Are you married?" I ask.

His mouth sets in a straight line. "I was. My wife died."

"Oh. I'm sorry." There's not much else I can say.

"So am I. She burnt to death. Someone set fire to our house one night when I was out at work. It was back in Birmingham."

"Was it a racist attack?" asks Jaz from the back seat.

"The papers reported it as a racist attack, yes, but the culprit denied it. Makes no difference to the outcome. I can't bring her back."

I think how I'd feel if Ma died and then we proved it was all Phelps's fault for contaminating the water. It wouldn't bring Ma back either.

PC CHOPRA DROPS Jaz back off at her mum's. She tries to persuade me to come in, but I want to go home.

"Are you sure you'll be okay, Arlo?"

"Sure."

"I'll call you later. I think you should stay at our house. Or at least stay with Clay?"

"Maybe. I'll think about it."

I wave at her as we drive off to Primrose Cottage, trying to make out I feel okay. Stupid really.

We pull up outside the cottage and PC Chopra gets out his notebook. He writes quickly and tears out the page to give to me. "Here's my number. Call me if you need anything, or if you feel ill at all. The slightest thing."

"Thanks."

"I'll be in touch if I have any news, and I'll call by in the morning. Maybe you should phone your friend Jazara back? I honestly think you should. It might be best if you're not on your own."

"I'll be fine. Really."

PC Chopra seems reluctant to leave. "Well, think about it, won't you?"

"Okay."

The truth is, I want to sit here by myself. My head aches from the effort of holding it all together.

Chapter 26

I T'S NOT EVEN four thirty, and it's been the longest day I can ever remember already. I look at my phone. I still haven't answered Clay or Hayden, and I already know I'm not going to. I turn off my phone and sit in the kitchen. The cup of tea I made for Ma is still on the table, half drunk. I get a lump in my throat looking at it, so I get up and open the back door and go down the garden instead.

The bees are upset. They buzz angrily around me as I approach the hives, probably wondering what's happened to Ma. Bees always know who looks after them, and although they tolerate me, they know I'm not her.

Jaz said she's never seen them behave like they did when she found Ma, and she was right. In an effort to calm them, I lie on my back on the grass, close to the hives.

Gradually, the buzzing returns to a normal level. They drone overhead, circling to make sure I'm still no threat before flying off towards the lavender and the sunflowers. I stare up at the sky, the blue of late afternoon. I stare at it for a long, long time, then close my eyes. I feel the tickle of flies that land on my face from time to time and scratch my ear to remove a curious ant.

Suddenly I get the sensation that there's someone else in the garden. The bees are still buzzing over the lavender, but the air has turned cooler. I hold my breath, waiting for Jaz or Clay to call out for me.

Nothing.

A shadow falls over my face, and I get a sudden waft of honeysuckle. I snap my eyes open. Andraste.

"Did you ring the bell? I didn't hear you."

She sits beside me on the grass and stares at me. She doesn't say anything. Her eyes flash green in the evening sunlight, and her tattoos seem to echo the pattern of the high cirrus clouds above. The honeysuckle smell is stronger as she reaches out to touch my face.

"We should talk," she says.

"Now isn't such a great time for me, Andraste."

"I know. That's why you need to come with me."

I look up at her, then make the effort to prop myself up on one elbow.

"I can't. I have to be here now, in case..." I don't bother to finish the sentence. I need to be here; she doesn't need to know why.

"Then I'll come back tomorrow," she says, still staring at me. "Remember, you know you can change what's happening."

I turn my head away and stare at the beehives. I don't feel like listening to some crap about changing stuff when there's nothing I can do to help Ma. In fact,

Andraste's made me angry. I turn back to say something sarcastic, but she's gone. I get up quickly. There's no sign of her anywhere. My pulse quickens.

Hearing footsteps on the path down the side of the cottage, I run to try and catch up with her.

But it's not her. It's Hayden. He appears in the garden before I reach the path, and I skid to a halt, then jump at the loud croak of a raven as it flies overhead.

"What are you doing here, Hayden?" Somehow it comes out more sharply than I meant it to.

"There was no answer at the front and I figured you might be out the back."

I stare at him blankly, still annoyed I didn't manage to catch up with Andraste.

"I heard about your mother. I came to see if you were okay."

"Of course I'm not," I snap.

Hayden looks at the ground and avoids my eye.

"Mum made you some food. She, well we both, wondered if there was anything else we could do. But there isn't, is there?"

I sigh. "No, not really. But that's very kind of your mum. I wasn't allowed to stay at the hospital, so..." My voice trails off, nothing else I can say.

Hayden takes the rucksack he's carrying off his back. I notice how sad he looks.

"I can leave it in the kitchen if you like?" He pulls out a Tupperware box and flinches slightly as the rucksack bangs against his arm. Something's wrong.

"No, wait...um, thanks. It was good of you to come over. I'm sorry." Suddenly I feel choked. I stop talking.

He attempts to smile as he hands me the Tupperware box, but he's pale and clearly unhappy. Whatever's going on for him, he doesn't deserve me being mean to him as well.

"Are you okay, Hayden? Have you seen Jaz and Clay? Please tell them you took the photos. I haven't had a chance—"

He shakes his head. "I haven't seen anybody. We only heard about your mum being in hospital when PC Chopra came to see us."

"PC Chopra? What did he want?"

"After he dropped you back here, he called by Spring Farm. The door was locked, but he found a way in through the window. Both the Suggeworths were in the house."

I stare at him, horrified. "Oh, no! Are they...?"

"Mary Suggeworth was okay. Well, alive at least."

"What about Harry?"

Hayden bites his lip. "Not good. Sorry."

"That's awful. I was there this morning...I wondered where they were. God, I wish I'd called the police then. I just took some of the eggs and left a note." I shake off the guilt. I wasn't to know they were inside. "What did PC Chopra want with your dad?"

"He was asking about St. Ann's Spring. He wanted to know how many people it supplied in case it's the cause of this illness. Dad was furious."

"Why? His test drilling caused the problem in the first place."

Hayden laughs bitterly. "Anger is Dad's first response to everything. You know that. As soon as he'd gone, Dad lost it completely."

"Is that why your arm hurts?"

Hayden stares at the ground, which I take as a yes. Yet his mum still took the trouble to make me food.

He breaks the short silence. "You know I see her too, don't you?"

I'm confused. "Who, Jaz?"

"No, I mean Andraste. I thought I saw her when I arrived, but then she was gone…"

I realise I'm holding my breath and nod to show I'm listening.

"I wonder sometimes if other people maybe don't see her. Like, she was at the meeting in the village hall, wasn't she?"

"Yeah, I thought I saw her too."

"Yet no one else seemed to notice her at all, even though she stands out a mile with those tattoos and the way she dresses."

I thought exactly the same thing but don't really want to admit it. "They probably ignore her because they don't like the way she looks," I say.

"It's more than that. She's so different from other people. Like, *very* different. The way she just appears and disappears…you know what I mean?" He hesitates for a moment. "Actually, your mum was asking me about her a couple of days ago."

"Seriously? How come?"

"Dunno. I ran into her in the village, and she said she was worried about you. She asked me what I knew— how often you saw her, that kind of thing. I said I had no idea."

I can't help being amazed Ma asked Hayden, of all people. "Why on earth didn't she ask me?"

"She told me she thought you'd been enchanted..."

"Yeah, right. Sounds like Ma."

"She thought...it wasn't a good thing..." His voice breaks off, and he shifts nervously. "She said it's happened to others before you. That Andraste appearing always means trouble."

"I wish she and Mary would stop coming out with that kind of stuff. And she really shouldn't have bothered you with it. I'm sorry."

"It's okay, I like your mum. I always have. She's just worried about you. I don't think it's weird at all. I told her I see Andraste about the place too. I thought it might make her feel better. Like you weren't being 'chosen', as she put it."

Suddenly I feel the pain of Ma not being here like a stab in the heart. Hayden's right: she was worried about me, and not without reason. Andraste *has* chosen me. I know it. And now there's no chance for me to talk to Ma about it or ask her what to do. I'm totally alone.

"Arlo, I have to get back to make sure everything's calmed down at home. But should you really be here on your own?"

"Yeah, don't worry. I'm going to head up to the Suggeworths' before it gets dark and lock the chickens up for the night. I feel kind of responsible for them."

Hayden pushes his glasses up his nose and blinks at me. "It's a shame your family lost the farm. You actually care about the land and the animals. Dad doesn't. For him it's about making a profit."

"Yeah, and look where caring gets you. You end up like my father."

Hayden frowns. "Seriously, ask Clay or Jaz over. You need company at a time like this."

"Yeah, maybe." I try to smile. "Thanks."

The truth is I need time to work out what to do. As soon as Hayden has gone, I leave the cottage to go and feed the chickens.

THE ENTRANCE TO Spring Farm is in deepening shadow when I arrive. An owl hoots in the pine tree by the sign. I open the gate and walk into the yard. Some of the chickens are still out, but most have gone back in. At the sight of me, the remaining chickens run back into the chicken shed, assuming my arrival means they're about to get more food.

It's dark in the shed, and I fumble along the rough, plank-built wall, feeling for the light switch. I find it, and the harsh fluorescent bulb flickers into life.

The chickens stare at me with beady, expectant eyes. I try to open the feed bin and can't prise the lid off. I try again and end up ripping a couple of nails. I kick the stupid bin in frustration.

Suddenly I'm so overwhelmed with sadness, I can hardly breathe. I sink to the ground, tears filling my eyes. I can't face it. I can't face anything. I can't even feed the stupid chickens. I sit on the rough concrete floor with my face buried in my hands, overcome with anger and raw grief.

When I finally stop myself crying, I stay slumped on the ground, breathing in the smell of straw and ammonia, staring at nothing.

EVENTUALLY, I HAVE to pull myself together. By the time I've finished in the shed, it's dark, the slightest hint of purple in the sky in the west. I drag my feet as I walk slowly back down the lane.

As I open the garden gate to the cottage, I see a familiar outline in the shadows. Clay.

"Where the hell have you been, Arlo? I was almost worried about you!"

I can't help smiling. "Hi Clay. Want to come in?" My voice sounds all scratchy.

"Of course. What did you think I was waiting for, bloody Christmas or something? I'm staying, by the way."

I have to admit, I'm really glad to see him.

Chapter 27

THE SECOND I wake up, I check my phone. No messages. I leave the cottage before Clay's even awake and go back to Spring Farm to see to the chickens. It's still only seven thirty when I get back, and Clay is just blundering down the stairs, complaining about how early it is.

Clay makes us toast and moans about the lack of bacon while I call the hospital. The nurse on the phone tells me there's no change in any of the patients on Ma's ward. She says they're not keen on too many visitors coming in as they still haven't got to the bottom of the illness and don't know how contagious it is. I tell her I'm coming in, whatever. She doesn't argue with me.

Clay switches on the TV. It's the local news, and it's all about the mystery illness. Of course it is. Nothing else happens around here.

"A further two deaths overnight of residents of Stanton were almost certainly caused by this unknown virus. Local MP Christopher Pheasant is demanding a public inquiry. Meanwhile, all houses in the area have been advised not to drink the water in the event that some kind of contamination is the cause of the illness."

The picture changes from the presenter's face to a group of people holding placards in the centre of Tytheford. I recognise a few faces.

"Local protesters claim that shale gas extraction, more commonly known as fracking, recently started on a nearby farm could be the cause, but Christopher Pheasant says there's no proof that this is the case."

The picture switches to the bug-eyed Christopher Pheasant, looking even more creased than usual, hair sticking up where he's scratched his head in irritation. He shouts at the camera.

"It's outrageous that these protesters are using an outbreak of a serious disease to further their minority concerns in this way!"

Then the picture cuts back to the studio where the newsreader glances at a sheet of paper in front of him. *"We've just been informed that the council have arranged for all drinking water in Stanton and the nearby village of Tytheford to be distributed by water truck today. The utility company are investigating the possibility of cutting off the supply to prevent further contagion."*

"I don't see any truck," Clay says, stuffing a piece of toast in his mouth and handing me a plate.

"Hope it rains. Otherwise, how the hell am I supposed to fill the water containers for Mary's chickens when the water butt is empty?"

"Like that's the most important thing?" Clay stares at me like I've gone mad.

"No, but it matters. Animals need water too."

"Then ask the truck to deliver extra when it arrives."
Clay stuffs the toast I left on my plate into his gob.

He's irritating me, and I go to look out of the window.
PC Chopra and PC Colenutt are getting out of the police
car on the other side of the garden wall. I feel sick with
anxiety as I run to open the door.

"What's up? Why are you here? Is Ma—"

"She's stable, Arlo," PC Colenutt says, walking up the
garden path and giving me what is probably meant to be
a reassuring smile.

"So why—" I don't get to finish the question.

"We wanted to make sure you weren't drinking the
water," PC Chopra says. "And if you like, we can give you
a lift to see your mother for a short while. We have to go
there anyway."

"Thanks. That would be great. Come in a minute.
I'll just get a few things."

The police officers follow me into the front room, and
I leave them chatting to Clay while I get some money
and hunt through Ma's room to see if there's anything
she might want. I can't think of anything apart from a
big T-shirt that she uses as a nightshirt. I glance out in
the garden and stare at the flowers. Flowers! I run back
downstairs, find a pair of scissors and nip out to the
garden. I cut a few roses and some lavender and hurry
back inside.

"Okay, I'm ready," I say, grabbing some paper to put
around the roses to stop the thorns piercing my skin.

No one says anything. I look at PC Colenutt, whose eyes have welled up. I wonder what's wrong, and my heart sinks. Ma.

"Have you heard from the hospital?"

"No, don't worry. It's nothing. I'm sorry. The flowers... are lovely, that's all." She smiles.

I don't know what to say, but I instantly know what this is about. Images of PC Colenutt's daughter flash into my mind. I look at the flowers I'm holding, and I remember. Roses. Her daughter's name was Rose.

"Any chance you can drop me in Tytheford on the way?" asks Clay. Sometimes his lack of sensitivity is stunning.

"Come on then. Let's all get in the car," PC Chopra says, and we all follow him outside.

THEY WON'T LET me in to see Ma. I want to push the ward sister out of the way and run in to see her, but this woman is built like a tank and I don't fancy my chances.

"Of course I understand you want to see her. What *you* need to understand is why I can't let you in there."

"I heard you. You think it's contagious. But I've been living with my mother the whole time. Surely I would have caught it by now?"

"It's not that simple. Things have become more... serious."

I glare at her.

"Serious in what way? What could be more serious than people dying?"

She sighs. "*More* people dying," she says. Suddenly I notice how tired this woman looks.

"Who? Who's died? Has Ma…is Ma okay?"

The ward sister doesn't say anything but glances over my shoulder. I turn to see Dave Benger coming out of one of the private rooms. He looks a broken man, tears streaming down his face. I don't need to be told.

Tracy's dead.

He notices me and stares for a minute like he wants to say something. He doesn't manage it, but I see the pity in his eyes. I know exactly what he's thinking. Ma will go too, the same way as Tracy. I stand unmoving until he's got into the lift and disappeared.

I turn back to the ward sister.

"They're all dying, aren't they? Can't I see her, just for a second? Please? I might never get the chance again."

"Be quick." That's all she says. I don't wait for her to change her mind. I push through the double doors onto the ward.

I rush straight to Ma's bed and take her hand. She's still breathing and her hand is warm. I grip it tightly, and for a moment, I imagine she squeezes mine back. It's probably reflex. She's not conscious at all.

"I can't stay, Ma. They won't let me. But if you can hear me, know that I love you—always. Sorry if I caused you any trouble. Say hi to Dad for me if you see him again."

I kiss her cheek. I can't let go of her hand, even when I see the ward sister coming towards me. She's not being unkind, I know. She's just obeying orders and I'm not supposed to be here. I only let go of Ma's hand when the ward sister pulls me gently away from the bedside. I can't look back at Ma. My eyes have welled up and I can't see anything. I stumble out through the doors and go straight to the lift. I have to get some air.

The automatic door at the hospital entrance opens as I approach. I don't see the crowd gathered until I'm outside. Some are waving anti-fracking placards. A man with blonde dreads spots me. He looks vaguely familiar, but it's only when he runs up and grabs my arm, dragging me in front of the crowd that I remember who he is. Dougie, the speaker from London who came to the meeting in Tytheford.

"Listen! Listen, everyone! This boy can tell you about the dangers of shale gas extraction, can't you... Arlo, isn't it?" He shoves the microphone he's holding towards my face.

I stare at the crowd, who have all turned to look at me expectantly.

"Sorry, I can't talk right now. My mother is in the hospital. She's very sick."

I see the glint of excitement in his eye before he can hide it. "Do you think her illness might have been caused by the mining operation in the area?"

"Yes. I think the fracking poisoned the water somehow. That's all I can say." I manage to blurt out the words before I'm overwhelmed and tears spill down my face. I turn away from him and push my way blindly through the crowd, desperate to escape.

Once I'm free of the crowd of demonstrators, I don't stop running. I pass quickly through the wide high street in the centre, dodging around the people shopping. I pass fruit stores and charity shops, and glance briefly at the White Horse bookshop, wondering if I can duck in there and hide from everyone for a while and catch my breath. I'm about to push the door open when I spot Caroline talking to someone behind the counter. I start running again, heading out past the posh school Hayden goes to and the straggling houses on the outskirts of town, making for the road that leads to Tytheford and Stanton.

It's only when I've left all the houses behind and I'm going past fields and hedgerows that I come to a stop by a field gate. I hang on to the wooden frame, gasping in air, feeling like I'm drowning. When I can finally breathe normally again, I climb up to sit on top of the gate, watching the butterflies flit over the brambles in the hedge, sometimes landing on the leaves to open and close their wings in the sunlight.

I'm not sure what to do next. I can't see the point in doing anything, so I sit where I am, watching the road.

I don't know how long I've been there when the police car drives past. It screeches to a halt, and reverses back to the gate. PC Chopra jumps out.

"Arlo? Are you all right?"

I nod. I'm not all right, but there's nothing he can do about it.

"Please get in the car. Let us take you back to Stanton. Come on."

I don't bother to answer. I stare at him for a moment, then jump down off the gate and do as he says. PC Colenutt is in the driving seat. She turns to face me. She looks grey, like she hasn't slept in weeks.

"Arlo, I know it's very difficult for you right now, but your mother is still alive. The hospital is trying everything to get to the bottom of this illness. Don't give up hope."

"Tracy Benger died. She was younger than Ma. And Harry Suggeworth died. Everyone is dying, and the hospital can't do anything."

"That may not be true."

"They won't even let me stay with her."

"That's because they don't want you becoming ill too."

"I won't. Not unless I drink the water, and I'm not going to."

She sighs. "It's a precaution. I'm sorry you can't stay with your mother, but the hospital will call if there's any change at all in her condition."

"So what am I supposed to do? Sit and twiddle my thumbs and let her die alone? I wouldn't do that to an animal. Why should I do that to my own mother?"

"It's different. If it was an outbreak of foot and mouth in cattle, we'd cull the herd. But it's people we're talking about. We do everything we can to find a cure, but we have to isolate those affected to avoid it spreading."

"I could stay in the hospital. That way if I caught it, I'd be isolated already."

"They can't let you do that, Arlo. If anything happened to you, they'd be held responsible. I know it seems unfair, and probably nothing would happen to you, but that's not the point."

I don't bother to argue with her anymore. I know she can't change or bend the rules. She's a police officer. She starts the car.

"You'd better fasten your seat belt," PC Chopra says.

I want to laugh. Right now I don't care if I die, so what's the point? But I fasten it anyway, to keep him happy.

They drop me back at the cottage and leave straight away. They have to get back and keep an eye on the demonstration outside the hospital. There isn't usually much crime around here, so these two represent half of the entire police force in the area.

I can tell PC Colenutt isn't happy about leaving me, though. She keeps telling me to call a friend and saying I shouldn't be on my own right now. I tell her I'll do as she says, but only to make her go away. I don't feel like seeing anyone.

Chapter 28

To KILL SOME time, I go up to Mary's chicken shed. I clean out the chicken bedding and put fresh straw down for them. I check my phone constantly. I get no messages from the hospital, and I don't feel like answering the ones from Jaz and Clay yet. It's still only midday. I don't know how to fill the time. Nothing distracts me from worrying about Ma.

Coming out of Spring Farm, I decide to visit the grove on the way home. I have some vague idea in my head about talking to Dad, to see if it helps.

I push my way under the hedge and into the woodland, and hurry though towards the clearing. I don't bother to keep quiet. If Phelps shows up, I'll enjoy punching him. The thought helps to give me focus.

But when I get there, the grove isn't the calm haven I was hoping for. It's just a space in the woodland. There's nothing here but dead grass and bracken, and the air is filled with the stink of stagnant water from the spring.

I duck under the oak and come out by the silent water. Staring at the ripple-free surface, I see myself reflected clearly, branches of oak and cloud-free blue sky above my head. Next to my reflection, there's something a bit blurry, and I stare at it for a moment, trying to work out what it is. Suddenly I realise and take a step back in surprise.

It's Andraste. Or at least, Andraste's reflection. She's looking down into the pool too, but when the image becomes clear, I see the trees above her head are different. The sky above her is almost dark.

She's not here next to me. She's in that other place. My heart starts racing, and I turn and run back through the grove, not stopping until I'm out of the woodland and on the lane.

Panting with exertion, I blink in the afternoon sunlight, trying to make sense of what I saw. As I gradually catch my breath, I get the feeling someone is watching me and look up. My skin goosebumps. Andraste is leaning against the gate opposite.

I instinctively step back and feel the hedge spiking my shoulder. "What are you doing here?"

"I came to find you. I said I'd come back."

"Yeah, I remember." I'm trying to be firm and assertive, but my voice is shaky.

"Do you remember your oath, Arlo?"

"Oath?" I'm stalling. Of course I remember the oath. My stomach feels like it's turned to liquid.

"Your oath to look after the grove and the spring. It's not your fault it was violated, but you have the power to change it back."

"I don't think so."

"I'm telling you, you do. But you don't have to be so afraid. You have a choice. Come with me now, and everything will become clear."

"Can't it wait?" I say, glancing at my phone to check for messages again.

"We're running out of time, Arlo. The damage is spreading fast now. In your world too. Tomorrow may be too late."

"Okay... I guess."

I try to calm myself by controlling my breathing. Her honeysuckle scent is overpowering, even from here.

Andraste turns and vaults easily over the field gate on the other side of the lane. I'm stunned, even though I'm all too aware how different she is from other people. I cross the road and scramble clumsily after her.

We stand next to each other on the grass. Wights Mound rises up in front of us a few hundred metres away.

Andraste starts walking slowly towards the Mound. I think maybe she wants us to climb it.

But she doesn't.

"Close your eyes, Arlo, and run with me," she says, reaching out and grabbing my hand.

The feel of her hand in mine sends a jolt through my body. As she starts to run, I try to do as she says and keep my eyes closed, but every so often, I stumble over tussocks in the grass and have to open them to check the lay of the land. We run faster and faster, until suddenly she stops. The momentum of running means I can't stop instantly like she did, and because she doesn't let go of my hand, my arm is practically wrenched out of the socket. I shake my hand free and turn to shout at her.

I close my eyes in shock. Then open them again. It's as weird as I first thought.

Wights Mound isn't there anymore. We're in the half light of dawn.

I shout at Andraste in panic. "What the hell have you done? Where are we?"

The largest Neolithic structure in the country has vanished. Only a second ago, it was afternoon. Here, the sun hasn't even risen.

All I can see in this light is rugged heathland covered in gorse and heather, surrounded in every direction by dark, tree-covered hills. A couple of startled hares leap away from us, running off in different directions.

Have I had another seizure and been out for hours? I turn, slowly, doing a complete 360° circuit until I'm looking at Andraste again. But there's still no Wights Mound

"Where's the Mound?"

"It doesn't exist in this place. This heath is where they built Wights Mound to separate our worlds."

"What are you talking about? What have you done to me? Did you spike me with something?" I'm so scared, I think I'm going to throw up.

"I've brought you through to the other side, that's all."

"Other side? What do you mean? Like, you mean, I'm *dead*?" The sound of my blood racing in my ears makes me think I'm still alive, but maybe that's what being dead feels like too?

"No. I've brought you through to my world. You've been here before—you know you have."

I feel the wolf fang hanging from my neck. My legs are shaking so much, I want to sit on the ground until they recover. The air smells so different here. Wild. Filled with unfamiliar scents. The confusion of unfamiliar sounds.

"But I didn't know for sure. I thought I was going mad..."

She comes closer, so she's standing right in front of me, and jabs me in the chest, directly over my heart.

"Deep down, you knew, Arlo. Your mother knew too, but you didn't want to hear her. Look around you." She jabs me again. "Look with your heart, not your mind. See where you are."

I tear my gaze away from hers. The first rays of the sun are rising above the forested hills in the east. Everything shimmers gold. My heartbeat steadies as my panic subsides. I realise I have never in my life been anywhere so beautiful, and I'm suddenly overcome with the wonder of this place. Everything is alive. It seems like the whole world is breathing. Rocks, plants, the earth— everything pulses with life.

I turn back to Andraste and gasp in surprise. Her eyes glow green *with no white showing*. Her tattoos move and shift over her skin like a living web. She could be any age. She's...*not human*. The vision only lasts a second. She smiles, and next thing I know, she's just a girl with long, red hair and too many tattoos.

"Who are you?"

"I'm the guardian of this place, Arlo. And I'm part of it. As much as everything else here."

"I don't understand."

"You're part of it too, but in your world. I've just been here longer."

"How much longer?"

"I don't know. It's not important. Here, we don't measure time like you do. You're trying to make yourself believe this place can't be real, but you know it is. You people have lost the way of seeing it. I had to bring you here to make you understand."

I stare at her, not knowing what to say. All the questions that form in my mind seem meaningless, so I don't voice them.

I look behind me, aware of loud growling and grunting coming from the edges of the nearest woodland. I've never heard anything like it. If it's an animal, it's big. Maybe I should run, but everything has taken on a dreamlike quality, so I gaze at the trees and watch as a large brown bear and her cubs leave the wood and lumber across the heathland, straight towards us.

Andraste yanks my arm, pulling me out of my reverie. The bear stops and sniffs the air. Despite the potential danger, I still don't feel afraid of them. All I can think is how incredible it all is. The cubs come running straight up to me and tussle with each other at my feet.

When I breathe in, I can smell bear. It's a bit like dry grass, but musty. Can this be real? It certainly feels like it is.

Andraste opens her mouth and growls, startling me. "I have to stop them getting closer to the spring," she says.

The mother bear eyes her curiously. Andraste growls more loudly. The bear raises its snout and sniffs the air again.

"That's right. You can smell the bad water now, can't you? So don't come any closer."

The bear turns away and lumbers back towards the trees, her cubs gambolling along behind her.

"Bad water?"

"The spring is in both worlds. It's a point of connection. And thanks to the mining activity in your world, it's poisoned here too. It's been like it since I first saw you out in the field. You saw me, too. And later, I watched you through the water and you picked up the token. That's how I knew you would pay the forfeit."

My heart freezes, and suddenly the place looks less beautiful. I stare at her in horror. Forfeit. Blood forfeit. Has she brought me here to kill me?

"Why me? I don't understand. Why not Phelps? This is all his fault, not mine!"

"You care. He doesn't. The agreement is with the land herself, and the sacrifice must be made by someone who is willing to pay the price. I'm not here to force you to do anything, just to help you as much as I can. You belong to the land, and Phelps does not."

Anger starts to bubble within me. "So nothing happens to Phelps, but me and my family lose everything, right? Is this what happened to Dad? Did you make him pay this stupid forfeit too? I know you were around back then, from things Mary and Ma said."

"No. It's true I was there at that time because the crows told me how things were changing. That the land was passing from your father to a new, dangerous guardian. I don't make bad things happen, Arlo. I come back because they're happening already. It was tragic that your father chose to end his life, but the only forfeit he paid was in his own head."

My mind is whirring, desperately seeking a way out. Does she believe I care enough for the land to sacrifice my life for it? She's wrong. Surely I can move away, live somewhere else?

Andraste is watching me. "You need to see more. Come to the spring with me. It's near the edge of the forest. Not that far." She starts walking and beckons for me to follow.

I have no choice but to do as she asks. Walking behind her, I wonder how long she'll make me stay here. All I want is to escape from her and get away from this place. I want to go home. I never want to see her again.

I stumble over some heather and stop a moment to look around the open heath. The dawn breeze is filled with the coconut scent of the gorse. I try to get my exact bearings from the contours of the surrounding hills, but this landscape is so different, I can't work it out. There's thick forest on the hills where I'd expect to see crops growing, and the heathland we're walking over should be pasture. Nothing looks like it should.

Soon we're ducking under trees and pushing through undergrowth in the forest. In places it's impenetrable. The only way through is to follow animal paths, and although Andraste seems to glide through with ease, my T-shirt keeps getting hooked on spiky blackthorn and brambles, and I'm scratched all over.

It's hard to see ahead, and I realise I can no longer see Andraste anywhere. I've no idea what direction she went in. The strange, primordial forest is full of sounds of rustling and grunting and loud birdsong in the branches above. I wonder what other animals live here. The scent of the thick leaf mould underfoot is intense. Every so often, I see pairs of eyes staring back at me through the undergrowth, watching, intelligent. Could it be the wolves? Some look different. Closer to human.

I start to panic. My chest tightens, and it's getting hard to breathe. Is this it? Do I pay the forfeit now, getting ripped apart by wild beasts? Speared by unseen people, or someone not human, like Andraste?

"Try to keep up, Arlo."

How did she get so close without making any noise? I'm startled but surprisingly relieved to see her. As we move on, I try to stick with her.

251

After a good half hour of battling through trees and undergrowth, we come to a halt. I breathe in sharply. All at once I recognise where we are. It's different and yet the same—a circular clearing in the forest, edged by oak, yew, ash and birch trees.

"Is this...?"

"The grove? Yes. Like the spring, it's in both places. At one time, your ancestors knew that and held the grove as sacred."

I stare around me. I try closing my eyes for a moment then opening them again, to see if I can force this vision back to my reality. I can't. Worse, I can see it clearly, touch it, smell it. This place is very real. I can't escape.

"Come and look at the spring."

Andraste's voice comes from beyond the oak tree. Not the same oak tree, but an oak tree nonetheless. I follow the sound and move quickly under the branches to find her.

The stench hits me immediately. Stagnant water. Rotting, dead things. It's enough to make me heave. I move gingerly through the swampy, reed-covered area around the side of the spring to find her. I can just see the top of her head, her red hair glinting in the morning sun above the tall rushes. There are far more reeds and marsh plants than back home, but the smell of the stagnant water and decaying plant life is far worse too.

"Animals are dying here, Arlo."

"I can smell them." As I'm saying it, I stumble over a pile of bones, the stinking, rotten flesh still attached, and barely stop myself falling into a pile of what looks like decomposing guts.

"Ugh! What the hell was this? It's massive!"

"Boar. Like my beloved wolf friend, it should have had enough sense to leave this water alone. Fortunately, that smell is deterring other animals for now. But until the blood price is paid, things will get worse. Everything here will die. My world will die."

I glare at her. I don't want to hear any more. It's not my fault this is happening. "Look, I know you want me to pay this forfeit, but maybe I want to stay alive! Why should I have to pay? There's mining in loads of places and this kind of crap doesn't happen!"

She looks at me carefully, as though she's deciding something. "I told you, Arlo, I didn't bring you here to scare you or force you to do anything. I brought you to show you how it is. This land here is like a pulse point in the earth. People always knew that, and so the agreement was made and sealed with earthlight. The Mound was built, and the great stones erected as signposts in the landscape, so people would never forget that this is sacred land."

"And Phelps has broken this agreement?"

"It's as if he's stabbed the earth herself. It has to be put right, or the illness will become airborne and spread like the black death once did through your world."

"The black death? You mean, like, the plague?"

"Yes. Here, it will be animals, the trees, everything. In your world, it will be people. You have too many. Millions will die, like they did back then."

"Aren't there any people here?" Even as I'm saying it, I get the feeling we're being watched.

"Most chose to stay in your world, back when the worlds separated. But there are... *others* here, yes."

Others? What does she mean, *others*? The hairs on the back of my neck rise thinking of the eyes watching me in the forest.

"When did this separation of worlds you're talking about actually happen?"

"Back when they started to farm the land. Before that, everything was like it is here."

I stare at her, wondering how long she's been here. She isn't part of our world at all; I realise that. I don't even know *what* she is.

I think about Ma, and how I've always poked fun at her and felt embarrassed when she talked about *the other place*. Suddenly I feel desolate. I have to find out if Ma is still alive.

"How long are we staying here? I need to get back."

"I know. You can go soon. I only wanted to show you how the mining affects both our worlds, to help you make your decision."

I can't stop shivering, even though it's warm.

"So if I choose to help save the land, how am I supposed to pay the forfeit? Do you get all the fun of killing me?"

She shakes her head. "No. My job is to make the path easier for you. I can guide you and keep you to your purpose. Death brings resolution."

My stomach knots, and I feel like I'm falling into a yawning abyss.

"That's easy for you to say. It's me who's expected to pay the price. What happens if I agree to this?"

"Then you must be on the land where the mine stands by dawn tomorrow."

"Dingle Hollow?"

She nods. "Head for the centre."

"The centre of what?"

"You'll see."

"What if I say no?"

"There's always a choice, Arlo. Sometimes it's not even down to you who makes it."

I don't get time to ask any more questions, as she grips onto my arm.

"Come, it's time to leave. Let's run."

She starts running, yanking me along with her. I crash clumsily through the undergrowth, heading back through the forest the way we came.

Brambles and creepers tear at my skin, and at one point I step in something that stinks like pig dirt. Probably wild boar. It squelches over my trainer, and the smell of excrement fills my nostrils, but Andraste won't let go or stop for a moment and there's no time to wipe it off. By the time we reach the gorse-covered heathland again, she's running much too fast for me to keep up. Inevitably, I end up tripping and falling.

I hit the ground hard and boil with rage at her for dragging me along like that.

"Why don't you let go and let me run by myself?"

I look up, expecting her to answer, but she's not there. The heathland has vanished and I'm back by the gate— exactly where Andraste appeared a few hours ago.

Overwhelmed with relief, I sit up shakily. My first thought is I have to find out about Ma. Looking up at the sky, my confusion returns. It looks more or less the same time as when we left, yet we've been gone for hours.

My head is spinning. I'm going mad. I must be. Maybe I'm getting the illness and I'm delirious. I feel my forehead. Seems normal.

Yet I'm out of breath from all the running and my heart's still thudding too fast. I'm covered in scratches and there's a disgusting stink of pig dirt coming from my trainer.

My heart sinks. It's real. There's no avoiding this. Ma was right to be worried. Andraste chose me. I'm the one she expects to pay the forfeit.

Chapter 29

A s I TRUDGE down the lane back towards the cottage, my mind is frozen in a kind of fog. Stupid little thoughts filter through, like who's going to look after the hens if I die? Should I leave a note about it for Clay? Or Jaz.

Thinking about Jaz opens such a well of sadness, I have to stop walking for a moment. Who cares about the stupid chickens? How can I possibly leave Jaz behind?

I wish I'd told her how I felt about her before she got together with Hayden. Too late now, though. But Hayden's sound. He'll look after her, whatever happens.

I'm feeling so low by the time I get home, for the first time in my life I understand what made Dad give up on everything that day. How it all became too much for him to take anymore. Maybe he felt he had to pay the price for losing the land to Phelps? I think about what Andraste told me and wonder briefly if Dad saw her too.

But he didn't have to pay a forfeit. It was his choice. And right now, selfishly, I'm finding it even harder to forgive him for choosing to die. Whatever Andraste says, it feels like I have no choice at all.

I push open the gate. The front door opens immediately. For a second I think it's Ma, miraculously better and back home. But it isn't.

"Why do you keep disappearing, dumb ass? Jaz has been worried sick! We've been to the grove and everything. Why isn't your bloody phone on?"

Despite the fact he's shouting at me, I guess Clay means well. I look at my phone. The screen's black. The battery's completely flat. My first thought is Ma.

"Crap. Get out of the way, Clay, I need to recharge it. You haven't heard from the hospital, have you?"

Jaz pushes past Clay to give me a hug. "No one's called the landline here while we've been waiting, Arlo. Don't worry. Are you okay?"

I'm really not okay. And having Jaz being so nice and so close to me is making it even harder to hide my emotion.

"I'm all right…well, y'know. Kind of. The hospital won't let me stay there. Ma's no better—how did you two get in the house?"

"You left the back door open," Jaz says. "We thought you wouldn't be long. PC Colenutt called me and told me the hospital sent you away."

"Did she? That was nice of her. I was just…" How much do I tell her? I decide to keep it simple. "Just cleaning out the hens. Look, if anything happens to me, will one of you make sure they're all right? Mary Suggeworth's still in hospital. Same ward as Ma. And Harry's already dead."

Clay stares at me. "Nothing's going to happen to you, mate. If you were going to catch this thing, it would have happened by now. But I'll take over the chickens, so you concentrate on getting your mum better—and being a media star."

Jaz grabs my arm. "We're so proud of you, Arlo. It was amazing what you said at that demonstration outside the hospital."

"Demonstration?" It takes me a moment to realise what they're talking about. I've been through so much since then. "How do you know about that? What do you mean, 'media star'?"

"You were on the news. It was so moving. They shouldn't have shown it without your permission, though!" Jaz is getting all indignant. I still don't understand.

"Eh?"

Clay butts in. "You're a sensation. The protest movement *loves* you."

"The news? What news? Are you joking?"

"No. We wouldn't joke about that. And it was obvious you were very upset." Jaz links her arm through mine. "Look, let's go through to the back garden, shall we? Phelps has driven past twice, and I don't fancy seeing him a third time."

"Phelps?"

"Mate, I know you're upset, but you're beginning to sound like a bloody parrot," Clay says. "Yeah, Phelps. He's probably pissed off about you being on TV.

Don't worry. If the bell rings, I'll answer it. I'd enjoy telling him where to stick himself. And maybe wash that mud off your trainer. You stink of pigs."

As we go through the house to the back garden, I'm still trying to remember exactly what I said to the protesters. It was about the water being poisoned by the mining; I remember that much. And if it's been on the news, it explains why Phelps is hanging around. I guess he's been looking for me to tell me the agreement is off and he's going to evict us. Like I care anymore.

I plug my phone in to charge and join Clay and Jaz down on the patch of grass by the beehives.

"What's up with the bees?" asks Clay.

I listen. There's an ominous silence around the hives.

"Guess they must have swarmed, though it's unusual for the whole hive to go."

The bees leaving is like a final straw. I mutter something about needing a drink and head back inside. Jaz follows me.

"It's the bees, isn't it? You think it's to do with your mum."

She's right. I have to bite my lip hard before I can answer. "I think maybe she's died."

"Don't be silly. The hospital would have phoned. The bees just swarmed, that's all. They probably haven't gone far. We have to find them and then we can get them back into a new hive, no problem. Your mum showed me how last year."

Strangely, even as Jaz is talking, I think I can hear buzzing. I signal her to keep quiet a minute. "Listen—can you hear them?"

The buzzing is coming from above us somewhere. I follow the sound and race up the stairs, with Jaz close behind me. The sound seems to be coming from Ma's room. Jaz and I look at each other. I open the door.

The bees have swarmed up against Ma's bedroom window.

Jaz's eyes widen in surprise. "Wow. Strange place to swarm. How can we reach them?"

I consider the problem for a second. "I'll fetch a cardboard box."

"It's like they're looking for her or something."

"Probably a coincidence. Won't be a minute," I say, but as I pound downstairs to get a box from the kitchen, I can't help thinking Jaz is right. They're looking for Ma. I have to get them back into the empty hive and hope they settle. It makes me feel better, though. If the bees are looking for her, she's probably still alive.

Finally, I find a box in the understairs cupboard, then fetch a ladder from the garden shed so I can reach the window from the outside. Jaz holds the bottom of the ladder while Clay stares at me like I'm mental. For once, he doesn't say anything sarcastic; he's probably humouring me because of Ma being so ill.

I knock the bees gently into the box and climb carefully back down the ladder holding the box in one hand. I take it over to an empty hive, open it, and talk to the bees to encourage them to go back in.

At first, they seem reluctant, but after ten minutes of me talking to them quietly, they pour slowly, like liquid amber, into the dark entrance at the bottom of the hive.

Jaz sighs. "It's amazing, the way they move like that. You can really see how they're all part of one thing."

Clay grunts. "You're both bloody nuts. You're lucky you haven't been stung to death."

"Shows how much you know about bees," I say. "They don't generally sting when they're swarming. Except idiots like you, maybe."

I realise how much I enjoy bantering with Clay. After tomorrow, I'll never be able to do this again. It's much too hard to take in.

"Are you okay, Arlo?" Jaz must have seen my expression.

Suddenly I want to reach out and hug her close to me, feel her warmth next to me. But I don't.

"Yeah, I'm fine. I need to check my phone and see if the hospital has rung," I say, hurrying back to the kitchen where I left it charging.

I haven't missed any calls from the hospital. All the missed calls are from Jaz and Clay from earlier this afternoon. And one from Hayden, saying he'll drop by this evening and how he hopes everything is okay.

I'm upset that he's coming over. This could be the last night ever when I can talk to Jaz, laugh with her, and maybe find an excuse to hug her before she goes home.

But maybe it's better that I don't. It's better if Hayden comes over and I don't dwell on how I feel about Jaz. If I think about it too much, it might make me change my mind about going to Dingle Hollow in the morning. As it is, Hayden can walk her home later tonight.

Clay comes into the kitchen.

"Any news?"

"Nothing from the hospital. Think I'll call them."

"No news is good news."

"Thanks, Clay, but all it means is that Ma's not dead yet."

"Well, that's better than the alternative, isn't it?"

Jaz sticks her head through the open doorway. "Clay, I seriously wonder about you sometimes."

Clay shrugs. "I'm hungry."

"Is that meant to be an excuse? Okay, for that, you're going to help me cook something. Arlo, you call the hospital."

"You don't have to cook, I'll be fine," I say. "You probably need to get home."

They look at me like I've gone mad, and I actually manage to laugh.

"Well, if you insist on cooking something, I got a message from Hayden to say he's coming too, but you probably knew that."

Before she can answer, someone knocks at the front door.

"I'll answer it," Clay says. "In case it's Phelps."

I'd forgotten about Phelps. Jaz and I wait in silence as Clay goes to the door.

Chapter 30

"OH. IT'S YOU."

"Is Arlo here?"

Hayden. I breathe a sigh of relief.

"Well, it's his house, so I guess he could be. Arlo? Are you in?"

"Stop being a moron, Clay," Jaz says. "Ignore him, Hayden. We're in the kitchen."

Hayden comes through to join us, carrying another Tupperware box. There's something not right about him.

Jaz notices immediately. "What's wrong with your eye, Hayden? You haven't been stung, have you?"

She goes over and touches his face gently. It looks red and puffy around his right eye. I'd bet anything it was Phelps.

"I'm okay, don't worry," says Hayden, flinching away from Jaz's touch. "Mum made an extra quiche. She wanted me to bring it for Arlo."

He plonks the Tupperware box on the table. Jaz opens it straight away.

"That's very nice of your mum, Hayden. I'll do some salad to go with it. It's plenty big enough for us all to share."

"I've had some already, thanks. And, er, I can't stop long. Just wanted to bring this..." He hesitates and looks at me. "Saw you on the news. Really sorry about your mum."

I can see he means it, and his puffy eye tells me exactly how Phelps reacted to the news. I've been harsh on Hayden. I should have known better. I want us to be friends again.

"You can stay a little while, though, can't you?"

"How do we know he's not here to report back to his dad?" asks Clay.

Jaz turns on him. "Shut up, Clay." She touches her forehead and frowns. "You're giving me a headache."

I know I should have told Clay it was Hayden who took the photos of the mining in Dingle Hollow by now.

"Clay, lighten up. You're way too hard on Hayden. Don't you realise he was the one who—"

I break off the sentence because I see Hayden shaking his head at me like he wants me to stop. I'm not sure why.

"It's not his fault that Phelps is his father," Jaz says. I smile at her gratefully. She always sticks up for people. She rubs her forehead again. It's not like her to get headaches. I start to feel uneasy.

Strange Hayden hasn't told her the truth, though. Maybe they still haven't had any time alone together since the meeting in the village hall.

Hayden stops with us for a while, but he looks uncomfortable the whole time, probably because Clay's here. Occasionally, he winces and touches his eye, and he keeps blinking. It must be painful. Eventually, he takes the opportunity to leave when Jaz suggests heating up the quiche his mum made.

"I must be heading back. Mum will be worrying I've stopped to eat all the food." He attempts a smile.

I wait a second to give Jaz a chance to see him to the door, but she's busy finding stuff in the fridge to make a salad, so I go. I walk to the garden gate with him, thinking how lovely the garden smells in the evening. The bees are back buzzing on the sunflowers. Everything seems so normal, and yet deep down it's all gone so wrong.

"Why don't you want them to know about the photos, Hayden?"

He shrugs. "I meant to tell Jaz but haven't had a chance. But I don't want Clay to know in case he starts shooting his mouth off about it. Dad's temper...y'know."

"Yeah, I know. Is your eye okay?"

"I'll live, but I can't risk leaving Mum with him for too long. Especially now."

Finally, I understand. He hasn't told them because he's protecting his mum from his dad. That's how it's been all along.

"I hope you can persuade her to move out very soon. Or throw him out. Definitely before he finds out about the baby. Take care, Hayden. Best of luck with it all."

I desperately want to ask him to look after Jaz for me too, but it would be too complicated to explain why.

He grimaces. "See you tomorrow. Hope you hear better news soon."

"Yeah, me too," I say. I'm sure we both know it's not going to happen. Everyone with this illness is dying. Soon it will be Ma's turn. Thinking about her having to die alone totally does my head in. I want to be there with her more than anything in the world.

I watch Hayden until the lane curves towards Home Farm and I can no longer see him, then go back to join the others. The smell of the heated quiche is delicious. I wish I felt hungry. But I'm not the only one. Jaz hardly touches her food.

"Are you okay, Jaz?"

"I just feel a bit sick and my headache's getting worse. I should get home."

Now I'm really worried. "Shall I call your mum? You look washed out."

Jaz flops down on the sofa. "I could walk, but I'm so tired. It's okay, I'll call her."

As Jaz reaches for her phone, Clay looks at me and raises an eyebrow. Even he's concerned. I think back to see if Jaz drank any water while she was here. My blood runs cold. That morning, when Caroline came with baby Laurel, they both drank some. Was that before or after the spring stopped bubbling?

JAZ'S MUM COMES to collect her about ten minutes later. As Jaz climbs into the car, I pull Caroline to one side.

"The symptoms Jaz has—probably nothing, but please keep an eye on her."

Caroline catches my drift immediately. "Should I take her to the hospital?"

"I don't know. Guess it can't hurt to get it checked?"

Caroline has gone white as a sheet. "I'll drive straight there before she can kick up a fuss."

"What are you two talking about? I'm fine. There's nothing wrong with me!"

"I think we should make sure," Caroline says firmly.

"Honestly, I haven't been sleeping well recently and I'm tired. That's all! And if you must know, my period's due. No way am I going to the blooming hospital!" She folds her arms and scowls defiantly.

Caroline rolls her eyes and sighs. "Okay, I'll take you home and give you some painkillers. For now."

"Tell me if you feel any worse, won't you?" I say.

Jaz grins at me. "I'm fine. I'll text you later to tell you I'm still fine, okay?"

"Okay."

But I notice she starts rubbing her forehead again as the car pulls off.

THE PHONE RINGS when we're eating. It's bound to be the hospital about Ma. I race to answer it, my heart thumping.

It's several seconds before I realise it's Jaz's mum again.

"Listen, I don't want to worry you, and Jaz insists she's perfectly well and she'll call you later, but now

Laurel is getting fretful and feverish too, so I'm taking them both to the hospital, to make sure."

"Thanks for telling me. Let me know what they say, won't you?"

"Of course. And Jaz says I shouldn't be calling you as you'll only worry and she's fine. She's taking Laurel out to the car."

I laugh. That's so like Jaz. But inside, it feels like my blood has turned to ice.

"Best to get it checked. Tell her I think you're right to be sensible."

Clay looks at me as I put the phone down. "Who was that?"

"Caroline. She's taking Jaz and Laurel to the hospital to get them checked, just in case."

"Bloody hell!"

"That's what I thought. But I could hear Jaz in the background, grumbling that her mum was making a fuss about nothing."

"Caroline's not the type to make a fuss about nothing."

"No."

"Let's watch a film. Take our minds off everything."

I'VE NO IDEA what the film was about. I couldn't stop thinking about Ma and wondering about Jaz. She hasn't called me like she said she would. No one has called. I'm no longer sure that's good news. It just means no one has died. Yet.

I hear Andraste's voice over and over in my head. *The illness will become airborne and spread like the Black Death...*

Clay says he's staying over. I try to tell him that it's okay if he wants to get home, but he's really stubborn.

"Don't be an idiot, Arlo. Of course I'm staying. Deal with it and shut up."

"Thanks, Clay... I guess."

I manage to persuade him to sleep in my room by saying I want to sleep downstairs in case the police call with news. Even he can't argue with that.

When the bedroom door shuts, I turn the light out quickly in case Clay comes back downstairs. I sit in the darkness for hours, listening to the owls hooting out in the garden, waiting for the hospital to ring, waiting for Jaz to text, feeling like the whole world is ending. Because tomorrow, for me, it will be.

What's happened to Jaz and Laurel has made my final decision for me. Jaz would have texted if she was okay, I know she would. I've never felt worse. Seems like everyone I care about is going to die if I don't do what Andraste says. There is no choice. I'm going to Dingle Hollow before dawn breaks.

Chapter 31

I WAKE UP SUDDENLY. I'm slumped on the sofa at an awkward angle and my neck feels cricked.

I sit up, rubbing my neck, amazed I fell asleep at all. I can't have been asleep for long. My gut twists at the thought of what lies ahead. I check my phone one last time. Still no word from Jaz. I glance out of the window and figure it's about to start getting light. I get up off the sofa as quietly as I can.

Out in the kitchen, I wash my face with water from the big container dropped outside the door by the lorry yesterday. My heart feels heavy as lead. I walk silently back to the front room and put my trainers on. I'm still wearing the same jeans and T-shirt I slept in.

As I slip out of the front door, the sky turns silver grey and the first birds start calling. I tread carefully, anxious not to make any sound until I'm out in the lane. Once on the road, I walk as quickly and quietly as I can.

A sudden sound behind me makes me jump, and I turn around to stare into the dark shadow of the lane, trying to see what it is. Nothing. Probably a deer or a badger.

I turn back and keep going. It's light enough to find my way with no problem. Besides, I could find the route blindfolded.

When I get to the spot, I duck under the hedge. The musty smell of fox scents the woodland as I push my way through.

The grove looks magical, silvered with early morning dew in the soft grey light of dawn. I stop a moment, thinking of Dad. Do I get to see him again when this is over? Is that what happens when you die? The thought brings no comfort. All I can think about is how much I'd rather stay alive.

Birds rustle in the woodland behind me and a twig cracks. I scan around quickly but can't see anything. Now my senses are on high alert. I tread as quietly as I can, out towards the spring, even though every part of me wants to turn and run home.

The plants around the spring are dank and dying, and the stagnant water stinks. It looks like everything's rotting. It was so beautiful here on Clay's birthday. How quickly things can change.

I glance back at the grove, hoping the trees aren't affected too. I catch a sudden movement by the oak. My heart skips a beat. I stand and stare into the grove, waiting.

A minute goes past. Two minutes. The smell of the water doesn't get any better, and it's making me feel sick. A barn owl swoops under the oak heading back to roost.

My heart rate steadies. It was nothing, but I'm really jumpy. I turn and look out across the field ahead.

A few hares are out. I see their long ears turn my way before they run at top speed towards the field borders.

There's no sign of anyone about, but I creep to the edge of the field where it's easier to hide if I have to. I need to get as far as Dingle Hollow undetected, where Andraste told me to go. I don't want Phelps or his security team preventing me getting there.

Dawn is breaking. As the light grows stronger, I feel that close connection with the earth that Ma says she gets in the garden in the early morning. And I teased her for being weird. I can't bear to think about it.

I wish I'd brought my phone with me, so I could check if the hospital had rung. I think about Jaz, in hospital with all the others who have this virus, and Clay back home, asleep for sure. Snoring too, probably. I've never wanted to hear Clay snoring as much as I do at this moment. The thought almost makes me smile.

I pass the spot where I made the wolf crop circle with Andraste, now totally ploughed over by Phelps. Then, reaching the far side of Spring Field, I climb carefully over the barbed wire that's wound around the top of the gate leading to Nine Acre. I'm closer to the farm here, though I can't see it because of the hedges. I hurry a little faster towards Dingle Hollow.

The top of the mine building comes into view, taking me by surprise. It's down in the dip, but it must be way taller than I thought. The pictures Hayden took didn't really give a sense of scale. No wonder Phelps placed it here; it's the part of the farm that's most difficult to see from anywhere else. He could keep the whole operation hidden until he knew for sure there was gas down there, without applying for planning permission.

I'm paying for his greed now, along with Ma and the rest of Stanton. It's all so unfair. I stumble over a clod of earth and practically fall over. Tears of anger prick my eyes, but I force myself to keep going.

As I reach the gate to Dingle Hollow, I slow down. My pulse thrums in my ears, making it hard to hear anything else. I stop and look down into the field.

In the hollow at the bottom left of the field, I recognise the squat mine building I saw in Hayden's photos, with the drilling tower stretching up to the sky next to it. There's a four-by-four parked by the building, but I can't see anyone about. The complex is surrounded by high chicken-wire fencing, topped with barbed wire and covered in signs. I can't make out what the signs say from here, but I hope it's not warnings from some security firm with guard dogs. Dogs would hear me coming from way off. I shudder at the thought of getting my throat ripped out.

Andraste said something about going to the centre. Did she mean the centre of the mine complex? I force myself to climb over the gate into Dingle Hollow. I catch my leg on the barbed wire going over the top and my jeans rip at the knee, tearing my skin. Without stopping to see how bad it is, I jump down from the gate and crouch low to the ground, keeping my eyes fixed on the building down below.

Something glints and moves on the side of the building. Security cameras. I'm not sure if they can pick me out at this distance, but I hope not. I try to visualise where Hayden would have been standing when he took those photos. Close enough for the cameras to have picked up on him, for sure, which means Phelps must have known it was him all along. My hatred for Phelps intensifies.

It's only when a flock of crows flies overhead and lands in the field to the right of the building that I see the crop circle.

Forgetting about dogs and cameras, I stand up so I can see it better, staring in amazement. The formation covers the entire field, stopping only about twenty metres short of the mine fence. I can't believe I didn't notice it straight away. I was too preoccupied with sussing out the mine.

The design is so stunning, it's hard to take it all in. Three gigantic ravens strut around after each other, beaks open, interwoven in a Celtic knot pattern. It's so good, for a second I almost forget why I'm here. The pattern weaves into a circle with no obvious beginning or end. That's the point of Celtic knots. They represent eternity. But there's a space at the heart of the design. The centre. I know immediately that's where I must go.

Chapter 32

I STUDY THE FORMATION for a few minutes, working out the best way to get to the centre without being seen by anyone at the mine. It's possible the CCTV cameras have picked up on me already.

I decide to edge around the field border, keeping close to the hedge. I pick out the best tramline to follow through the crop to reach the centre, about two-thirds of the way down the field. I calculate the fastest route to get to it, counting the number of tramlines I'll need to pass first. I know from experience it'll be much harder to see where I'm going when I'm down the field at ground level.

I take a deep breath. It's now or never. Hearing the harsh croak of a raven, I look up. The huge bird flies down the field, following exactly the route I was about to take, before flying off over the crop formation. It crosses my mind that the raven and Andraste must be connected in some way; I'm not sure why it didn't occur to me earlier.

Following the raven's flight path, I pick my way around, trying to keep in the shadow of the hedgerow. I count the tramlines as I walk over them, the odd beetle scurrying for safety as I approach. The crop is high enough for me to stop worrying about being caught and stopped by security men after a while. I'll be lost in the landscape.

I reach the ninth tramline, turn and start walking along it towards the centre of the circle, my heart hammering. This is it.

The earth smells damp with the early morning dew as the first shafts of sunlight hit the field. For a moment, everything turns gold. I reach the centre just as the sun rises above the hedge boundary, and the light bounces off the woven corn. I can't believe how beautiful the world looks. I stand still, legs shaking. I've no idea what to expect.

Then I see her, Andraste, on the outer edge of the circle, weaving her way through the formation. Even at this distance, I can see she's fixed her gaze on me. Her long, red hair is woven through with black feathers, which flutter in the breeze as she moves. What I can see of her dress above the corn is raven black. My pulse races. Everything goes into slow motion.

Suddenly I hear a clicking sound coming from somewhere behind me. Andraste freezes, and the look on her face terrifies me. What the hell's going on? I turn around, searching for an answer.

My brain has worked it out even before I spot him. Phelps. I recognised the sound. It was the shotgun being loaded, and now he's pointing it at me. He's already trampled into the edge of the circle to make sure he's close enough.

In that instant, I know exactly what he's thinking. His shotgun is so powerful he could probably kill an elephant at this range. He's going to pretend he can't see me. His words come back to me in a flash. *"You're trespassing on my land, Arlo Fry. I might have shot you 'by mistake'. Would have got away with it too..."*

Then I catch some movement from the corner of my eye, and I hear someone shouting, *"NOOOO, STOP!"*

Before I can work out what's happening, something slams into me so hard that I fall, face first, into the dry soil. My ears ring with the explosion of gunfire, and as I turn my face to spit out dirt, I feel the weight of someone holding me down.

The dry earth is splattered with fresh blood, pooling, sinking into the ground. My thoughts jumble. So much blood... Am I dying? How come I still feel alive? Who the hell is holding me down against the earth like this? Far away, I hear shouting and swearing.

Sounds a bit like Clay. But it can't be. He's asleep...

I push myself up, using all my strength. An arm flops down beside me, running with blood. I flip sideways, panicked out of my mind, forcing the thing off my back. The body rolls to the ground next to me. And I see who it is.

"Hayden! Oh my God, Hayden! Please God, no!" I scrabble at the body to turn him to face me. His eyelids flutter, and he looks up at me. His chest is a total mess. Fresh blood pumps out from the wound, soaking his shirt, staining his jeans dark red. I try to hide my shock.

"Hayden, what on earth...?" As I'm saying it, I rip my T-shirt off over my head, and try to push it into the wound. It turns from white to red immediately.

Hayden's lips move, but I can barely hear him. "Dad. Shot me."

I sit up and cradle Hayden's head in my arms. I can't believe what's happening.

"He meant to shoot me, Hayden, not you! Why are you even here?" I lean in closer, pushing my saturated rag of T-shirt against his wound, desperate to keep him alive.

"Followed you," he whispers. "Saw Andraste..." His breath is ragged.

"Andraste? Did she tell you I was here?" He blinks at me. I take it as yes. "Hayden, I'm so sorry. It wasn't supposed to be like this!"

His lips try to form words. I only just make them out. "Yes, it was. Had to be...my choice."

"But why...*why*? Why did you do it?"

"Love you. Couldn't let you die..."

I stare at him. "What? But...?"

His look tells me everything he feels.

"Love me? Oh, Hayden! You never said..."

He reaches up and touches my face. "Always. Ask Jaz..." I grasp his hand and hold it tight. His eyes are growing dim.

The truth hits hard.

It was never about Jaz. It was about me. And I wasn't even that nice to him because I was jealous. *Jealous*! How could I have been so stupid?

279

I cradle him closer, whispering. "Hayden, I didn't know! Sorry, I'm so sorry, please don't die, Hayden, please don't die... *hang in there, stay with me...*"

He's trying to say something. I stop ranting and listen. He can hardly move his lips.

He coughs painfully with the effort of talking, and a trickle of blood runs down his chin. I quickly wipe the blood from his mouth with my thumb.

"We can always be friends," he whispers and smiles.

He actually smiles.

"Of course, we will be. Best friends. Always, forever," I croak, watching the light fading from his eyes.

"Look after... Mum... tell her... I love her..."

And then he's gone.

My heart breaks.

For him, for Ma, for Jaz, for the whole stupid mess of life. I wish Phelps had shot me like he meant to. I wish I was dead.

"THIS IS ALL YOUR FAULT, YOU WORTHLESS PIECE OF SHIT! WHY COULDN'T YOU STAY AWAY FROM MY LAND?"

Phelps wrenches Hayden away from me. He's still shouting, clutching Hayden's body, covering himself in his son's blood. He screams the same thing over and over, how it's all my fault, if I hadn't come here, it wouldn't have happened... how I've killed his son.

I'm unable to do anything except curl up on the ground, feeling the earth spin beneath me, wanting it to swallow me, trying to accept that I'll never see

Hayden alive again. Or Ma. Or Jaz. Yet I'm still here. It should have been me, not Hayden.

I hear a voice shouting at Phelps, "Just shut up!" Then I feel someone shaking me.

"Arlo! Mate, can you hear me? God, so much blood everywhere... are you hurt? Please tell me you're okay!"

Clay. So it *was* him I heard. I blink. Time stands still while images flash in front of me, scarring my retinae. Hayden's blood soaking into the ground. Clay crying and swearing, begging me to be alive. Phelps standing there, holding Hayden's lifeless body, shouting that it's all my fault.

Then everything goes dark.

Chapter 33

IT'S THE WEIRDEST thing. People keep talking to me, but I can't seem to turn to look at them and I can't make sense of what they're saying. It's like I'm in some place where I'm blanketed in cotton wool. I see nothing clearly, just shapes in a fog, sounds muffled by thick walls.

Then suddenly, through the wooliness, a face appears right in front of me, and stares into my eyes.

"Try and find your brain, nut job. Jaz needs you. Hell, even I need you. Stop it with the staring into space crap, can't you?"

This time I understand perfectly, and I even want to laugh. But I can't make my mouth move, and I can't see him clearly. But at least I know it's Clay.

"Do you think he's getting better? I'm sure he heard you."

"Looks exactly the same to me. Like a dumb vegetable."

"I saw his eye twitch like he wanted to look at you."

"Wishful thinking, Jaz."

Hearing Jaz in this place, wherever this place is, makes me feel a bit better. She's alive! But I can't move my head to turn to look at her. I can't move at all. Somehow it's easier this way. I drift back into the cotton-wool space for a while.

I'm lying on my side. When I open my eyes, I see green. Gradually, I make sense of the green. It's part of a piece of clothing. A skirt maybe. It moves away, and a face swims into view. I can't quite place it for a minute.

"Arlo? Are you awake? I wanted to come and see you. I don't know if you can hear me or not, but I need to tell you. It's not your fault what happened. I understand how you feel. But for what it's worth, it's all my fault, not yours. I should have divorced his father years ago. If I'd left like I wanted to... Hayden kept telling me to, and we were going to get out before the baby... I'm so sorry..."

The voice falters and cracks, and I hear the sound of someone softly crying. It goes on for a long time, occasionally punctuated by louder sobs as she takes a breath. The bed is shuddering in time with her crying, and I want to reach out and say no, it's not your fault. I try to remember her name. Emily. Emily Phelps. Poor woman. Her Hayden is dead. And I feel like it's my fault, not hers, whatever she says. I want to cry too, but I can't. I'm frozen.

This time, I know I'm dreaming. I see a rainbow of knitting.

"Arlo, you have to come back to us soon. Everything will be okay, you'll see. The bees know it too."

Ma. Funny how it feels like she's here. Wherever here is. I still can't work it out, but I smile at the memory of her.

"See, I knew you'd come round. You're smiling!"

I try to work out how my face feels. Strangely, I think it could be true. I might be smiling. Then I'm back in the fuzzy place, where everything is white and I don't have to think at all.

"Arlo? It's me again. Emily. Hayden's mum. Your mother told me she thinks you can hear now. I hope so." There's a pause where her breath catches in a sob.

"Arlo, I want you to know you don't have to worry about the cottage. Norman...Mr. Phelps didn't get bail. The estate is my responsibility. You can stay in your home."

She breaks off talking, and there's silence for a moment, but I feel her pain. She sniffs and blows her nose. Her voice is shaky, but I can sense how much she wants me to understand what she's telling me.

"Hayden told me about your father, remember? His ashes are scattered in the grove, aren't they? You can go there whenever you want now."

I have to look at her. I try my hardest to focus, to make myself look at her. I want to say something, but all the words have gone.

"I hope you get well again soon. Come and see me, won't you? You're the only link I have left..."

She's crying again, and I want to reach out. This time, the cotton wool doesn't save me. I think I'm crying too. I feel the water trickling down my face.

Then I feel her gently touch my cheek with her fingers, brushing the tears away. I'm a well of darkness.

WHEN I OPEN my eyes, the knitted rainbow is there again. Then the rainbow moves and a familiar face appears.

"Are you awake, Arlo?"

I move my lips. "Ma?" I don't think any sound comes out, but she still hears me. She hugs me until I feel like I'm suffocating.

"I knew you'd be okay," she says.

She lets go and moves back slightly. "Oh. Sorry, love. You've got a mouthful of knitting."

The sensation of fur in my mouth goes away, and I find I can smile after all. And then I find my voice.

"Colours."

"Yes, Jaz bought me the wool. She said I should knit a rainbow for a change. I'm not sure about it, to be honest. What do you think?"

I look at the long, shapeless rainbow of knitting that trails from Ma's knitting needles.

"Nice," I manage. Then I start to laugh, and it sounds so weird in my ears, I laugh even more.

"I don't know what's so funny," Ma says. She's trying to sound offended, but she's grinning at me. "I suppose you think I should knit something useful, like a sweater?"

In the background, I hear a door opening and shutting, and a waft of hospital food smells reach my nostrils.

"Is he awake?" It's Jaz. With a mega effort, I manage to turn my head and look at her. Her dark eyes light up like lanterns as she smiles at me, and for a moment, the world seems okay again.

"The doctor will be here in a minute, but I can tell you now, they're letting you go home, Arlo!" The nurse is called Poppy. She's been great.

"But I still can't move properly," I say.

"You will. I've seen a few cases like yours before. Trauma paralysis is temporary, and you're already recovering. You'll be fine. Being back home with your mum and your girlfriend should help."

I'm about to say *she's not my girlfriend* but stop myself. Jaz is amazing and beautiful, and I love her, but right now, there's no way because practically every time I shut my eyes, I see Hayden dying in my arms. Every night since I came round, I've woken up from nightmares filled with screaming and blood.

I don't think I'll ever get over that.

My attention is brought back into the starkly painted hospital room by the arrival of the doctor. She smiles.

"Do you want the good news or the bad news first?" she says.

I instantly feel wary. I hope they haven't changed their minds about me leaving. "Bad news first."

"Don't look so worried. It's not that bad, but it's serious. The scan we gave you when you came in has shown up a small cyst on your brain. It's probably what's been causing your recent seizures."

I force myself to ask.

"Is it, like, cancer or something?"

"No, we believe it's just a cyst—and not in a difficult place. It should be easy to remove, and it's unlikely to grow back."

"So it's not cancer. That's the good news?"

"Yes. But it means if we let you out now, you'll have to come back for the operation. We'll put you on a waiting list. That's the bad news."

"What if I don't?"

"You'll quite possibly have more seizures. But we can prescribe you medication to help prevent that."

"No. I don't want medication. I'll have the op."

"Do you want time to think about it?"

"No. Put me on the waiting list. Please."

287

Chapter 34

M A AND I eat our tea together on the sofa, watching some programme about the moon landings. I'm too tired to move.

It's strange being back home again. When I left to go to Dingle Hollow a couple of weeks ago, I thought I was leaving the cottage behind forever. Of course, it's great to be back home with Ma and the bees, but underlying everything, there's a constant ache in my heart that never goes away. I can't shake the image of those last moments before Hayden died. I can never apologise for not realising how he felt or make things work out so we really could be friends again, the way we should have been all along. Basically, I can't put it right. Ever.

The astronaut they're interviewing on TV is saying how strange he finds it thinking about the moon, the intensity of longing he feels to be there again yet knowing he can never go back.

And that's another thing. It's not just Hayden. I think a lot about Andraste and the whole weird, intense experience of being in her world. It's something I can't talk about to anyone in case they think I've gone mad. But I know exactly how the astronaut feels. I can't go back there either.

"We should talk about it." Ma puts down the rainbow knitting and stares at me.

"What do you mean?" I haven't mentioned Andraste once, so for a second, I wonder if she means my operation, the *other place*, Hayden, my paralysis—have I mentioned Andraste in my sleep?

"About Hayden. How you feel. You haven't talked about it yet."

I see the worry in her eyes.

"Yeah." That's all I can manage. I don't know how to begin to express how I feel.

"It never goes away, Arlo. We both know that. But the pain fades in time. Like with your dad—remember the nightmares you used to have?"

"What about them?"

"They got better, or at least you had fewer of them after a while."

I hesitate a moment before plucking up the courage to ask. "About those nightmares. Dad's always in the grove when I see him in those dreams. Something Mary said made me wonder."

Tears start rolling down Ma's cheeks, and she quickly wipes them away with her hand. "I should have told you the truth at the time. That's where I found him. It felt so sad because it was his favourite place, and I knew you loved it there too. I didn't want people to know, so Mary helped me bring him back in the pickup truck and we said it had happened in the barn. I'm so sorry, Arlo."

"That's okay. I understand."

She wipes her eyes again and attempts a smile. "So, how you feel now about Hayden—it'll fade in time too."

"I wish."

"It will, I'm sure of it." She fiddles with her knitting a moment, as if there's more she wants to say.

"Spit it out," I say.

"What?"

"Whatever it is you're not telling me."

She looks at me carefully. "Guess it's better I tell you now because it's bound to be in the papers. Phelps is up in court for the preliminary hearing next week."

I wasn't expecting that. A wave of panic washes over me at the thought of seeing Phelps again.

"Do I have to go?"

"No, not for this. It's just the start."

"But I do later?" My heart's beating faster, and I get that sensation of falling into the earth again. The feeling I might have a seizure. My pulse is racing so fast, I can't even talk.

"Calm down, love. I'm sorry. I didn't want to upset you. You're still only sixteen, so I think you can give evidence by video link."

"But I have to talk about it?"

She nods. "But they have trained professionals to deal with this kind of thing. You'll be needing counselling, of course. Clay will too. And Jaz."

I've stopped listening. Thinking about Phelps has brought the whole thing straight back. I get up off the sofa, trying not to let Ma see I'm shaking like a leaf.

"Think I'll go up to bed, Ma. Feel knackered."

I lie in bed for a long time, listening to the owls hooting in the garden, trying not to fall asleep. Because every time I do, the nightmares take over.

CLAY CALLS IN a few days later. He's furious with me for leaving without him that morning. "I suppose that whacko woman told you about the crop circle. How come you didn't wake me up?"

"It's not that simple."

"But she told you about it, she must have. Did she make it? I saw her there."

"You saw Andraste?"

Clay shudders. "She's bad news, Arlo. There's something bloody weird about her."

"I didn't know you'd seen her too."

"I told the police. They're looking for her." He sounds bitter, and I'm not surprised.

"They won't find her," I say. "Not now."

"How do you know?"

"I mean...she's gone." I can't explain to Clay. I don't even know where to start.

"I told them she was making the crop circles you were getting blamed for, and I reckoned you went to the field because you'd heard she'd made a new one. I shouldn't be telling you this, by the way. I'm not supposed to talk to you until after you've testified."

I still can't think about that morning without coming out in a cold sweat, or speak about it without crying, but I owe it to Clay to say something. "No one but Phelps is to blame for what happened, Clay. For all of it."

"Yeah, I know. I guess. But I should have caught up with you that morning. Would have, but when I saw Hayden was following you, I wanted to find out what he was up to. I didn't trust him, and now I know better, and I feel like crap."

Clay is all hunched up, obviously deeply unhappy. Reckon Ma was right about him needing counselling too.

"Yeah, I wasn't that nice to him either. Sorry, I haven't been much help to you, have I? PC Chopra tells me you're the key witness. It must have been the worst day of your life. I know it was mine. Even worse than when Dad…well, you know."

He grimaces. "Yeah. Definitely up there in my top three. Anyway, I'd better go. Like I said, I'm not supposed to talk to you about this, so you haven't seen me, okay?"

I squeeze his shoulder. "Of course I haven't. Thanks for coming though, mate. Soon be over and we can talk more then."

When Clay's gone, I find myself crying again. I wish things were getting easier, but they're not.

JAZ SITS ON the step by the kitchen door, next to me. "Your mum says you're really churned up about having to testify."

I don't say anything, just gaze out at the bees on the lavender. After a few moments, I feel the weight of silence and turn to look at her. Her eyes are filled with tears.

I reach my hand across to cover hers. "What's wrong, Jaz? Why are you so upset?"

"You're not the only one!" She sounds angry with me too.

"No, I realise that. Sorry."

"And that's not all!"

For a second, I'm mystified and stare at her blankly.

She scowls at me. "What were you thinking? Going into the fracking site that morning? Was it because *she* asked you to? Did she want you to see her precious crop circle? If so, it's her fault almost as much as Phelps's, what happened."

"I didn't go to see her, Jaz, honestly. I didn't even know she'd be there. I only went because...I didn't care what happened to me any longer. I thought everyone I cared about was going to die. You, Ma, Laurel—everyone."

She stares at me. "What? You don't mean...surely you didn't think *I* was going to die?"

"Okay, I know it was stupid and I should have called. But when you didn't text, I thought it meant you must be...like Ma."

She looks horrified. "God, I'm so sorry! They gave me such strong painkillers at the hospital, I fell asleep." Her eyes well over and tears spill down her face.

I squeeze her arm. "It's okay, it's not your fault!"

"But you probably wouldn't have gone out at all that morning if I'd texted you. I should have stayed here that night when you thought your mum was dying. Now I feel so guilty…"

She sniffs and searches her pocket for a tissue.

It's one of the few times I've seen Jaz actually cry. She's really sobbing her heart out. Before I have time to think what I'm doing, I pull her into my arms, close to my chest. I stroke her hair. She smells like cinnamon. The tight little plaits she's put in her hair feel soft against my cheek. I keep holding her until her tears subside. I don't want to let her go.

"We can all get through this, Jaz. Don't worry, I'll look after you."

She pulls away slightly and looks up at me. She is so beautiful to me, even though there's mascara running down her cheeks.

"What, *you*? Look after *me*? Are you serious?" She sounds incredulous. Then suddenly she grins, and her eyes light up.

I smile back. "Of course! I'm really stable, me. Totally on top of the situation."

And then, despite everything being so terrible right now, we both crack up laughing.

Chapter 35

JAZ AND I decide we should go together to see Emily, Hayden's mum. Hayden's funeral is coming up soon, having been delayed by all the legal proceedings. I want to see her before it happens, even though I'm dreading it.

I'm nervous as hell walking up the track to Home Farm but try not let Jaz see. She knows, of course. Since that day in the kitchen, we've become really close—sort of different from before. We haven't talked about it yet, but I think she feels the same.

I turn to ask her if she's okay and notice the rigid set of her jaw and her tense expression. I probably look similar. On impulse, I grab her hand, like it's a perfectly normal thing to do and I do it all the time, even though I've never done it before.

"Don't worry. Emily Phelps came to see me while I was in hospital, when I wasn't able to move."

"Really? You never said."

"I still wasn't conscious most of the time. But when she came, it was practically the first time I was aware of someone being there, even though I couldn't speak or anything. She thinks what happened was all her fault."

"Why? She wasn't even there!"

"She said she should have divorced Phelps years ago and then it wouldn't have happened. I really wanted to tell her it wasn't her fault, but I couldn't."

"Poor woman."

"She's pregnant, you know. Hayden told me."

"Yes, he told me too. I only hope no one's told Phelps."

We stop talking because we've reached the farmyard. Oddly, there's a smell of baking in the air...and hardly a hint of pig dirt. I look up at the vast piggery across the yard. It's quiet and feels different.

"She must have got rid of the pigs," I say.

Jaz stares at the piggery and sniffs. "Yes, she must have done."

I haven't been here since the day Phelps caught me in the field after the seizure. I remember how jumpy Hayden was around his dad. Thinking about him makes me feel all hollow inside again, and I let go of Jaz's hand as we go up to ring the front doorbell.

I can hear my heart thumping as we stand and wait for someone to answer. The door opens a crack, and the smell of baking gets stronger.

"Is that you, Arlo?" She sounds hesitant.

"Mrs. Phelps? Yes, it is. I'm here with Jaz."

The door opens wide, and Emily blinks in the sunlight. Her eyes are deep blue, like Hayden's. She attempts a smile.

"Thanks for coming, both of you. It can't have been easy for you. But please, call me Emily like you always used to. And I'm changing my name back to Waters, my maiden name."

I totally get why she'd want to do that. "Okay, Emily," I say.

She holds the door open. "Come inside. I made you some cake. It was...um, it was Hayden's favourite." Her voice fades to a whisper.

She sounds so sad when she mentions Hayden, I feel all twisted up inside. Jaz looks like she wants to cry. We follow Emily through to the farmhouse kitchen.

"It's lemon drizzle cake. Hope you like it. I'll put the kettle on—or would you rather have lemonade?"

"Tea, please," Jaz says.

I don't trust myself to speak, so I smile and nod. When Emily turns to fill the kettle, Jaz and I look at each other. She seems as anxious as I am; I grab her hand and press it quickly.

Being in this kitchen is a weird experience for me. The last time I saw it was the day Ma and I had to leave the farm after Dad died. I never thought I'd feel worse than I did that day, but I was wrong. Today feels even sadder.

The room hasn't changed that much in some ways. The old range is still there and the beams in the ceiling. But new, expensive-looking kitchen units have been fitted, and it's bright, with spotlights over the countertops. I wonder what Ma would make of it.

Emily cuts the cake and hands us both plates with massive slices on. I wish I felt like eating it. It smells amazing. I struggle to think of something to say.

"Have you sold the pigs?" It's all I can manage.

"Yes. I hated the piggery anyway. I'm having the whole thing taken down."

"Are you going to stay living here then?" asks Jaz.

"Yes...maybe. It's a link to Hayden. I feel like he's still around somehow. I'll have to get a farm manager in, of course, especially when the baby comes. I was thinking you might want to manage it one day, Arlo. If I do stay on here, you'd be welcome. Hayden always said you were great with animals and really cared about the land, but that'll be a while off yet. I guess you need to finish college and then maybe university first."

It takes me a moment to stammer out a reply. "Thank you. I'd like that...one day maybe, if you're still here..." There's a moment of silence. A bee buzzes outside on the roses. Dad planted them, and I'm glad they've survived all that's happened. I force myself to speak.

"Um, it was good of you to visit me in hospital, by the way."

She looks surprised. "You remember me coming to the hospital?"

"Yes. Every so often, I heard people come in and I understood what they were saying, but I couldn't move at all. To be honest, I wasn't entirely sure if they were actually there or not." I hesitate. "But now we're talking about it, what happened to Hayden—it wasn't your fault either."

She seems shocked. "Oh. You heard me? I didn't realise...I thought you were in a coma."

"I kind of was a lot of the time. But thanks for telling me I wasn't to blame. I really believed it was my fault, so it meant a lot."

"That's okay. He'd have hated you to think that, Arlo. I know how he felt about you. He'd have wanted you to know."

I wonder if she really does know how Hayden felt about me, but I'm too overwhelmed to say anything.

She catches my expression and puts her hand to my cheek. "Of course I knew how he felt about you. I always knew. He was so upset when Norman bought the farm so cheap, and heartbroken when he stopped you coming here anymore. It wasn't Hayden's fault, you know..." She breaks off.

There's a big lump in my throat and I can't speak. I feel terrible. Poor Hayden. I wish I'd known how violent his father was back then, so maybe I'd have understood. And now it's too late.

"I think Norman sensed how he felt about you too, and that's another reason he stopped you from coming. Although all Hayden wanted, more than anything, was for you two to be friends again. Not being allowed to be your friend was the thing that hurt him most."

I can't hold it together any longer. It's too much for me to take. My breath comes in ragged gasps as I bury my face in my hands, unable to prevent myself from breaking down. The raw pain of the grief is so intense, I feel I'm going to choke with the effort of trying to stop crying.

How come everyone in the whole damn world knew how Hayden felt, except me? My heart feels like it's being squashed in a vice.

I feel the gentle pressure of Jaz's hand squeezing mine, and when I force myself to look up, Emily hands me a box of tissues. Neither of them says anything as I try to pull myself together. Finally, I find my voice and look at Emily. "There's something I have to tell you. About Hayden. His last words..." I try to block the vision of Hayden, dying in my arms, so I can still speak.

Emily's voice is barely audible. "Go on..."

"He said, 'Tell Mum I love her.'"

I can't see Emily properly through my tears, but I can hear her crying. When she speaks again at last, her voice is shaky. "Thank you, Arlo. That means more than you can ever know."

She gets up, I think mostly to hide her sadness, and makes another pot of tea. She refills our cups before she sits down again.

"Actually, there are things I need to say to you too, Arlo, if that's okay?"

I nod and take a gulp of tea.

"About the cottage. I'm giving it to you and your mother. The piece of land with the grove and the spring too. In memory of Hayden. It's what he would have wanted..."

Emily's lip quivers, and Jaz puts her arm around her. I feel miserable and broken and like there's nothing I can do to help. It's too late.

"Thank you. It's far more than I deserve," I croak, digging my nails into my palm to try and stop the tide of emotion that threatens to swamp me again.

"It's not more than you deserve, Arlo, believe me," she says. "Norman cheated your family back when he bought this place. He paid far too little for it. You know that. I always thought maybe that was the final straw for your father."

As we finish our tea, the silence is filled with the memory of Hayden and wishing things could be different.

"I know it can't be much fun, but...please come again, won't you?" asks Emily when we leave. Jaz immediately gives her a hug.

"Of course! We want to share time with you and talk about Hayden," she says. "Seriously. He was a very good friend. He loved you so much, and he'd want us to care for you too. I know he would. And the baby."

I nod and wonder if all girls are so much better at saying stuff than I am, or if it's just Jaz. She's amazing.

As we walk back down the farm track, I'm not sure whether I should hold Jaz's hand again. Before I can decide, she links her arm through mine.

"So are we going to talk about it?"

"What, about Emily?"

"About how Hayden felt about you."

I don't say anything.

"You knew, right?" she says.

"Only at the end. In the field. When he was dying… he told me. That's why he pushed me out of the way—to stop his dad shooting. Only it didn't stop him, did it?" I'm trying so hard not to cry again, I'm almost shouting.

"That's not your fault."

"However many times you say that, I still wish I hadn't been so blind. We could have been friends again, all that time, and I realised too late. Too bloody late. All this might not have happened if I'd realised sooner."

I turn to look at Jaz. "I thought he was in love with *you*. I was jealous of him! Can you believe it? I feel so bloody guilty." I sniff and attempt to wipe my eyes and nose with the bottom of my T-shirt.

Jaz doesn't say anything for a minute. She scrabbles in her shoulder bag and hands me a tissue.

"Cheers," I say.

"That's okay. Snot on your T-shirt isn't such a great look."

We walk on a bit, both too busy thinking to speak.

Jaz breaks the silence. "You were jealous?"

"Yes. Stupidly jealous."

"You're such an idiot."

On impulse, I pull her to me. She puts her arms around my waist, and we hold each other for ages, saying nothing. Eventually, she pulls away and looks up at me. Then, for a moment, all the pain and pent-up grief dissipates as we tentatively, gently kiss.

We start walking again, and I put my arm around her. I keep it there, all the way back to mine.

302

Chapter 36

CLAY WALKS STRAIGHT through to the kitchen like he lives here. He hasn't been around much since I came out of hospital because of the legalities of the court case, and I'm glad to see him.

He looks at me expectantly. "Mine's a Coke if you're offering."

I grin. "Don't be dumb, Clay. Remember where you are. The choice is organic apple juice, or possibly carrot and orange if you need your immune system boosted."

He grimaces. "I was hoping things might have changed with everything that's happened, but guess it was too much to expect. Got any coffee?"

"I can manage that for you. We even have sugar."

"Brown sugar?"

"Obviously. We only do wholesome."

I make us both a coffee, and we sit at the kitchen table, looking out at the garden.

"How's things going with the brain tumour?"

"It's not a tumour. It's a cyst."

"Whatever. The thing that sent you mental."

"Thanks."

"S'okay. So when's the op?"

"I'm on a list. Could be any time. Apparently, it's not life-threatening, so they don't think it's a priority."

"But the seizures?"

I put my hand down on the tabletop. "Touch wood, haven't had one since, well...y'know...hospital and everything."

"That's not wood, mate. It's a plastic tablecloth."

I grin at him and touch his head instead. "Yeah, I know."

"Gerroff!" He grins back. "Want to come up and see the chickens in a bit?"

"Spring Farm?"

"Yep. I'm still helping out, thanks to you."

"That's good of you. Meant to say cheers for taking that on. Mary needs all the help she can get, now Harry's died."

"She'd like to see you. She said so."

"I should have been up before now, really. We can go up when we've drunk our coffee if you like."

"Yeah, as soon as Jaz arrives." He gives me a meaningful look.

"What's that for?"

He smirks. "Well, y'know, since you've finally seen a bit of sense in your choice of girlfriends, thought you might want to talk about it."

"She's not...well, okay I guess she is, but not kind of, officially..." Crap. I'm blushing.

"That's cleared that up then."

The doorbell rings before I can say anything.

"I'll go," he says.

"Hey, move in, why don't you?"

Clay ignores me and goes to answer the door. He reappears in the kitchen with Jaz. Seeing her makes me feel all kind of warm inside, and I smile. But I quickly realise from her expression that something's up.

"What's wrong?"

"Nothing." She sits down and looks at me, then gives me a half smile. "Really, nothing that bad. I ran into Emily earlier. We talked about Hayden's funeral. She said she'd love it if we could say something at the service."

"What, all of us?"

"Well, you and me, yes."

My head starts buzzing with anxiety. I'm not sure I'm ready to say anything at Hayden's funeral. It all feels far too raw. But the bottom line is he saved my life. It's the very least I can do for him. And Jaz will be there with me.

"I guess we have to, in that case," I say.

Chapter 37

WE DECIDE TO all go up to Spring Farm together. We walk slowly up the lane, none of us saying much. The road is filled with strands of straw at the edges, dropped from all the passing tractors with trailers laden with bales. Harvest is nearly all finished now. Eventually, I break the silence.

"Where's the funeral being held?"

Jaz kicks a stone to the side of the road. "Chapel in Tytheford." She avoids looking at either of us. "So how would you feel about saying something at the service, Clay?"

Clay shakes his head. "I've not got a lot to say. I wasn't that friendly to him, so I don't feel too great about the whole thing."

Jaz and I glance at each other.

"Guess the funeral's not going to be easy for any of us," I say.

"I asked Mum about the possibility of Phelps himself being there,' Jaz says.

I feel myself tensing. "You don't think...surely there's no way Phelps would be there? What did your mum say?"

"She said Phelps hasn't gone to trial yet. He's officially innocent until proven guilty, even though he's being held in custody until then. And it could be up to a year away."

"Which means?"

"If he hears about it, he can ask to be there. It's a service for his son, after all."

That sends me seething with anger. "His son? Oh, yes, the son he shot in cold blood."

Clay shrugs. "To be fair, he was actually aiming at you, mate."

Clay has a knack of making us all laugh despite ourselves. But even while I'm laughing, I'm thinking how I can't possibly face being in the same room as Phelps, ever again. At the same, time I can't avoid being at Hayden's funeral. None of us can.

WE REACH THE entrance to Spring Farm, and the air is tinged with the smell of the chicken run. I can hear the hens clucking contentedly.

"Sounds like you've been doing a good job, Clay. They're still alive."

"Amazing, huh?" He grins.

Being at the farm gates immediately takes me back to the last time I was here, when I went to the spring on the way back and saw Andraste reflected in the water. In the other place.

"You're very quiet." Jaz touches my arm gently. "Are you okay?"

I smile at her. "Yeah, I'm fine."

I'm still thinking about Andraste. I doubt I'll ever see her again. When I did see her, she scared me stupid, but I keep getting a strange, nostalgic feeling about the other place, like that astronaut had about the moon. I can't ever forget what it felt like to be there.

Mary has spotted us through the window and comes out into the yard.

"Hello, young Arlo! I believe I have a lot to thank you for. It's good to see you again. Are you recovered now?"

"Yeah, I think so, Mary." I smile. "But I was very sorry to hear about Harry."

She gazes at me through old, misted eyes. "'Appens to us all in the end, Arlo. I'll be joining him soon enough." She laughs wheezily for a moment, then stops abruptly and stares into my eyes. "I was sad to hear about that young lad Hayden at Home Farm, mind. Funeral coming up soon. We should all go and pay our respects."

"Yes, we're definitely going," Jaz says.

"Good job. The whole village should go. We owe him. Paid the forfeit for us."

"Forfeit?" Clay looks mystified. "What forfeit?"

Mary smiles enigmatically and shuffles back towards the open farm door.

"You best come in and have some tea. I reckon the chickens can wait a bit, Clay."

We troop into the house after her. The dark interior smells of a mixture of chickens, tobacco and cake. Out in the kitchen, a Victoria sponge rests on a wire rack to cool. It smells good. Mary fetches plates and cuts a slice for each of us, then pours our tea from a large copper teapot resting on the Aga. The tea is so strong, it's almost undrinkable. I know from experience that she makes a pot and keeps it warm all day. You could practically stand a teaspoon in it.

Clay stuffs in a mouthful of cake approvingly, then looks at Mary.

"So what was that you said about Hayden paying a forfeit for us, Mary? What did you mean, exactly?"

I cringe, wondering what Mary's going to say. I know she and Ma have been talking.

"You youngsters know nothing these days. No one tells you the old stories anymore. But since you've asked me, I'll tell you. She's always been there, under Wights Mound. The story goes that if anything bad happens to her land, she returns. It takes a blood sacrifice to put things right again." She cuts into the cake again and looks at Clay. "Would you like another slice, deary?"

I can see Jaz looks uncomfortable, like she doesn't know what to say. Clay holds out his plate for the cake. I hope he's going to drop the subject, but I know him too well. Of course he's not.

"So who's this 'she' you're talking about?"

"No one's sure exactly who she is. There's stories about her. She appears when things go bad. She's like a guardian of the land."

"So you believe there's some ghost woman under Wights Mound who demands blood? I don't buy that, sorry, Mary. Hayden died because his father's a total psycho and he shot him. End of story."

Mary pauses before she says anything. "That's as maybe. It's true he's a nasty piece of work, that Norman Phelps. Always thought so. But me and Melissa, we saw things. We've talked on this. We started to get better the minute that young man got shot. He paid the forfeit and the curse was lifted."

Clay stares at her and swallows his mouthful of cake. "Seriously, you got better because they found the right antibiotics in time, more like," he mutters. He stuffs more cake in his mouth.

"Why are women always the bad guys in these stories, do you think?" Jaz asks.

"I never said she was bad. She's just a part of the land here. She looks after it."

Mary catches my eye. She winks at me as if we're co-conspirators.

"Young Arlo knows I'm right," she says.

Fortunately, I don't have to answer because Clay gets in first.

"Well, everyone knows he's mental. Though apparently he's got a brain tumour, so it's probably not his fault."

"I told you. It's not a tumour, it's a cyst."

"Whatever."

Mary chuckles. "Nothing wrong with him if you ask me." She reaches for her tobacco and starts rolling herself a cigarette. "But he's lucky to be alive, I'd say."

Chapter 38

JAZ AND I leave Clay at Mary's, feeding the chickens and sorting out the eggs. We head back to my place. Jaz goes down the garden to call her mum, and Ma and I are left in the kitchen.

"Ma? Can I ask you something?"

"Yes, of course." Ma puts down the bunch of herbs she's holding and looks at me.

"Mary was telling us you saw things when you were in hospital. Before you started to get better."

"Oh, that."

"Well?"

"We both saw the girl. Strange, isn't it?"

I wait for her to say more, but she doesn't.

"What girl?"

"You know... The one from *the other place*."

My heart starts racing.

"Where?"

"In the hospital. She came out of the mist to release me. Or that's how I saw it. Don't know about Mary."

"There was a mist in the hospital?"

"No, stupid. That's the first thing I remember before I started to recover." She looks at me. "She was the girl you were seeing. Andraste. Seen her hanging about

311

Stanton a few times, so I know it was her. Long, red hair. Lots of woad."

"Woad?"

"Plant dye. The blue tattoos."

"Oh. So Andraste was in the hospital?"

"How should I know? I was in a coma."

Ma can be so exasperating.

"But you said you saw her."

"There's seeing and seeing. It wasn't the kind of seeing that means she was actually there and other people could see her. Well, except maybe Mary, of course."

"Who was also in a coma..."

"But it's strange we both saw her around the same time. We reckon it was about when Hayden was shot."

"It's probably best you don't tell people that."

"I know. I'm not daft."

Suddenly I'm aware of Jaz, standing at the kitchen door. I'm not sure how long she's been there, but she must have heard some of the conversation.

Ma still hasn't noticed her standing there. "So do you miss seeing her, Arlo? I imagine she's gone back where she came from."

I look at Jaz. I'm not sure how much to say.

"To be honest, it wasn't romance, Ma, whatever you thought. Would you like a drink, Jaz?"

Ma gets all flustered and is clearly embarrassed. I pour some orange juice and hand Jaz a glass.

"Let's go and drink this outside in the sun, shall we?" I suggest.

Jaz nods gratefully and we head off down the garden.

As soon as we're out of earshot, she turns to me. "Sorry, I didn't mean to listen in."

"That's okay. It was my fault. I asked her to tell me more about what Mary said to us earlier."

"Can we talk about it?"

"You mean about Andraste?"

Jaz nods and takes a swig of orange juice. I can tell she's nervous, and I reach out to squeeze her arm.

"Look, Jaz, I know everyone thinks I was getting together with her, but it really wasn't like that. Most of the time, she scared the crap out of me."

Jaz smiles. "Like when she took you to 'the other place' that time?"

"I know what you thought about that. But what I told you was the truth. It was so weird and so frightening being there, I blacked out and lost a lot of time. And time is very different there anyway." I glance at Jaz to see how she's taking this.

She's looking at me, listening intently. "Go on."

"So, the day before Hayden died, Andraste appeared after I'd been up at Mary's farm. She wanted me to go back to her world with her, so she could explain why someone had to pay the forfeit."

I notice Jaz is trying hard to keep her expression neutral. She's not doing too well. My heart melts as I look at her.

"Is that the blood sacrifice Mary mentioned?" she asks.

"Exactly. I sort of knew that I was the one she'd chosen to pay it, but I still hoped there might be some way out. Even though I thought I was losing everything—Ma, the cottage, you—I wanted to stay alive. But when she took me back there, I got it. I could see what she was saying."

"Does her world feel like a real place when you're there?"

"Totally real. It *is* real. It's kind of like here, but how it would have been here before they built Wights Mound. I didn't see any people, or at least, I don't think so. Mostly wild animals. Bears."

"Bears? Are you serious?"

"There must have been bears here once. Around Stanton. And wolves. And thick forest. In the other place, it's like nothing changed." I hesitate. "This all makes me sound like I'm mental, right?"

Jaz smiles. "Frankly, yes. But I can see you believe it, so I guess in some way it must be true. What did Andraste say about the forfeit?"

"She told me someone had to pay it to stop all the bad stuff happening. You know how Phelps poisoned the spring? The spring is in both places. It's like some kind of connecting point. But the damage caused by the explosion was even worse there. Everything was dying." I glance at Jaz. "I can see what you're thinking, but it felt so real, Jaz. And I was bricking it."

Jaz looks deep in thought for a moment before she says anything. "Whether the other place exists or

314

not—and I totally believe you think it does—is kind of irrelevant. What you're saying is that when you went out to Dingle Hollow that morning, you seriously thought you were going to die. So why on earth did you go?"

It's hard to find words to explain. "I thought if I didn't, more people would die. You getting the headache and going to the hospital was the final straw. I know now it turned out to be nothing, but I didn't at the time. Harry Suggeworth and Tracy Benger had died. I believed Ma was as good as dead too. Andraste told me if the forfeit wasn't paid, everything that was happening would get worse. It would be like the plague—the black death. She said there'd be no escape, but I had the power to change all that if I paid the forfeit."

"But because Phelps shot Hayden, he ended up paying the forfeit—this blood-sacrifice thing—instead of you?"

Talking about it, even with Jaz, is making me feel very shaky again. But I have to tell her. I have to tell someone how guilty I feel. I force myself to answer her.

"I don't think he knew what was going to happen when he set out, but yes, that's how it turned out. He said Andraste had told him where to find me, or that's what I think he was trying to say. He *chose* to pay it for me because of how he felt about me. And I know how crazy that sounds." I pause for a moment. The memory of it makes it hard to talk. "But it should have been me, Jaz. It was *meant* to be me..." My voice trails off in the pain of remembering.

"But if Andraste told him where to find you...did he tell you how much time she spent with him?"

"No. No, he didn't. But he did talk about her once to me. He said he saw her too, and he thought maybe other people didn't."

We stare at each other for a moment. I hesitate. "You don't think...?"

"He was the one chosen to pay the forfeit all along? I guess it's possible." Jaz reaches out and holds my face gently in her hands. She looks into my eyes. "None of it was your fault, Arlo, so stop beating yourself up. Whichever way you look at it, Phelps is to blame for all of it. Everything. He was doing something illegal and he was prepared to kill to protect his interests. If it wasn't for Phelps, Hayden would be alive and you'd be close friends again."

I put my arms around her and kiss her, tasting the sweet orange juice on her tongue.

Then I stare at her for a moment.

"However guilty I feel, I'm so glad to be alive right now," I say.

She pulls me to her again and kisses me. We hold each other close, and she sighs. "Sorry I made you talk about it like this. I didn't want to upset you, but I really needed to know."

"We should have talked about it before, Jaz, I know... but, well, I couldn't."

We hold each other without speaking, for a long time, both lost in thought.

As soon as Jaz has gone home, Ma corners me before I go over to Clay's.

"Was Jaz okay about earlier? I felt terrible. I should never have started talking about that girl when she was here."

"It's all right, Ma. Jaz and I needed to talk about it. I just hadn't been able to until now."

Ma looks worried. "I know it must be so hard after everything that happened. Before I got ill, I was convinced Andraste had chosen you to pay the blood price and I might never see you again."

"She did. She did choose me..." I stutter. "At least, I think so. But when it came to it, Hayden paid the forfeit instead. He saved my life."

Ma goes very still, like she's frozen or something. "I knew it. I felt it in my bones." She grabs her knitting. "You must keep paying your respects from now on, Arlo. Make it clear that you haven't forgotten her."

"How am I supposed to do that?"

"Maybe a little offering at the spring or in the grove. That's what people always used to do."

"You never said before. How do you know?"

"My granddad told me his mother used to leave little offerings there when he was a boy. She told him they'd always done it, since before people could remember."

"What kind of offerings? And why don't people do it anymore?" Even as I'm asking her, I put my hand in my pocket and feel the tiny coin I found in the spring. I've kept it with me, like some kind of lucky charm, ever since I found it. Maybe that was an offering once, like Jaz said at the time.

"It's a different world, Arlo. People don't stick to traditions anymore. But there's no harm in doing it. Just leave a flower or some token in the grove like you do for your dad—or maybe by the spring."

I nod. There's so much I haven't told Ma about what happened with Andraste, and I never will. But what she's said about the offerings feels right somehow.

Ma's knitting needles clack over the rainbow wool. "Just do it every now and then when you remember. She'll be around long after we've all gone."

Chapter 39

I T LOOKS LIKE the whole population of Tytheford is crammed into the chapel. I start having flashbacks to the last time I saw them all together like this, back in the village hall. The night of the meeting.

Clay glances at me. "Hope they've changed minds about the benefits of mining by now."

"Keep your voice down, for Pete's sake!" Jaz says, but I notice she's smiling.

Jaz and I have spent much of the past week preparing short speeches to read at the service, about Hayden and what he meant to us. I still think my speech is a cop-out, with no mention of Phelps or the mining, but Jaz and Ma both insisted I keep it just about Hayden.

I know they're right. Phelps's case hasn't gone to trial yet, and no one wants to say or do anything that jeopardises the chances of him getting a life sentence. At the same time, not being able to mention Hayden taking a hit to save me from his own father made it hard for me to think of anything to say at all.

The three of us are ushered to the front to sit in the pew right behind Emily Phelps—or Emily Waters, as she now wants to be known. There's a couple next to her along with two kids. When Emily turns and sees us, she introduces them as her sister, brother-in-law, niece and nephew. I'm glad she's got some family here to support her.

I twist around to look at all the other pews behind us and check to see who's here. Ma's near the back, sitting on the end of a row next to PC Chopra. PC Colenutt is next to them, chatting to Dave Benger in the row in front. Neither of the police officers is wearing uniform, I notice. PC Chopra looks like he's deep in conversation with Ma.

"I reckon those two really like each other," Jaz says. "Your mum and PC Chopra, I mean. They get on so well. He was great at giving her lifts when you were in hospital."

"Really? I had no idea."

"What, you hadn't noticed anything?"

"No, not really. He's been to the cottage a few times since I got back, but I thought that was because of what happened. Like, he took my initial statement."

"It probably was, you idiot. After all, he is a policeman. But I reckon he was pleased to have the opportunity to visit your mum as well."

I turn back to look at Ma again. Now Jaz has mentioned it, she and PC Chopra do seem kind of close, but it's hard to tell at this distance; I can't hear what anyone's saying clearly because everyone's keeping their voices down.

I scan the rest of the pews quickly. There are loads of familiar faces, most of whom I haven't seen since that night in the village hall. I get sympathetic looks and smiles from a few people, which is a bit embarrassing. I guess times change. I see Mary at the back, and she waves to me. I smile back at her, then quickly scan the entrance to see if anyone else is coming in.

"He's not here," Clay says.

"Who?"

"Phelps. That's who you're looking for, isn't it?"

"Yeah," I admit. "Didn't think he would be, but it's good to be sure."

Once I've established Phelps isn't here, I force myself to look at the coffin, up on a plinth at the front. It isn't what I was expecting at all. The last funeral I went to was Dad's. We'd gone bankrupt, but the village had clubbed together to get him a pine coffin. I don't remember any flowers in the chapel at the service, only the ones me and Ma picked and left for him in the grove afterwards.

Hayden's coffin is very different. It's made of wicker, and someone has carefully threaded wild flowers and berries all through the weave of the basket. It's beautiful but immediately makes me think of those Moses baskets people buy for newborn babies. I look at Emily Phelps in the row in front and wonder if she chose it—a final cradle for her Hayden. Life can be so unfair. I stare straight ahead, trying unsuccessfully to stop my eyes welling up with sadness.

Jaz hands me a tissue from a packet she's got in her shoulder bag and takes one for herself at the same time. I even hear Clay asking for one, but I avoid looking to see if he's crying.

The service begins, and after an introductory speech from the vicar to tell us the service is to be a celebration of Hayden's life, Jaz is first up to give her eulogy. She nervously pushes her hair behind her ears and stares at her notes for a minute. Then she looks up at the room and starts to speak. Her eulogy is short but it's from the heart—about what a good friend Hayden was to her, and how they became friends at primary school when she came back from Africa; how no one else would play with her at first except for Hayden because she was new and she looked different. She talks about some of the things they did together, how kind he was, and how much she'll miss him.

When she comes back to sit down next to me, I grab her hand and squeeze her fingers.

"Was I okay?" she whispers.

"More than okay. You were brilliant."

A few hymns and a couple of eulogies later, it's my turn. My legs feel like jelly as I go up to the pulpit. Crap. I shouldn't have agreed to this. I see Jaz looking at me, willing me to keep going. I look at my notes. Then I put them down. I don't know what makes me do it, but I have to say something more than the stuff I've jotted down in the notes. I cough nervously, then start speaking.

"Um, we've heard some great things about Hayden, and they're all true. He was a lovely person. But to me, he was far more than that. I wasn't such a great friend to him recently, and I let him down on more than one occasion. I wish I hadn't. But the thing is with Hayden, his opinion of me didn't change because of that. He cared. I'm not able to say much about what happened, but many of you must be aware that it's because of Hayden I'm able to stand here and talk to you today. I didn't appreciate how good a friend he really was to me until..." I hesitate. The door of the chapel opens, and a group of people walk in. They stand close together. My heart starts beating faster. Surely it can't be...then one of them looks up.

Phelps. He stands at the back, flanked by two men I guess are prison wardens.

He stares straight at me, and even from here I can see the hatred in his eyes and the anger on his face. And suddenly it's as if I'm back in the cornfield, Phelps pointing his gun at me, aiming to kill. My heart's racing so much, it feels like the walls are closing in on me. I start getting the weird déjà vu thing, and all my senses go into overdrive. I catch the scent of Hayden's mum's perfume in the air. And Jaz. The sweet smell of her cinnamon hair oil. The tobacco breath of David Clutterbuck two rows back. I see Ma craning her neck to see who came in, and I even hear her sharp intake of breath when she realises what's wrong with me.

The air is being sucked out of the room. All eyes are on me, waiting for me to continue. Sweat trickles down the back of my neck. I open my mouth to speak but find I'm unable to say anything.

Suddenly Jaz is beside me, clutching my hand and pulling me gently down from the pulpit. I walk shakily down the few steps,

"Go and sit down, and just breathe slowly," she whispers in my ear. I do as she says, stumbling quickly back to the end of our pew. Jaz has stepped up to the pulpit again. I have to lean forward and put my head between my knees.

"Everyone knows what happened that day," Jaz says. Despite the ringing sound that's started in my ears, I can still hear her, but I can't trust myself to lift my head to look at her. I'm going to have a seizure, I know it.

"I'm sure you all understand why Arlo found it hard to keep talking. But I know what he wanted to say most was what a great friend Hayden was to us, and such a sweet, lovely person. Thank you." I hear the sudden crack in her voice, and I bet she's spotted Phelps.

I hear her moving down from the pulpit. She pushes me gently to make me slide along and make room for her.

The vicar announces the next hymn, and I hear everyone shuffling to stand up, rustling the handouts we were given with the order of service. I can't stand, so I stay where I am.

"Arlo? What's wrong, mate?" Even Clay sounds concerned.

"Phelps."

"Phelps? What, you mean he's here? He had the nerve to—"

"Shhh! Keep your voice down, Clay!" Jaz hisses. "Hold it together until after the service."

I keep my head down and my eyes closed to try and stop the sensation that the ground is shifting under my feet. It's not working. I feel the wave of movement like an earthquake when everyone stands to sing the final hymn. Although my eyes are tight shut, the image of Phelps staring at me is seared onto my eyeballs. I stay bent double in my seat.

The hymn ends and everyone sits down.

"Do you need to go outside? Shall I take you?" asks Jaz.

"S'okay," I say. I can't face walking out past all those people and giving Phelps the satisfaction of seeing me like this. Besides, I'm not even sure I can stand, let alone walk.

"Breathe in slowly, counting to three... Hold your breath, and count to three again... Now release your breath, counting slowly... Good. Now do that ten more times. Keep concentrating on your breathing."

I try to do as Jaz tells me. It feels like an eternity goes by. Tiny sounds in the room start to echo in my head, magnified a thousand times.

I hear Ronnie shout from the back of the church. "It's okay, he's gone now!"

Jaz is talking to me again, but it's as though she's far away and under water.

"Ronnie says they've taken Phelps away. Are you okay to walk?"

I force myself to raise my head. A small crowd of people including Ma and PC Chopra are standing in the aisle next to our pew. Ma looks so anxious it makes me feel even worse.

"I'm fine," I say and stand up as quickly as I can, so embarrassed.

Then the chapel goes dark and I'm falling.

Chapter 40

I STRUGGLE TO OPEN my eyes. They feel like lead and I can only half open them. I see Clay staring back at me. He grins.

"Hi, slap-head! Nice of you to wake up!"

I try to make sense of the words. "Slap-head? What are you talking about?" My mouth feels dry as sandpaper when I speak.

I reach up to feel my head. It's smooth, no hair, and a wodge of some soft, fabric stuff is wound around above my ears. I sit up and look around the room, and the movement makes my head really hurt. Hospital ward. Smells like disinfectant. What the hell?

"How did I get here?"

"Ambulance. They took you straight from the chapel and kept you sedated until the op."

"Op?"

"Yeah. They took your brains out. You probably won't notice much difference, mind."

I manage a smile. "Cheers for that." Behind him, I see Ma and Jaz coming through the swing door at the end of the ward.

Jaz runs towards the bed I'm lying on.

"Arlo! You're awake!"

"So it would seem. And someone stole my hair."

"Yeah, but you look fine. Honest. It'll soon grow back—I can almost see the stubble already."

"What happened?"

"It was that cyst they told you about. You got treated as an emergency."

"How come?"

"You were out cold for hours. They thought it was a good idea in case it kept happening."

"See? I told you they took your brains out."

"Shut up, Clay. Try to be serious. How do you feel, Arlo?"

"Confused. And my head hurts a bit. Quite a lot, actually." I feel my head tentatively and pat the dressing. It's like a small pillow stuck to one side of my head. "What is this thing? Has anyone got a mirror?"

"It's the plug to keep the stuffing in."

"Clay, really!" Jaz says.

"Here you are, love." Ma hands me a tiny mirror that she keeps in her make-up bag. I hold it up. Can't see much. Just a bald me with a massive dressing and a bandage wound around to keep it in place. I pan down to see my face. Two heavily bruised, puffy eyes stare back at me.

"Bloody hell. I look awful."

"True."

"Clay, for crying out loud! The doctor said the swelling around your eyes should go down in a few days."

"Cheers, Jaz. That's very reassuring."

Ma looks worried. "At least it's done now, love. One less thing to worry about."

And suddenly everything comes flooding back to me. Phelps.

"When's the trial?"

"Sanj tells me it'll be a good few months. But your evidence will be recorded as soon as you're fit enough."

"Oh."

"It'll be fine. Don't worry. You don't have to see him. Your evidence is televised to the court when the trial starts. Clay's too."

"So how long do I have to stay in here?"

"Only until tomorrow, so long as everything's okay today. You have to take it easy for a few weeks, though."

I wonder how I'm going to take it easy when my brain's still exploding from the sight of Phelps in the chapel. I feel shaky again and lie back against the pillows.

"He looks tired. We should probably let him rest."

"I can hear you, Ma. I haven't gone deaf."

"I know, son. But I don't want you overdoing it. We need you back at home."

I try to smile. I feel so tired. I close my eyes.

PHELPS POINTS HIS gun in my face. He's so close I can smell him.

I flick my eyes open. Ma, Jaz and Clay are just pushing their way out through the double doors of the ward.

I try not to shut my eyes again.

I've been prescribed sedatives for the next few weeks.

"Don't want you to get overexcited," the doctor says.

Overexcited? Terrified, more like. I try to smile at her. PC Chopra and Ma have come to pick me up. PC Chopra is looking at me intently.

"Are you sure you're okay?" he asks.

"Yeah, I'm fine," I lie.

We go down in the lift to the car park. PC Chopra has parked the police car close by. I'm not supposed to walk too far to start with.

I climb in the back and Ma gets in next to me.

PC Chopra turns around from the driving seat before he starts the car. "Arlo, I feel you're not telling the entire truth. What's worrying you? Is it Phelps?"

I'm irritated with PC Chopra for being so direct. But I guess he means well. I nod.

"Thought so. You need victim support. It's a very scary thing having some idiot try to kill you. It's perfectly reasonable to feel like you do."

Chapter 41

THANKS TO PC Chopra, Doctor Bill has prescribed me a course of trauma counselling, but unfortunately, the counsellor doesn't have space at the moment. Doctor Bill's amazing, though. It's almost like having a counsellor before I start having counselling.

"Now are you sure you can handle the recorded video interview, Arlo?"

"I think so, yes. I don't have to see him. I think I'll be okay."

"I can stay with you, alongside the child psychologist the police are sending."

"Yes, you said. Thank you."

"So would you like me to stay with you?"

"Maybe..."

"Do you still see Phelps every time you close your eyes?"

"No. Not always. Usually at night just before I go to sleep."

Doctor Bill looks worried. "I wish they'd put this off until you've recovered."

"But they can't, can they?"

"I guess not. Still, I think you can do it. I believe in you!"

I'm glad someone does. Inside, I feel like I'm hollow.

FINALLY, THE FIRST interview is over. I got through it.

I told them exactly what happened. Except, of course, I left so much out. I told them about the fracking. The photographs. The threats from Phelps.

And that day.

I told them I'd gone early to check out what Phelps was hiding in Dingle Hollow. About seeing the corn circle and going to look at it. How he was waiting for me. Yes, he saw me. Yes, he was looking straight at me. In my opinion, he definitely had every intention of shooting me, and he'd threatened it before.

He killed his son. Yes, by mistake.

But he meant to kill me. In cold blood.

The whole time, I say nothing about Andraste. Of course I don't.

But I think about her, as the last of the honeysuckle scents the air and the autumn mists rise each dawn covering the cottage and the garden in a soft blanket.

THERE'S A LOT more coming and going. Apparently, Phelps is going to plead temporary insanity, brought on by righteous anger at the destruction of his crops.

I stick to my story. Clay and Jaz are being interviewed separately, and we've been advised not to talk to each other while the police are recording evidence. It's lonely not seeing them. I feel so isolated, and I miss Jaz so much.

Doctor Bill comes with me every time I'm interviewed, worried that the counsellor still hasn't been able to see me. Everyone expects me to be sad about Hayden, so it's okay that I can't talk about it without sometimes breaking down.

JAZ IS FINALLY allowed to come over again. It's such a relief to see her again, I hold her like I never want to let go.

The Crown Court refuses to grant Phelps bail. The weight of evidence against him is very strong, and he's considered too dangerous to let out. The police are charging him with murder.

For the first time since it happened, I feel like I can breathe.

PC CHOPRA IS very concerned for us. He comes over to explain to me and Ma that even if Phelps gets a life sentence, it doesn't mean he won't ever be let out. In fact, he might serve as little as ten years.

"I want to make sure you understand that, so you know what to expect."

Ma shakes her head sadly. "Ten years? Is that all you get for killing your own son, Sanj? Poor Hayden. He was worth so much more than that."

PC Chopra looks at her, his dark eyes filled with sadness. "I know. My wife was worth more too. The arsonist who killed her was charged with manslaughter. He'll serve less than ten years."

I feel for him. It's obvious he still finds it very painful to talk about. I know what that's like.

Then he forces a smile. "But if it hadn't happened, I wouldn't have moved to Tytheford," he says.

I notice he looks at Ma when he says that.

I DECIDE IT's time I went back to the grove. It's been a while since we finished giving evidence, and I haven't been there since Hayden died. Ma hears me opening the front door.

"Arlo? Have you finished your coursework for Monday?"

"Just going out for a bit, Ma. Don't fuss. I'm going to Jaz's later and she's helping me."

Truth is, I'm finding it hard to get back into college work this term. It's probably a good thing Ma and Jaz are around to nag me.

I choose a perfect red rose for Dad and wonder what to take as an offering for Andraste. I think about it for a bit, then pick a few late flowers from the honeysuckle growing by the front door. It feels right. The smell makes me think of her, every time.

I know it's stupid, but my legs start shaking when I get close to the grove. So much has happened since I was last here, it feels like eons ago. In fact, it's been only a few months.

I push my way to the centre and stand in the clearing for a few minutes, listening to the wind in the trees and the chatter of the rooks. I find the spot where we scattered Dad's ashes and lay the rose on the ground. I always used to talk to him while I was here, but today I can't think of anything to say. Not yet. Too much has happened.

I leave the grove and duck under the branches of the hollow oak to come out by the spring.

The air smells clean. A faint hint of wood smoke drifting on the breeze.

I stare into the water, and my heart lifts as I watch the bubbles rising to the surface. Ma told me it was recovering. She's right.

I place the honeysuckle carefully on the water.

For Andraste. Like Ma told me.

Down in the depths of the pool, I see a hint of green light. I stand stock-still and watch as it grows stronger, bending through the water, weaving a perfect circle of earthlight. It's her. I know it. My pulse starts racing.

The harsh croak of a raven distracts me, and I look up to see the bird circling above. It's watching me. The hairs on the back of my neck prickle. I look back down into the water, but the light has disappeared.

Was it the sunlight playing tricks on my eyes? I stare at the reflections on the surface. It takes a second to realise. The honeysuckle has gone too.

Suddenly I picture Hayden, the person I owe my life to, and my heart aches. I scrabble in my pocket to find the tiny gold coin, and after taking one last look at it, I flick it into the spring.

"That's for you, Hayden. I wish..."

I can't think what else to say. I wish things had been different. I wish he was still alive. Words aren't enough. I watch the coin through a blur of tears as it flashes in the clear, sunlit water, spirals down through the bubbles and disappears.

The raven above me croaks and flaps off over the grove.

I wipe my eyes on the sleeve of my hoodie and think of Jaz, who would find a tissue to give me to stop me from doing that. And I smile.

Guess it's time to go back home to collect my books and head over to her place.

ENDS

Acknowledgements

Broken Ground took so long to write, I managed to complete a few other books in between drafts. For some reason, the original plot didn't quite hang together, and so I shelved it for a while, waiting for inspiration. But the story stayed with me, and Andraste, the ancient land goddess, nagged away at my subconscious. She's a hard taskmistress. Over the years, it's gone through edit after edit until finally both I and, hopefully, the land goddess, are happy with it.

Many people have helped, in different ways, with the numerous drafts of *Broken Ground*. I'll try to thank them all here, starting with my partner, my family and my very ancient cat, for all the background support and encouragement. (Though to be fair, the cat wasn't much use. He merely walked over the laptop at all the wrong moments.)

Various writer friends have been incredibly helpful on this journey. Lottie Sweeney took the time to help me pick up and rearrange the pieces after the first year, when the original draft didn't quite work; SF Said was kind and encouraging about draft two (or maybe it was three?), tactfully pointing out places that still needed redrafting; writers Paul Magrs, Eugene Lambert,

337

Liz Flanagan, Sara Crowe and Mel Darbon read later, better drafts and offered kind and helpful feedback. By the time it reached what I thought was the final draft, my writing group friend, Helenka Stachera, suggested a missed plot opportunity – so yet another final edit followed.

Underlying the story in *Broken Ground* is all the knowledge I've gained about folklore and magic over many years, filtered from numerous books and a lot of time spent with wise and magical women: Laura Daligan, for sharing everything she knew about the Morrigan and other land goddesses; Val Thomas, who has an incredible knowledge of herbs and magical working; Rae Beth, the hedge witch, who experienced a real-life visit to 'the other place' with her fae guide; Dee Banton, for (among many things) the happy hours we spent exploring crop circles in Wiltshire; Marian Green, for holding the annual Quest conferences in Bristol – a space where people feel safe to speak openly about their paranormal experiences.

For practical advice, thanks go to crop circle maker John Lundberg, for all the detail on making a crop circle; my lovely agent, Ben Illis, for always being ready to listen to my plot ideas and having flashes of insight that invariably give them more substance; Rachel Hamilton, for reading a final draft and giving me fresh hope; Rhi Wynter, for creating the amazing cover design; and finally to Debbie McGowan at Beaten Track, for her wonderful editing, and believing *Broken Ground* is a novel worth publishing.

About the Author

Lu Hersey worked as an advertising copywriter until she escaped to become a librarian and study for an MA in writing for young people at Bath Spa University. Her debut book, *Deep Water*, won the Mslexia Children's Novel Award and was originally published by Usborne. In theory, her four children have all left home but are mostly still around, busy depleting her food cupboards. She currently lives in the heart of the West Country.

Twitter: @LuWrites

Also by Lu Hersey:

Deep Water
(current edition: Tangent Books Ltd)

When her mum vanishes, Danni moves to a tiny Cornish fishing village with Dad—where the locals treat her like a monster. As the village's dark, disturbing past bubbles to the surface, Danni discovers that she's not who—or what—she thought she was. And the only way to save her family from a bitter curse is to embrace her incredible new gift.

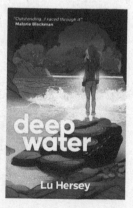

Beaten Track Publishing

For more titles from Beaten Track Publishing,
please visit our website:

https://www.beatentrackpublishing.com

Thanks for reading!